W9-AWV-934

"I thought you had no intention of following up on this thing between us."

"That was what I said, and I meant it. Then." Jed narrowed his eyes. "But I'm changing my mind. Fast."

"Like I don't have a say?" Julianne's words came fast and furious. "I have more taste than to get involved with an insufferable baboon."

"I'm giving you a say. I'm also giving you the responsibility. I'm about through fighting this attraction between us. If you don't want us to end up in bed, you'd better stay a good distance from me."

He'd left her speechless. Her voice was strangled when she finally managed, "Believe me, it won't require much sacrifice." She went inside, slamming the door behind her.

Jed made no attempt to follow. He'd given her fair warning, and some damn good advice. He hoped to hell she'd take it.

For both their sakes.

Dear Reader,

Once again, we've rounded up the best romantic reading for you right here in Silhouette Intimate Moments. Start off with Maggie Shayne's *The Baddest Bride in Texas,* part of her top-selling miniseries THE TEXAS BRAND, and you'll see what I mean. Secrets, steam and romance…this book has everything.

And how many of you have been following that baby? A lot, I'll bet. And this month our FOLLOW THAT BABY cross-line miniseries concludes with *The Mercenary and the New Mom,* by Merline Lovelace. At last the baby's found—and there's romance in the air, as well.

If Western loving's your thing, we've got a trio of books to keep you happy. *Home Is Where the Cowboy Is,* by Doreen Roberts, launches a terrific new miniseries called RODEO MEN. THE SULLIVAN BROTHERS continue their wickedly sexy ways in *Heartbreak Ranch,* by Kylie Brant. And Cheryl Biggs's *The Cowboy She Never Forgot*—a book *you'll* find totally memorable—sports our WAY OUT WEST flash. Then complete your month's reading with *Suddenly a Family,* by Leann Harris. This FAMILIES ARE FOREVER title features an adorable set of twins, their delicious dad and the woman who captures all three of their hearts.

Enjoy them all—then come back next month for six more wonderful Intimate Moments novels, the most exciting romantic reading around.

Yours,

Leslie J. Wainger
Executive Senior Editor

Please address questions and book requests to:
Silhouette Reader Service
U.S.: 3010 Walden Ave., P.O. Box 1325, Buffalo, NY 14269
Canadian: P.O. Box 609, Fort Erie, Ont. L2A 5X3

HEARTBREAK RANCH

KYLIE BRANT

Published by Silhouette Books

America's Publisher of Contemporary Romance

SILHOUETTE BOOKS

ISBN 0-373-07910-9

HEARTBREAK RANCH

Books by Kylie Brant

Silhouette Intimate Moments

McLain's Law #528
Rancher's Choice #552
An Irresistible Man #622
Guarding Raine #693
Bringing Benjy Home #735
Friday's Child #862
*Undercover Lover #882
*Heartbreak Ranch #910

*The Sullivan Brothers

KYLIE BRANT

lives with her husband and five children in Iowa. She works full-time as a teacher of learning disabled students. Much of her free time is spent in her role as professional spectator at her kids' sporting events.

An avid reader, Kylie enjoys stories of love, mystery and suspense—and she insists on happy endings! When her youngest children, a set of twins, turned four, she decided to try her hand at writing. Now most weekends and all summer she can be found at the computer, spinning her own tales of romance and happily-ever-afters.

Kylie invites readers to write to her at P.O. Box 231, Charles City, IA 50616.

For Aunt Della, with many thanks

Prologue

So, she was finally coming home.

Jed Sullivan narrowed his eyes against the thin stream of smoke trailing from the cigarette in his hand. He propped his arms against the fence post, one booted foot crossed in front of the other. Unaccustomed to indolence, he swept his gaze over the cattle, mentally estimating how much longer this pasture could be grazed before the herd would need to be moved.

He brought the cigarette to his lips, inhaled deeply. He couldn't help but wonder what Julianne would think of the changes at the ranch. She'd have an opinion. Julianne Marie Buchanan Richfield always did. He should have been used to the quick twist in the gut her name brought him. Since it couldn't be controlled, it was best ignored.

Had she dropped that weasel's last name when she'd had the good sense to divorce him? At one time he'd thought he'd known her inside and out, but that had been before she'd stunned the family by eloping with the playboy heir to a shipping empire. He hadn't been able to figure out Julianne for a very long time.

Taking a deep draw, he let the smoke filter through his lungs before exhaling again. Once this ranch had been the most important thing in Julianne's life. Their love for the place had bound them together in a way their parents' marriage never could. She hadn't been back but one time since her wedding, and that trip hadn't gone real well. The ranch obviously didn't mean what it once had to her.

He didn't bother to analyze the mingled regret and relief that accompanied the thought. He'd expected her to ask his help when her marriage had ended in a spectacular media scandal, but he'd been wrong about that, too. It seemed he couldn't predict Julianne's actions anymore. But he was still certain about one thing. She wouldn't stay.

He took another puff before meticulously stubbing the cigarette out against the fence post.

He'd be willing to lay odds on it.

Chapter 1

The long drive from the airport was soothing. Julianne could have used that time to think, to devise answers to the inevitable questions that would accompany her homecoming. But she was short on answers these days. Hopefully, moving back to the ranch would help supply some of them.

She'd been purposely vague about her arrival date. She hadn't wanted Jed to have to free up one of the hands to come after her. And to be honest, she especially hadn't wanted to chance Jed showing up himself.

Her fingers clenched the steering wheel before she made a conscious effort to relax them. She'd managed to avoid him for another few hours by renting a Blazer at the airport. Once she arrived at the ranch there would be plenty of time to unpack and rest before dinner. She'd need all her wits about her to deal with the man who was technically her stepbrother. Their relationship had always been a verbal and mental two-step, with each of them fighting for the lead.

The analogy brought a quick curve to her lips. Fencing with Jed had been her greatest joy, once upon a time. Childish, really, but simple pleasures sometimes were. He'd always been so darn controlled, even when he'd come to the ranch as a boy of twelve. Trying to get a rise out of him had quickly become her favorite sport, one that hadn't succeeded often enough to satisfy.

She reached up to push back a strand of blond hair that had escaped from the braid she'd confined it in. There was no reason to believe that after all this time she and Jed couldn't get along like two adults. She liked to think she'd matured some since she was seven, although admittedly, the process had been completed only recently. That thought had the slight smile fading from her face. There was nothing like an ill-conceived marriage, a public scandal and a messy divorce to build character.

She'd been driving alongside Buchanan property for the last twenty minutes. Slowing the Blazer, she swung onto the road that would lead to the ranch house. From here everything looked exactly the same. A part of her marveled at the fact, while another part was steeped in gratitude. There was something soothing about the endless sea of land that stretched farther than the naked eye could see. Something comforting in the knowledge that the land had been here long before humans began their foolishness, and would remain long after they'd ceased to exist.

Her eyes focused on the sign arching over the road, and her heart hitched once in her chest. She slowed the vehicle to a stop. The H/B Ranch had been named by her father, unabashedly after himself. After winning it in a high stakes card game, Harley Buchanan had lost no time making the ranch a home for himself and his daughter. She was aware that it was often referred to by the neighbors as the Heartbreak Ranch, just as she was aware of the reasons for it. But despite her father's constant roller coaster of luck, her home had remained secure. Harley had promised that he'd always keep it safe for her. It was one of the few promises he'd ever made that he'd kept.

The emotion she'd struggled to hold at bay for the last few weeks slammed into her then. She rested her brow against the steering wheel, her eyes sliding shut. When things had gone so horribly wrong with Andrew, her first instinct had been to run for the shelter of the ranch. But if she'd learned one valuable lesson from her life with her husband, it was that need wasn't always an emotion to be acted on. She'd been married to a man who refused to assume responsibility for his life. It was past time, she'd thought, to take charge of her own. So she'd faced the media, the police and the federal agents alone. However frightening it had seemed at the time, there had been a measure of satisfaction in regaining control of her life.

She pressed on the accelerator, unmindful of the plumes of dust trailing in the Blazer's wake, but it was another five minutes before the ranch house came into sight. She pulled to a stop, pride and happiness tangling in her chest. *Home.*

It was a sprawling structure of wood, stone and glass, and, she was told, it bore little resemblance to the original house. She'd only been three when she'd moved here with her father, and too young to remember the place before Harley had ordered the remodeling. Acres of glistening wood and shiny squares of tile covered the floors. The huge open staircase was of gleaming oak. There were four fireplaces, fashioned of wood and stone natural to the area, and enough space to keep Annie, their housekeeper for as long as Julianne could remember, busy full-time. Julianne knew every inch of it, loved every square foot.

She turned off the ignition and jumped down from the Blazer, running lightly up the steps to the huge porch that stretched across the front of the house. She slipped in the front door and paused, letting herself become immersed in the quiet peace that always seemed to linger in the air here. Just breathing it brought her comfort. For several moments she stood and did just that.

As she walked through the hallway to the kitchen, she noted that nothing seemed to have changed in the house. The same pictures graced the walls, the same framed photos adorned tabletops. She hadn't realized until that minute how much she'd needed that unswerving consistency. Especially now.

She poked her head into the kitchen. "What's a person have to do to get offered a glass of lemonade around here?"

Annie didn't startle; Julianne never had been able to surprise the woman. She just looked over her shoulder as if she'd been expecting company, her voice matter-of-fact. "A guest would have one fixed for her. A woman without the sense to let us know when to expect her will just have to pour her own. There's a fresh pitcher in the refrigerator."

Unfooled by her tone, Julianne put her arms around the woman's shoulders and squeezed. "How are you, Annie?"

The housekeeper took her hands from the dough she'd been kneading and wiped them on a towel. Then she turned around and gave Julianne a fierce hug, her dark head barely reaching the younger woman's chin. Though it hadn't been quite a year since their last reunion, Annie's hair was threaded with even more silver. Julianne tried not to feel guilty for being the cause of the gray hairs, and failed.

"About time you came home, girl."

Julianne loosened her arms and stepped back. "I just finalized my flight yesterday."

Undaunted by the verbal dodging, Annie said, "I meant after that business in Florida."

Julianne took a glass from the cupboard and went to the refrigerator, as much to avoid the woman's steady gaze as from thirst. "Oh. That."

"Yes, that," the woman mimicked. She followed Julianne to the table and sat beside her. "We read a little about it in the papers." She went on, despite Julianne's wince. "You should have let us know you were in trouble."

Julianne brought the glass to her lips and drank to cool a throat that had gone suddenly dry. "I wanted to come," she murmured. "You can't know how much. But it's getting past time for me to learn to clean up my own messes, hasn't it? And I didn't want Jed thinking he had to ride to the rescue." She particularly hadn't wanted that.

The other woman opened her mouth, then pressed her lips firmly together again. After a moment she said briskly, "Well, you're home now, even if you did take your own sweet time getting here. Things will get better, you'll see. Have you talked to Harley lately?"

Julianne nodded, the tightness easing from her muscles at the change of topic. "Tracked him down through his service about ten days ago. He was in Vegas. Sounded like he was having quite a string of luck."

Annie raised an eyebrow when Julianne didn't go on. "That's all he had to say?"

"Pretty much. I told him I was coming back to the ranch, and he mentioned something about having a bodacious babe waiting for him. He had to run." She smiled at the obvious disapproval on the housekeeper's face. "What did you think, Annie? That he would suddenly go all fatherly on me? I've long since given up expecting that. So should you."

Giving a sniff, the woman replied, "It shouldn't be too much to hope that the man would just once do his duty by you."

Julianne stifled the pang the words brought. She'd long ago accepted Harley's shortcomings. Loving her father didn't prevent her from seeing him with realistic eyes. The reality might have fostered bitterness if there hadn't been other people in her life who had given her what Harley couldn't. The woman standing before her was one of them. Julianne didn't remember the mother who'd died shortly after her birth. Annie had always served as that figure for her, despite the fact that Harley had married Jed's mother. The beautiful Kimberley hadn't been much of a parent to the son she'd adopted with her first husband, and she and Julianne had done little more than co-exist. When the marriage had broken up after five years or so, Kimberley had left and Jed had chosen to stay. Her leaving hadn't mattered to Julianne. Annie had been the constant in her life, providing advice, admonitions and support with equanimity.

Rising, she went to the sink, rinsed her glass and set it in the dishwasher. Habits drilled into her a lifetime ago by this woman were still with her. "I think I'll go upstairs and rest a bit. Dinner's at six?"

The woman nodded, then a frown formed between her brows. "How did you get here? I didn't think to ask."

"Rented a Blazer." Julianne waved away the next words Annie would have spoken. "I didn't want to put anyone out."

"Well, just leave your bags. I'll get one of the men to take them up for you later."

Glad to agree, Julianne reached out to give the woman another tight hug. "It's good to be home, Annie."

The housekeeper's eyes were suspiciously bright when Julianne stepped away. "About time, too. Get on with you. I've got just enough time to whip up something special for dinner. Isn't Jed going to be surprised?"

Smiling weakly, Julianne agreed. Jed was surely going to be surprised.

Once she was out of Annie's sight, Julianne took the steps two at a time. Her old bedroom had always seemed an oasis of tranquillity. Peace had been in short supply recently, and she was going to enjoy having it here. She was going to enjoy every aspect of being home.

Flinging open the door of the room that had always been hers, she stepped back in time. It was the only room in the house to have carpet covering the hardwood floor. She'd complained about its icy surface too many winter mornings, and for her sixteenth birthday it had been covered in a soft, plush forest green. The rest of the room had been redecorated at that time, as well, with the pale yellow walls and the tiny floral print in the matching curtains and bedspread. It had always reminded her of a corner of the forest, with its warm colors and quiet serenity.

But the serenity she'd been expecting was missing. As soon as she stepped into the room and saw the man bending over her luggage, she knew the reason why.

"Jed."

Her voice was a whisper trapped in her throat, but he dropped the bags he'd been carrying and straightened, as if he'd known she was there. Perhaps he had. Jed had always seemed to know all manner of things.

"Jules." His voice was inflectionless, his face, below the brim of his hat, more so. He nodded to the mound of luggage at his feet. "Is this all you've brought?"

If there was a hint of sarcasm in his tone, she chose to ignore it. "I'm traveling light," she said, moving into the room and facing him.

Time had always been very good to Jed. If anything, his shoulders had grown broader, his thighs harder, his jaw firmer. Though his hat shielded his eyes, she knew they were a cool, direct gray, a startling contrast to the tan he acquired from working outdoors. Beneath the hat, his dark hair curled a bit in back of his ears, telling her better than words that it had been too long since it had last been cut. His nose had a slight bump in it, a legacy of the time he'd lost a battle of wills with a half-wild stallion. He carried an aura of simple male confidence, and a maddening arrogance, glossed with a sheen of unmistakable danger.

She'd long since recovered from her adolescent fascination with that aura, just as she'd long since given up trying to impress him. So she blamed the sudden tripping of her pulse and the knot in her throat on a justifiable appearance of nerves. Jed Sullivan was the last person with whom she wanted to discuss the excruciating details of her marriage. The last to whom she'd admit just how alone she felt right now, how uncertain about her future.

She tossed him a careless little smile and crossed to the bed, dropping down on it in a studiedly casual pose. "Does Annie know you're wearing your boots in the house?"

His mouth curled a fraction. "What she doesn't know won't hurt her."

"Well." She aimed a bright smile at him and wished with all her might that he'd stayed outside, wherever he'd been. She'd counted on a few hours in which to gather her defenses before facing him. How like Jed to make that impossible. "Thanks so much for the service." She nodded toward the suitcases. "You didn't have to do that. How did you know I was home?"

"Hard to miss the dust you kicked up. You always did drive like a bat out of hell."

Shoving down her annoyance at his words, she replied smoothly, "I didn't figure I'd see you until dinner."

He gave a negligent shrug, one twitch of a massive shoulder. "I was at the bunkhouse talking to Gabe. Saw the Blazer tearing up the road and figured it was you. I expected you to call when your plane got in. I would have come and gotten you."

"I didn't see any point in you wasting an entire day away from the ranch."

"Wouldn't have taken me long. I bought a little four-seater Cessna a few years back. I could have picked you up at the airport. There was no need for you to rent a car."

She looked at him in surprise. "You bought a plane? Do you fly it yourself?"

She didn't need his nod to have her answer. Of course he did. She had never known a man so completely self-sufficient. She doubted he'd ever failed at anything in his life. Somehow, right now, that knowledge seemed particularly intolerable.

Her eyes widened when he took a pack of cigarettes out of his pocket, shook one out and lit it. *In the house.* "Oh, man, you are going straight to hell. Annie will see to it personally."

"It's your bedroom," he reasoned. "Who do you think she's going to blame?"

"Jerk. Put that out before she tracks you down like the dog you are."

He shook his head and crossed the room, sitting down on the bed beside her. He picked up a pretty little painted clay bowl she'd made when she was about nine. Sensing his intent, she leaned over to make a grab for it. "Oh, no, you don't. You're not turning that into an ashtray."

With a rare flash of teeth, Jed grinned and held the bowl out of her reach.

Julianne stretched farther. "You're still a bully. I see some things haven't changed."

"And you've still got a temper like quicksilver. That hasn't changed, either."

She sent him an annoyed look, and their proximity finally registered. Their struggle had had her reaching across him, and for an instant she let herself inhale the aroma of tobacco, horses and the raw, elemental male scent of Jed. His firm mouth was still curved in amusement, at her expense, and was too close to hers for comfort. Belatedly, questioning the wisdom of their little tug-of-war, she dropped her hand and straightened. Prudence would have had her moving off the bed and putting some needed distance between them. Pride wouldn't allow it.

"Don't say I didn't warn you. I just hope I'm there to see Annie take the big wooden spoon to your ornery hide."

Utterly relaxed, he brought the cigarette to his lips and inhaled. "As I recall, you were much better acquainted with the big bad spoon than I was."

"Only because you started perfecting your sneaky streak at a shockingly young age."

"Stealthy," he corrected her, blowing a smoke ring and admiring it as it hung in the air. "And your problem was you were all flash and impulse. Always tried to grab what you wanted without putting any forethought into it." His voice sobered and he added, "Which pretty well describes how you got mixed up in that crazy marriage of yours, doesn't it?"

Pride be damned, there was no way she was going to sit inches away from Jed Sullivan while having this particular conversation. Rising, she crossed to her luggage, picked up a bag and carried it to the dresser. Setting it on top of the surface, she unzipped it and began to empty its contents into drawers.

With a casualness she was far from feeling, she said, "Oh, I won't bore you with the tedious details of my marriage."

"No need. The tabloids were full of them. Not to mention the segments on 'Who's News' and 'First Copy.' The media has always had an uncommon interest in millionaire orphan, Andrew Richfield." Derision laced his voice. "He never seemed to mind the attention until recently."

She winced. She'd deliberately stopped watching TV and reading the newspapers. As usual, the rumors and speculation had been even worse than the facts. Whenever she'd called the ranch, she'd been deliberately vague about the mess, hoping that Montana was far enough removed from the playground of the rich in the Florida Keys to keep most of the story from filtering this far. Apparently she'd been overly optimistic.

One suitcase emptied, she zipped it up and put it aside, moving to another. "How bad was it?"

He took his time answering. "Actually, after the first couple of stories your name wasn't mentioned much. Just Richfield's. There was plenty about his appetite for women, drugs and gambling. Quite a prince you had there."

There was no mistaking the contempt in his tone. Julianne wondered miserably if it was all directed at Andrew, or if some of it was pointed at her. She didn't dare ask. Right now she wasn't sure she could deal with his answer.

"Well." She was relieved to note that her voice

sounded steady. "Sounds like you got all the highlights. You'll understand why I felt the need for a change of scenery." And then, because she couldn't help herself, she asked, "Was Annie very worried?"

She hadn't realized he'd moved until she heard him behind her, felt his knuckle brush her jaw. Swinging around, she found herself caught between the surface of the dresser and Jed's hard body. He crooked a finger beneath her chin, tilted it up.

"We both were."

She squeezed her eyes shut for a moment, regret washing up in waves. "I would have given anything to avoid that. I hoped the whole mess would blow over. I didn't want anyone here to be touched by it."

For a moment, his thumb grazed the soft skin below her jawline. "Anything that affects you touches us, too, Jules. You should know that."

His unexpected gentleness was almost her undoing. It would be so easy to lean on him, to let his solid strength take her weight, to let him absorb some of the hurt and desperation that had ridden her for so long. It was tempting to just let go, to allow someone else to take care of her for a change. The strength of that temptation frightened her.

She strove for lightness. "God, Jed, you're not going to be sweet, are you? I can handle anything but that."

His hand dropped away, and, blessedly, he took a step back. "Just tell me that you're okay now."

That, at least, she could answer honestly. "I am, now that I'm home. You don't know how much I needed to see the ranch again."

His brooding gaze held hers for a long, steady minute. "Makes it hard to figure, then, why you took your own sweet time coming home."

The moment of danger had passed. She turned back to her unpacking. "Well, I had things to do. Dodging the media was top of my list."

"Not to mention the police."

"They were tenacious, too," she replied carelessly. "But they listened to reason soon enough."

"Pretty understanding, were they?" The sarcasm in his voice was thinly veiled.

"Once they had the facts. I wasn't even on the ship the night it was raided."

"I understand that some said otherwise."

Her mouth twisted bitterly. "Times like these you find out who your friends are, don't you?"

"Yeah, you do. But if it took you this long to figure out that your best friends are right here, you're a bigger fool than I ever thought."

She whirled to see him stalking away, and he didn't bother to stop the door from slamming behind him. Weakly, she propped her weight against the dresser, a rueful smile curving her lips. That abrupt, blunt statement was so like Jed. Apparently there were some fences to be mended before she could settle in to life at the ranch again. She didn't mind. Although she and Jed had had their share of spats, they'd always gotten along fairly well. She'd obviously ruffled his male pride by not asking for his help at the first sign of trouble in Florida.

She took a deep breath and strove to calm the fluttering in her stomach. It must surely be due to some quirk in her nature that she preferred his temper to that uncustomary gentleness. Facing Jed in a temper was like riding into a storm: exhilarating, bracing and a little scary.

But tenderness from him...

That was nothing short of terrifying.

Chapter 2

"Hope you've got time for an old friend before this slave driver starts cracking the whip."

Jed watched impassively as Julianne launched herself into Gabe Hathaway's open arms. The older man was their senior hand. Harley had inherited him with the ranch. But he'd been much more than that to Julianne, and to Jed, too. He'd taught them both how to ride, shoot and rope. He'd been full of wisdom and encouragement when they'd needed it, and hadn't been above a bit of butt-chewing when they'd needed that. If Annie was general of the house, Gabe was admiral of the ranch.

Right now the man's seamed, weathered face was split in a wide grin. "About time we had you home again. You're looking good, Julianne. Real good."

Silently, Jed agreed. Her curling swing of hair was the color of polished gold, impossibly shiny and bright. Although the color hadn't changed since she'd lived at the ranch, the style had. Instead of a brilliant spill down her back, it was cut to curve below her jaw, framing that fancy face. With her elegant cheekbones and short, straight nose, she would have looked haughty if not for those wide, expressive brown eyes. At an early age she'd learned that it took only one soulful look from those big eyes to turn an unsuspecting man's brain to mush. She'd used the skill shamelessly. Though her bones were small, nothing about her suggested fragility. Her personality was too damn strong for her to ever be considered weak.

Maybe that's what was bothering him now, he thought, turning away from the reunion before him. He was too used to Julianne flaring up or steaming full ahead when trouble brewed. That hint of vulnerability he'd observed yesterday in her room had had an unexpected knot of tension coiling in his gut. He wished he hadn't recognized it; wished instead he could believe the nonchalant air she'd worn at dinner. Despite her efforts to convince them otherwise, it was plain that Julianne had taken some hard knocks in the last few years.

And she'd never once let on to him about any of them.

The thought had his hands clenching at his sides. Maybe that's what had made him fire up at her so quickly yesterday. God knows, he'd like to shake the little fool for not telling him or Annie about the depth of trouble she'd found herself in. When that idiot she'd married had seemed intent on descending into a pit of self-destruction, he'd almost managed to pull Julianne down with him.

Consciously, Jed uncurled his fingers. That was over now. She was free of Andrew Richfield and back at the ranch. Gabe and Annie wouldn't be the only ones welcoming her home. She'd been a favorite with the neighbors; most of them, at least. He seemed to recall some of her pranks in high school earning her a couple of enemies. An unwilling smile tugged at his lips. She'd always been a handful, but life around her stayed interesting.

"Ain't that right, Jed?"

He turned to face Gabe, who was beaming at him. "What's that?"

"I was telling Julie girl that there's been big changes at the ranch since she was here last."

"Since she's barely been home for the last seven years, I imagine it's going to seem that way to her."

"Well, it certainly wasn't the prospect of your charming personality that drew me home, big guy," Julianne drawled. He slanted a glance her way. The light amusement on her face was a kick in the ego. Sarcasm was wasted on her; she skated right by it. It was one of her more annoying traits.

"Are you planning on showing her around, Jed?" Gabe asked.

Before he could open his mouth, Julianne answered quickly, "I'm just going to wander around by myself, see what's new."

"She can tag along with me today," Jed replied. He felt a flicker of satisfaction at the visible start she gave at his words.

Gabe nodded, as if it had been all decided. "Well, I gotta get to work and earn my paycheck." He winked at Julianne. "See ya later, won't I?"

She smiled at the older man, that punch-in-the-gut smile of hers, the one she rarely wasted on Jed. "You know you will. Can I get in on a game of poker some night?"

Guffawing, Gabe nodded. "You betcha. Got plenty of new hands since you've been here last. They'll be easy pigeons."

The sunlight slanted and bounced over her hair when

she tossed her head back and laughed. "That's what I like to hear."

Jed got a mental image of Julianne in the bunkhouse playing cards with the hands, and for some reason it didn't set well. She'd done so in the past, he remembered, when she'd still been in high school. Before the men had figured out that those batting eyes and sunny smile disguised the soul of a cardsharp, they'd been cleaned out several times. Cards were the one thing Harley had taken the time to teach his daughter, and she was ruthless. Not to mention being a consummate bluffer. But she wasn't a kid anymore, and some of these hands weren't men she'd grown up with.

"C'mon," Jed said abruptly, turning on his heel. "I'll show you our new foaling barn, then we'll take the truck. I need to check on the herd in the north pasture. You can ride along."

"No, you go ahead. I'm just going to poke around on my own."

He stopped and turned back to her. She slipped her fingertips into the back pockets of her jeans and smiled winningly. With the back of his hand, he pushed up his hat and surveyed her. "It's not like you to pass up an opportunity to tag along and pester me with a thousand questions."

She gave a shrug, and her smile never faltered. Only someone who knew her well would have seen the hint of nerves in her eyes, and wondered at it.

His gaze narrowed. He figured he knew Julianne better than most. At least he once had. "Like Gabe said, we made some improvements around here. If you want to know what they are, come with me. Otherwise, get yourself back to the house and stay out of the way."

Her gold hair swirled as she angled her chin, and her

eyes spit sparks. "You don't give me orders, Jed. You never did."

The corner of his mouth tilted. Despite any other changes Julianne might have undergone, her temper had remained the same. She flared up as easily as dry twigs in a campfire. "The way I remember it, I gave plenty of orders. You just didn't follow them."

"And what makes you think anything is different now?"

"Everything's different," he said, suddenly serious. "Isn't that why you came back?"

Emotion flashed across her face so quickly he couldn't be sure he'd seen it at all. For a moment, he thought she'd turn away without a word. Then that slow, mocking smile, the one she seemed to reserve especially for him, curved those full lips, and she sauntered toward him.

"You win. Lead on, O Mighty One."

His eyes slit. He didn't know why it should continually surprise him that inside that luscious-looking mouth lurked the tongue of a baby viper. He strode toward the foaling barn, leaving her to catch up to him. Not that she tried, of course. She strolled along behind him at a hip-swinging pace set by some senseless god and entered the barn a good five minutes after him.

By that time he was already deep in a discussion with Les, the hand in charge of the foals and yearlings, leaving Julianne to roam the place on her own.

When he joined her again, she was holding a colt's muzzle in her hands, petting the velvety softness and cooing to it in a lilting voice. "Oh, you're a precious one, aren't you? You're a sweet thing, yes, you are. Who's your daddy, hmm? I'll bet it's one of those mean old stallions who breed champions and get the better of Jed occasionally. Is that what you're going to do, pretty boy? Are you going to get big and love the ladies and whip up on mean, old Jed?''

"Don't give him any ideas," he said dryly. "His sire has the worst temper on the ranch. I'm hoping this one's got his dam's temperament."

She aimed an innocent look at him. "Isn't it a coincidence that the males have the orneriest dispositions, in both the animal and human worlds?"

He ignored the gibe and reached out to smooth a hand down the colt's smooth brown neck. "This one's not going to get a chance for much of a love life, I'm afraid. In another few months he'll be a gelding."

"Shh!" She covered the colt's ears with her hands and fixed Jed with a reproachful look. "Don't talk like that in front of the baby."

Her teasing tone lightened something inside him. He reached out and tugged at a strand of her bright gold hair. "A soft heart doesn't go far on a working ranch, Jules. You know that."

She wrinkled her nose at him, much as she had when she was a kid. For a moment he was transported back to the time he'd first come to the ranch. Five years his junior, she'd been a precocious one. She'd had the run of the place and had been miserably spoiled by most of the adults on it. That is, with the exception of the one whose attention she'd most craved—her father's.

That had been another bond between them, one he'd never put into words. He hadn't known his real father, and his adoptive one, Luther Templeton III, had never had much interest in a family. As a stepfather, Harley had treated Jed just as he did his own daughter, alternating between sporadic, careless indulgence and long periods of inattentiveness. The ranch had been the first solid thing in Jed's life that he could hold on to, and at one time it had represented the same for Julianne. He wondered how much it still did.

"Annie said you'd talked to Harley."

She nodded, giggling when the colt nuzzled her shirt pocket, unashamedly begging for treats. "It wasn't much of a conversation. I reached his service, then he called me back from Las Vegas. Sounded like he'd run into some good luck. He had to rush out to continue his streak."

Jed reached down to a bag of oats propped next to the stall door and distracted the colt from Julianne's chest with a handful. "He was in Reno when I spoke to him a couple weeks ago. He said he was going to speak to you." Had been promising to for weeks, as a matter of fact. He should be used to broken promises from Harley, but he didn't remember a time when one had bothered him as much as this one did.

She lifted a shoulder. "You know Harley. I only had him on the phone two minutes before he had to run to the next card game."

"Yeah," Jed said grimly. "I know Harley." Any other father would have been concerned about the situation his daughter had found herself in. Most would insist on flying to her side, to try to shelter her from the worst of the fallout from that mess in Florida. But not Julianne's father.

"How come this guy's in the foaling barn?" she asked.

Jed fed the colt one last handful of oats, then shook his head at the horse. The beast would eat all day if allowed. "He snagged a back fetlock on the barbed wire. Got a nasty gash. The vet came and took care of him, but we need to keep it clean for a few days. Then he can go back to the fields with his mama."

They walked through the nearly empty barn. Although it was usually full in spring, most of the foals were pastured with their mothers when they were a few weeks old.

When they exited, Jed led her to a gleaming red, half-ton pickup. "Hop in. I want to take you to the new cattle barn we're building, and it's a ways from here." He could see the slight stiffening in her shoulders before she shook her head.

"I don't mind walking."

He stopped in his tracks and looked hard at her. He wasn't used to seeing her this edgy, and a sudden thought bloomed and twisted through him viciously. He strode over to her and took her elbow, forced her to face him. "What's going on, Julianne?"

Her eyes met his, startled, wary. "What do you mean?"

"You've been nothing but nerves every time I'm within two feet of you. Is it me? Or any man?" His voice went lethal as he voiced the questions, and his fingers tightened unconsciously. "Was it Richfield? Did he hurt you?"

Her gaze widened as she caught his meaning, and she shook her head vehemently. "No, Jed, nothing like that. Andrew had more than his share of vices, but hitting women wasn't one of them."

He dropped his hand as relief coursed through him. "Then what?"

She lifted a shoulder. "I guess you're right. I've been a little nerved-up lately. But it doesn't have anything to do with you."

Unconvinced, he continued to watch her, but her eyes were cool and dark, revealing nothing. Out of patience, he turned away. If there was something riding Julianne, he wouldn't find out about it until she was good and ready to tell him. The last several months had proved that.

"Get in the truck, then," he said brusquely. "I'll show you the barn we've got going up. It was supposed to be done last week, but they ran into some supply problems and missed the deadline." He opened the door and swung into the truck. After the briefest of hesitations, she complied. He drove the quarter of a mile to the structure.

The building was little more than a massive skeleton. As they walked up to the framed building, she said disbelievingly, "Good Lord, it's going to be huge. What in heaven's name is it for?"

"We've added to the herd, and we'll be expanding more." He pointed to a far corner that had been framed off. "I have plans to leave space there for a veterinary office. When there's a problem, we'll have some basic equipment right here."

"That will be convenient. Is Mike Lytrell still the vet around here?"

Jed nodded. "He's got an assistant now. He wanted to take it a little easier. Haven't noticed that he's slowed down much, though. We'll still be using the old barn, too. We're going to need them both."

"This is wonderful," she said, turning a shining gaze on him. The sincerity in her voice uncurled a ribbon of pride deep inside him. Then she continued, and just as quickly the feeling withered. "I can't believe that Harley is finally taking an interest in the ranch again. All these changes…" She indicated the structure with one hand. "He must be planning to come back here for good."

He chose his words with care. "I don't really know what Harley's immediate plans are. I know he wants to see you, though. I was surprised when you said he didn't show up in Florida."

She tilted her head back to examine the high ceiling. "I'd much rather see him here. I'm glad he didn't choose to put up another metal building. We have enough of those, and I think a wooden structure adds character, don't you?"

"Jules…"

"I wonder why Harley didn't mention his plans for the

ranch when I talked to him.'' Then, just as quickly, she shook her head, laughed a little. ''What am I saying? I couldn't keep him on the phone long enough to say much more than hello.'' She looked at Jed. ''Did he give you any indication of when he'd be moving back?''

Jed stared hard at those wide brown eyes, that expressive face, and silently cursed. Not for the first time, he damned Harley Buchanan to hell. ''Jules, listen to me. Your father isn't coming home. At least, not to stay.''

She blinked slowly, and a feeling of guilt pooled in Jed's chest, sprouting fangs as the hope faded from her eyes.

''But…why would he do all this, then? Why would he care about expanding the herd and improving the conditions here, if…''

''Harley isn't making all these improvements. I am.'' He looked away, wished for a cigarette. He didn't reach for one though. They were too close to the new structure, and caution on a ranch was ingrained in him. ''My adoptive father, Luther Templeton, died last year.''

She nodded slowly. ''You mentioned that on one of your visits to Florida.''

''He left me everything.'' Even now, the knowledge gave him no pleasure. The man had never been Jed's father in any real sense of the word. Being named his heir had seemed the height of irony. ''I guess he didn't want his estate to go to one of his ex-wives.'' He gave a shrug, as if it didn't matter. And it didn't. Not anymore.

He consciously gentled his voice when he looked back at Julianne. ''But that's the money being poured into the ranch, Jules. Not Harley's.''

Her face went smooth and blank. ''Well, that makes sense, I guess. It was foolish to think he was going to change his priorities at this point in his life, wasn't it?''

She turned and walked back toward the entrance, and Jed followed reluctantly. Although he knew it was illogical, he couldn't help feeling responsible for this latest disappointment of hers.

Harley, he thought grimly, *you're lucky you're not close enough for me to get my hands around your throat.* The first thing he was going to do after supper, he vowed, was to call the man again and demand that he hop the next plane out here. There was a great deal he owed his daughter. It was time someone forced him to live up to his obligations.

Julianne didn't mention her father for the rest of the day. She rode with Jed, inspecting the various outbuildings, listening and asking questions when he filled her in on the changes that had been made, and the reasons for them. As he pulled up in the ranch yard, he reflected that he'd talked more that afternoon than he had in a week. The ranch was one subject that he and Julianne had never had problems communicating about.

He stopped in the mudroom off the kitchen to get rid of his dusty boots, and Julianne went to her room to change for dinner. It was just too damn bad, he thought grimly, as he grasped the heel of a boot and tugged, that the two of them couldn't seem to talk about any other subject as calmly.

The second boot joined the first, then he headed upstairs for a shower and change. Like it or not, the time was rapidly approaching when they were going to have to broach some ticklish subjects.

The certainty of the fireworks to follow made his temples thud in painful anticipation.

"Great meal, as usual, Annie." Julianne placed the last dish in the dishwasher, filled the receptacle with soap and turned it on. The other woman finished wiping off the table, and Julianne sat down again, a sense of comfortable familiarity flowing through her.

After Harley's failed marriage, his gambling excursions had grown more frequent and longer in duration. He'd failed to return at all from one trip he took when Julianne had been sixteen. With single-minded focus, he'd chased one streak after another: cards, horses, casinos. There had really been no one moment when the realization had hit her that her father, such as he was, wasn't coming back to live at the ranch. Certainly, he'd never come right out and said so. But there had always been another game, another race, another high stakes purse to go after. Life on the ranch had moved seamlessly on.

One night, instead of eating in the dining room with its mile-long walnut table and formal wallpaper, Annie had set their places in the kitchen with her. Jed and Julianne had eaten there ever since. She remembered many dark winter nights when she and Annie had sat here after dinner playing rummy or just talking, while the savage Montana wind had blown snowdrifts up to the eaves of the house. There was still a cozy feel to the kitchen; still a sense of coming home.

"Sit down, Annie. Everything's done. Just relax."

The woman closed the cupboard she'd been wiping out. "Easy for you to say," she replied, with no sting in her voice. "This blasted house doesn't clean itself, you know, and it's not getting any smaller." She started to scrub at the counter with brisk movements. When Julianne rose to help, she was waved away, so she sank back into her chair.

Once dinner was over, Jed had retired to the study, a habit Julianne remembered from her teen years. After putting in a twelve-hour day on the ranch, there were always markets to be checked, a mound of paperwork to be done.

With a start, she realized that he had taken over the role of running the ranch long before Harley had left. Certainly he'd played a part in its daily operations since he'd first come here. Harley had always been content to leave the major decisions to Gabe, who acted as the ranch foreman. When Jed had shown the interest and the knowledge, he'd gradually been given more authority. She supposed she would have been jealous if she didn't recognize exactly where the ranch would be today without Jed's management.

When she thought of how much he had invested in the place, financially, physically and emotionally, she felt the initial tuggings of guilt. She'd never thought about how her plans for coming back here might affect Jed. Even as a young child she'd been aware of Harley's pendulum of luck. He'd made and lost more fortunes than even he could keep track of. But after years of pestering, she'd gotten his promise that he'd hang on to the ranch for her, and she'd made certain he'd kept his vow.

This place was a part of her, as it was a part of Jed. He'd been the one to keep it running in her absence; he'd been the one to expand its operations. She stroked the wood grain on the table absently. She should have known better than to assume that Harley was responsible for the latest improvements at the ranch. He'd always been more anxious to siphon money away than to sink any into it. Jed must have had to work some magic on the man over the years to keep him from bankrupting the place. And now it was his own money he was sinking into it to keep it running.

She pushed aside the sense of unease. Nothing had to change; surely they could co-exist here peacefully enough. Today had proved that they could get along remarkably well, when they were talking about the ranch. And that was all she was willing to talk to him about.

She almost winced as she remembered the conclusion he'd drawn about the reason for her edginess. There were a great many things she could and did blame Andrew for, but he wasn't the cause of her show of nerves today. The cause had been Jed himself.

Julianne raised an unsteady hand to push her hair back from her face. It must be the recent stress that had her so unnaturally aware of the man, so skittish around him. Whatever the cause, she was anxious to return to the soothing routine of life on the ranch. There was safety in resuming the old familiar relationship with Jed. Her lips quirked. However that was defined.

Annie finished scrubbing the kitchen spotless and laid the washrag over the faucet with a sigh. "Should I get the cards out?"

"Go ahead, if you're that anxious to get fleeced."

She took a deck of cards, a pen and paper from a drawer and seated herself across from Julianne. "As I recollect, I cleaned you out more often than not."

Grinning, Julianne shook her head. "Age will do that to a person's memory, I hear. But if it makes you feel better to think so…" She dodged the pencil Annie flicked in her direction.

"Age, is it? We'll see about that, miss. Same stakes as usual—a penny a point. Go ahead and deal those cards. And none from the bottom, mind you. I was on to your tricks long ago."

Expertly, Julianne shuffled and dealt the cards. She picked them up and arranged them, and the two settled down for some friendly competition.

"I talked to Gabe today," Julianne said, drawing a card and discarding another.

"Good. He's missed you something fierce, just like the rest of us. I know you called him when you could, but he didn't get down to Florida to see you like Jed and I did. He's going to enjoy having you back."

Memories of those trips to Florida had discomfort flickering. Jed had brought Annie out at least twice a year. After the first couple of years of her marriage, it had gotten more and more difficult to hide her dissatisfaction with it. And certainly impossible to admit that the dire warnings Jed had uttered about her choice in husbands had proved true.

Annie picked up one of Julianne's discards with a sound of satisfaction, and Julianne made a mental note of what the woman was collecting. "Did you roam the ranch over today?"

Julianne nodded, then corrected herself. "Well, I got a start, anyway. Sounds like Jed has some big plans for changes."

The other woman nodded. "He's determined, our Jed is. I don't think there's anything he can't do once he sets his mind to it. He's a good man—takes care of his own." Studying her cards, she clucked her tongue absently. A sign, if Julianne remembered correctly, that the woman was close to gin.

Annie drew another card. "You might be surprised to find out how much folks around these parts have started depending on him. Looking up to him."

She managed, barely, to avoid rolling her eyes. "I'm sure he enjoys that. I know he always expected me to treat his opinion as if it had been brought down from a mountain, chiseled on stone tablets."

"Now, Julianne," Annie scolded, "that's just not true. Jed's got some mighty fine qualities, if you'd just take the time to remember."

Tilting her head, she pretended to try to summon those memories Annie spoke of. ''I remember that his blood runs hot, and so does his temper. But it's when he's the coolest, the quietest, that he's the most dangerous.'' She remembered other things, too, memories much more recent. The way his hair still fell across his forehead despite his efforts to comb it back severely; the flex of the muscles in his arms when he'd dragged the heavy gates open so the truck could enter the north pasture; the heat that had transferred from his hands to her skin when she'd been unable to avoid his help getting back into the pickup.

She ducked her head to hide the color she could feel blooming in her cheeks. Those certainly weren't the type of memories to be shared with Annie. Or harbored herself, for that matter.

''Neither of you ever did give the other an ounce of credit if it could be helped. But try as you might to deny it, you always looked up to Jed, just as he watched out for you. That protective streak of his is still a mile wide. Why, after he and his lawyer visited a few of those newspapers down there in Florida, they stopped including you in that trash they were printing soon enough.''

The air clogged in Julianne's lungs, and for a moment she forgot to breathe. Forcing the words through stiffened lips, Julianne said, ''Jed…was in Florida…before the divorce?''

Annie looked up quickly, regret shimmering in her dark eyes. ''Oh, I'm sorry, honey, I meant not to tell you. Jed thought it best if we kept it to ourselves.''

''Did he?'' Emotion bubbled and churned just beneath the surface. Through the tangle of sick feelings circling in her stomach, she plucked out anger and focused on it. It was infinitely more comfortable to fix on her fury than the shamed panic that arose when she thought of Jed hearing

all the messy details of the scandal that had rocked her
life. Details that she'd gone to considerable length to be
sure no one here would have to know. "I don't suppose
it occurred to him that if I'd needed his help I would have
called."

Annie gave up all pretense of playing cards, her discom-
fiture apparent. "I don't know how he got wind of it,
honey. But you know he takes all those newspapers for
the stock reports. He must have read something about it in
one of them. And I have to tell you, I've never seen the
man more enraged than he was that day. He just stomped
upstairs, threw some clothes into a bag and hopped on a
plane."

"Without a word to me," Julianne murmured. The cards
dropped from her nerveless fingers. That entire scene yesterday in her bedroom took on new meaning. He'd led her
to believe that the facts he knew of the debacle with Andrew had been gleaned from the media. The thought of
him down there, in the midst of all the rumors and innu-
endoes, made nausea roll greasily in her stomach.

Reaching across the table, Annie grasped her hand. "He
was in a temper, Julianne, some of it aimed at you for not
telling him. I've never seen him in such a state. It was
better he handled it the way he did."

She concentrated on moving air in and out of her lungs.
That single act seemed to require a great deal of attention.
"Maybe you ought to tell me what else you know."

Annie sat back in her chair. "I don't think…"

"I do," she interrupted flatly.

Annie regarded her steadily, her gaze reflecting all the
wisdom and compassion she'd drawn on to raise Julianne
to adulthood. "He hired a fancy lawyer out there, and they
paid some visits to a few of the newspapers, threatening
libel lawsuits. Since most of the details they were writing

about you were speculation, they backed off quickly enough. And then he went to see Andrew.''

Shock held her still. ''Andrew? Why?''

Annie shook her head. ''Jed didn't share the details with me. But there was murder in his eye when he left here. I don't think things went too well for your ex.''

Julianne closed her eyes, embarrassment clawing up inside her. Sir Jed, riding to the rescue. He wouldn't have trusted that she would be capable of dealing with the mess on her own. No, he'd just figured that spoiled, frivolous Julianne, party girl of the Keys, lacked the intelligence to extricate herself from the situation.

She welcomed the anger boiling in her veins. ''What could he possibly have hoped to gain by seeing Andrew?''

''I don't know, honey. I've said too much already. You'll just have to take that up with Jed.''

Julianne rose, her fingers clutching the edge of the table tightly. ''Yes,'' she agreed grimly. ''I think that's exactly what I'm going to have to do.''

Chapter 3

When the door to his study banged open, Jed looked up, annoyed. But seeing Julianne sailing toward him with fire in her eyes and fingers curled had him rising, immediately wary. He rounded the desk toward her, involuntarily admiring the sight of her in a storm. Quick reflexes had him dodging the fist she aimed at his chin. He didn't quite manage to avoid the one she sent into his midsection. Air hissed out between his clenched teeth before he could prevent it. The little wildcat had always had a hell of a right. He sidestepped to evade the knee aimed to damage his chances for future offspring and caught her fists in his hands. Pulling her toward him off balance, he gave her a shake. "What the hell is the matter with you?"

"You...low-down, scum-sucking...sneak!" She threw the hair out of her eyes with a toss of her head and attempted to tug free. "Let me go! I'd like to break your stubborn, know-it-all jaw for you!"

He knew from experience she'd try to do just that, so

he gave her another shake. "Settle down. I'm not letting go until you promise to stop taking shots at me."

She gave another mighty jerk, but he held firm, his gaze locked with her murderous one. At first she remained stubbornly silent, reluctant to give her word. Once she did, he knew he could trust her to keep it. A promise from Julianne had always been gold. It came, he supposed, from a lifetime of disappointment over the ones her father had broken.

"Let me go." Some of the fury had dissipated from her voice, but her eyes remained hot. When his grip didn't loosen, she added sulkily, "I promise that no matter how much you deserve it, I won't knock your block off."

He released her hands and propped his hips against the edge of the desk. "You'd try, anyway."

Her eyes narrowed at his deliberately nonchalant tone, and she asked, too sweetly, "How's your stomach? Did I puncture anything important?"

Because a nagging ache still lingered where she'd caught him off guard, he gave her a pitying smile. "Did you get lucky and land a punch? I didn't notice."

Normally he would have enjoyed the sight of her heating up all over again. Right now he was too busy wondering what had lit a match to her temper this time. "Mind telling me what brought on this tantrum?"

"This 'tantrum,'" she said, in a measured tone that left no doubts about her lingering fury, "was brought on by discovering you went behind my back. Did you think I wouldn't find out?"

He went still, every muscle in his body drawing up in tension. His voice inflectionless, he asked, "Find out what, exactly?"

Her eyes glittered, and he could tell she was longing to throw something. "That you'd leaped on your white horse and gone charging to the rescue in Florida! What did you think you were going to do, I wonder, make it all disappear by taking on the police and media in one fell swoop?''

He released a breath, and his body relaxed, a fraction at a time. "It worked, didn't it?"

His quiet words effectively silenced her, and he could read the instant distress in her eyes. Remorse flared, only to be ruthlessly pushed aside. Somehow he'd known she'd react this way. That's why he'd done his best to ensure she never discovered the part he'd played in untangling that mess in Florida. But damned if he was going to apologize for it. If truth be known, he'd just as soon have it out in the open. There were a few home truths Julianne Buchanan needed to hear.

"I've gotten friendly with a cattle buyer in Florida. I usually visit him when I'm in the state. When the scandal broke, he recognized your name and called me, in case I hadn't heard about it from you." He made no attempt to mask the bitterness in his voice when he added, "Of course, I hadn't."

"There was a reason for that."

"There was no reason for that," he disputed, letting the anger that had simmered inside him for the past several weeks rise to the surface. "And no excuse for it. It was a slap at the people who care about you the most. How were we supposed to feel, to hear that you were in that kind of trouble and never bothered to let us know?"

She looked at him, her eyes troubled. "I told you, I didn't want my problems to hurt anyone here."

"You hurt us by shutting us out." His words scored a direct hit. For a moment, Julianne's full lips fought a tremble, before she made a visible effort to firm them. A kinder man might have stopped to soothe. Jed had never pretended to be kind.

"You might think you were trying to spare us, but it looked like you just didn't give a damn. I went to Florida to haul your butt out of trouble, because I knew Annie and Gabe would be worried sick about you when the news reached them. So if you want to come flying in here begging for a fight because I saved you from most of the misery you found yourself in, I just might oblige you."

The hand that she reached behind her was not quite steady as she pulled a chair close enough to sink into it. Once he'd finished with the cops and the press, his next urge had been to go after her and bring her home. It had taken more self-control than he'd known he'd possessed not to do so. He didn't ever remember being as cold-bloodedly furious as he had been on that trip. She was lucky he'd realized the depth of the emotion and had returned without seeing her.

She moistened her lips. "What...exactly how much do you know?"

"Everything," he said flatly. "I got a lawyer to take on the media, and we hired a private investigator to track your whereabouts that night. It took him about six hours to line up witnesses who could positively state you'd been in St. Petersburg on the night of the raid, and that satisfied the police. After another few days, he discovered there were no witnesses willing to testify to seeing you that night on the yacht Richfield was running the drugs in on."

Because he knew her so well, he could see the faint wince at his words.

"Heroin's a nasty business, Jules."

Her eyes were wide and sober. "I knew about Andrew's problems with drinking and gambling. But I swear to you, finding out that he was involved in drug smuggling was a shock."

"I figured that." Julianne had a deep-seated honesty

about her that would never have allowed her to be a part of something so contemptible. Even in his deepest fury, he'd never questioned her involvement. "One of the reasons it was so easy for the investigator to verify your movements was because you hadn't just been in St. Petersburg for a day or two. You'd been living there for over four months. Alone."

Her hands smoothed down her jeans-clad thighs, but she didn't look away. "Yes."

That single word, offered with no other explanation, sent little bubbles of anger firing through his veins. "You'd left your husband, but never saw fit to let us in on that, either. For someone who claims to care, that's pretty shabby treatment."

Her temper, always easily stoked, blazed anew. "It was my decision, my life. I don't have to report in to you. Did you let me know about every single thing that was happening in your life? Did you fill me in on every change you made here—probably without Harley's knowledge? Not hardly. So back off. I was trying to do the best I could, and things got out of control in a way I never dreamed possible."

He clenched his hands to keep from reaching for her. "Those 'things' could have sucked you in with them. Damn near did, as a matter of fact."

She bounced out of her chair, started to pace. "So what are you looking for? A thank-you for butting into my business? Well, thanks." The sneer in her voice was unmistakable. "Forgive me if I happen to think that the police just might have discovered my innocence in their own time."

"Sure," he jeered. "Maybe even before you spent a couple of days in the cell next to your beloved ex. Maybe the media would have arrived at the same conclusion, or maybe you could have just batted those pretty brown eyes at the reporters and convinced them to stop slandering you, regardless.''

She whirled on him, chest heaving with emotion, hands fisted at her sides. He paused a moment to enjoy the sight. He wondered if there was another woman born who looked as good with a snarl on her lips, the flush of anger on her face.

''I don't like secrets being kept that concern me.''

''We're even then,'' he retorted. ''I didn't much care for the secrets I learned you'd been keeping from us.'' Then, because he couldn't help himself, he asked, ''Why did you, Julianne? Why didn't you get rid of Richfield for good years ago? It surely didn't take you this long to see what he was.''

For a moment he thought she wouldn't answer. Or, if she did, that it would be only to wish him a speedy departure to hell. But then she jammed her hands in her pockets, pulling the denim tight against those long, slender thighs, and gave a sigh. ''I made a promise. That's what a marriage vow is supposed to be, isn't it? And I guess I didn't want to admit I'd failed.''

The simple emotion in her words hit him like a brick. Yeah, that was Julianne. Loyal to a fault, unwilling to break her word once she'd given it. He remembered when she'd been about fourteen, and he'd presented her with front-row tickets to see some singer she was all gooey-eyed about. She'd already promised to attend a friend's dance recital and have dinner with her afterward. Watching her fret over the decision had been almost painful to watch. But in the end, she'd accompanied her friend, as she'd said she would.

Something unfamiliar settled in the pit of his stomach and gentled his voice. ''You didn't fail. Loyalty can only be pushed so far. I never understood what you saw in Richfield, anyway.''

"He needed me." Her simple words struck hard at his chest. "I'd never been needed before. Not like that." She shook her head when he would have spoken. "Oh, I know that on the surface it looked like he had everything. His father was a shipping magnate, his mother a film star. When they died in that plane crash, he inherited a fortune, but he was emotionally adrift. He was searching for something to stabilize his life, and he thought I could anchor it. I thought so, too." Her fingers pleated the denim covering her knee, the act seeming to require a great deal of attention. "Even after I found out about the booze and the gambling, I still thought I could help him.''

"And when you found out about the other women?''

Her gaze slowly rose to meet his, and something in those wide brown eyes made him feel small. "That's when I moved out.''

He looked away. "I wish now that I'd broken more than his nose.''

Acerbically she observed, "Now, why didn't I think of that? There's nothing like a good beating to make someone straighten up, is there?''

His fingers flexed in memory. "What it lacked in finesse it made up for in sheer satisfaction.''

She regarded him for a moment, visibly torn between the urge to argue and the need to explain. He didn't know which of them was more surprised when the need won out. "I don't know how to make you understand. But I felt sorry for him. I guess, in a way, I still do.''

That had his gaze jerking back to hers, incredulity filling his voice. "What's to feel sorry for? A poor little rich boy who couldn't find the strength to face his life without a series of crutches to help him? He's no kind of man at all.''

She smiled crookedly. "Not everyone has your strength, Jed.''

"Or yours, Jules. You're the strongest woman I know, and that leech knew it, too. Like a parasite, he latched onto you as if he could force you to be strong for him. I saw that the first time I met him. I'm only sorry it took you this long to see it as well.''

She shoved a hand through her hair, pushing it away from her face. "Well, it must be immensely gratifying for you to be proved right. I'm not a fool, Jed. I know it was the start of the gambling that clouded my judgment. Harley will never want to stop, but I thought there was a chance to help Andrew....'' When he turned away with a softly muttered curse, her voice went wry. "Correction. I *am* a fool. But I had to try. I've seen firsthand the kind of havoc gambling can wreak on a life. I lost my father to it. This time I wasn't going to surrender without a fight.''

Each of her words stabbed at him like darts of pain. He, better than most, knew just how much Julianne had lost to Harley's addiction. It had cost her her childhood, and a man who should have learned long ago how to act like a father. Recalling the phone call he'd had with Harley minutes before Julianne had come into the room, he felt certain doubt about whether things would ever change. A man couldn't be forced into becoming a decent parent and doing right by his daughter.

"Is it going to be a problem for you, Jed? Me coming home?''

He turned back to look at her, leaning his weight against the edge of the desk. "No. It's not a problem for me.''

She released a breath, and he imagined he could see a little tension seep out of her limbs. "Good. I came back because I've missed this place. All I want to do for the next few days is ride all over the ranch and get reacquainted with my favorite spots.'' Wistfulness traced through her words. ''I didn't do much riding in Florida. It just seemed to make me homesick. And I haven't even been on a horse since I've gotten back. Maybe I'll ride out with Gabe.''

''Gabe doesn't do a lot of riding anymore. At least, not on a horse. He'd be the last to admit it, but arthritis has settled in one hip pretty bad. Some days he has a tough enough time getting in and out of the pickup.''

His words brought a hint of a frown to her face, but she lifted a shoulder. ''Well, I know my way around.''

''You're not riding out by yourself for a couple of days,'' he said flatly.

She arched a brow at him, unimpressed. ''Says who?''

With a notable lack of success, he tried for patience. ''It would be one thing if you just intended to go for a ride, but you don't. You'll be all over the ranch, gone from dawn to sunset, and riding that long by yourself when you're not used to it is just plain foolish. I won't be around, and I don't want to have to worry about you getting yourself into trouble while I'm away.''

''Where are you going?''

''The state Cattlemen's Association is having their annual bash in Helena tomorrow night. Dinner and a band afterward, I guess.'' His voice trailing off to a mutter he added, ''Never did figure why they needed some fancy shindig to talk about business.''

She said nothing, just looked at him quizzically.

Uncomfortably, he shifted his weight against the desk. ''I'm the president this year.'' She didn't have to look so damn amazed, he thought, affronted. He'd been involved in one form or another with raising cattle since he was twelve. He figured he knew as much about it as most ranchers, more than some.

Her lips curved, and dread spiraled in anticipation of her reaction. It wasn't long coming.

"Well, la-di-da. Jed Sullivan has gone and gotten civilized somewhere along the way. Who'd have thought it?"

He glared at her. "I know cattle."

She nodded, her amusement still visible. "I realize that. I also know that being elected state president means a lot of other folks around here realize it, too. Congratulations, Jed. I never would have guessed that you'd grow to be this…"

His voice was a dare. "This what?"

Tilting her head, she contemplated the ceiling, clearly enjoying herself. "I guess…*staid*…is the word I'm looking for."

"Staid?"

Her eyes sparkled with mirth. "I mean that in a positive way, of course."

"Yeah, right." The muscle in his jaw tightened as he ground his teeth. "I realize you don't have a great deal of experience with responsibility, but it's a trait most of us try to cultivate as we get older."

"Well, there you go." She nodded sagely. "Since you're five years my senior, you've got a head start on being responsible. I'm sure that when I get to be your age I'll be just as decorous."

He snorted. "And pigs will grow wings."

Her blinding smile went straight to his gut like a well-honed arrow. It took a moment for his brain to remind his lungs to breathe again. He'd watched Julianne perfect that smile on every male this side of ninety from the time she was seven. Obviously, he wasn't as immune as he'd thought. The realization would have been troubling if he hadn't decided in the next moment that he much preferred to see that smile on her face than the despair she'd worn earlier. Even if her amusement *was* at his expense.

He folded his arms and crossed his booted feet at the ankle. "Actually, it's exactly the kind of affair you've always liked. It'll be a big crowd. Four or five hundred people."

If he hadn't been watching her so closely, he might have missed her sudden pallor at his words. "I used to like that kind of affair. Right now I'm more interested in isolating myself at the ranch for a while."

He went still at the word. "Isolating?"

She gave a careless wave of her hand. "You know what I mean. Resting up. Getting my life in order again."

He studied her long enough to have her fidgeting in her seat. Her words sounded nothing like the Julianne he knew. She'd always had a boundless store of confidence, of energy for life. He wondered just how deeply the rumors from the scandal had wounded her.

"Maybe," he said slowly, testing her, "you'd be interested to see firsthand just how…staid…I've become."

She settled back in the armchair. "Are you selling tickets?"

"Something like that. I can bring a guest to this thing tomorrow night. Why don't I take you along?"

"Me?" His offer dimmed her smile considerably.

"Why not? It will give you a chance to get out and socialize, as well as a perfect opportunity to do what you've always done best."

"And what might that be?"

"Show off. You must have something in that heap of luggage that would be suitable to wear."

"Don't be offensive. I can assure you, should I put my mind to it, I could find something that would give those ranchers plenty to discuss with their cattle for decades to come.''

He sprung the trap neatly. ''It's settled then. You'll come along. I know this is still Montana, after all, not Florida high society. But you should find it entertaining enough. You've always liked a party.''

A flicker of something suspiciously close to panic showed in her eyes, and she shook her head. ''As much as I enjoy getting dressed up and showing off, I'm going to say no thanks. I just got here, and I'm not ready to leave the ranch just yet.''

All his protective instincts rose to the surface, and he was suddenly, illogically angry. Angry at a turn of events that had the power to sap Julianne of that bold self-assurance that was so much a part of her. Angry at her for letting it happen, and angry at himself for not being able to prevent it. He made sure none of the furious emotion sounded in his voice. ''You wouldn't be gone long. I'll fly us to Helena after lunch tomorrow, and we'll return the next day.''

Her tone was lazy. ''I don't think so. Maybe another time.''

His eyes narrowed consideringly. Damn, she was good. Her yawn and sleepy smile almost convinced him that all she wanted to do was spend the next month loafing and poking around the ranch. He stared at her, long enough to cause her to shift in her chair, before she rose, announcing her intentions of heading to bed.

The old Julianne would have accepted in a minute. He wasn't being totally sarcastic when he'd said this event would be just the sort of thing she used to like. There was nothing Julianne had enjoyed more than getting all dolled up and making an entrance at a party. And, if memory served correctly, being its focal point while she was there.

His gaze bored a hole in her retreating back.

She was nearing the door. Her hand reached for the knob. He let her open it, move through it, before saying coolly, "Well, this is one for the books. Julianne Buchanan…running scared."

He could have predicted her reaction time to the second. One instant…two…before she backed through the door again to look at him challengingly.

"Pardon me?"

He let a sardonic grin curl his mouth. The haughty tone was familiar—princess to peasant. It had never failed to get a rise out of him when they were kids. But they weren't kids anymore.

"I said you're running scared." He shrugged. "You've got a right, God knows. No one would blame you for not wanting to face a ballroom full of people, all the time wondering how much of the Florida scandal had reached here, what they know, what they think they do. If you want to hide out at the ranch awhile longer and lick your wounds in private, hell, you're entitled."

The look she aimed at him should have singed off a layer of skin, but then she sauntered toward him, slow and nonchalant. He pushed away from the desk, his weight coming to rest on the balls of his feet. Deliberately baiting Julianne could be an unpredictable business, and it was best to be prepared.

She stopped in front of him, a dangerous little smile on her face. Brushing a piece of lint from the shoulder of his denim shirt, she patted his cheek, a little more forcefully than necessary. "Jed. Dear. If this is a pathetic attempt at reverse psychology, you'd better leave it to the pros. You need more practice. The day that I'm afraid to face people is the day they eat lemon Popsicles in hell."

He caught her wrist in his hand and moved it away,

smiling mockingly. "Sure. Whatever you need to believe, Jules."

Their gazes clashed for a long moment, her eyes expressing every emotion she was feeling...irritation, disdain, uncertainty. It was the last of those emotions that drew his chest tight, that made him sure he was right.

Then she was tugging her hand free, as cool as you please, and tucking it into her back pocket. She rolled one shoulder in magnificent indifference. "Since it seems so important to you, I'll come along. A night in Helena might be amusing, if only to see you forced to wear a suit." She turned her back on him and strolled toward the door. Before she exited the room, she looked back and drawled, "Who knows, this might turn out to be fun, after all. If we put our minds to it, we just might give the Montana cattle ranchers something to remember for years to come."

Her parting shot succeeding in splintering the satisfaction that had formed at her acceptance. With a sense of unease, he thought about the upcoming twenty-four hours and wondered just what he'd managed to get himself into.

Chapter 4

Ordinarily, there was nothing Julianne liked better than a party. Surrounding herself with music, food, dancing and plenty of people was, in an odd way, both relaxing and exhilarating. She was comfortable in a crowd of strangers because she enjoyed people. She liked talking to them, hearing about their lives, and in some instances, making up pasts about them for her own amusement. She wasn't above making up a past for herself just for the sheer entertainment of it. She doubted Jed would approve.

She pursed her lips slightly and outlined them with a lipstick pencil. Not that pleasing Jed was going to be high on her list of priorities tonight. It still rankled that she'd allowed him to buffalo her into attending this evening, but he'd had plenty of years to learn which buttons to push, and he knew she'd never let him call her a coward. Realizing how blatantly she'd been manipulated hadn't changed her response.

He'd been right, damn him, though she'd rather waltz

naked through Yankee Stadium than admit it aloud. Her first reaction when he'd invited her to come with him had been pure, unadulterated panic. The feeling had been totally out of character, not to mention irrational. The people who mattered most to her, like Annie and Gabe, were very forgiving when it came to her mistakes. Jed had never let her get away with much, of course. When it came to support, however, he could always be counted on, whether his help was asked for or not.

Her hand trembled, and she paused in the middle of applying her lipstick. And his help most definitely had not been asked for in Florida. Through the media circus and the endless interrogations, the only shred of pride she'd been left with had come from the knowledge that she was fighting her own battles. When she'd been cleared of suspicion, she'd congratulated herself for standing alone. Others might sneer at the amount of strength that had taken, but it had been a personal victory of sorts for her.

Now she had to share that victory with Jed. She'd never know how much his involvement had helped to clear her, and not knowing robbed the situation of most of the satisfaction she'd gained from it. She finished applying her lipstick and blotted her lips on a tissue. If he'd been down in the middle of that mess, an idea that still had the power to make her shudder, then she'd been lucky that the scene in his office hadn't gotten uglier. Jed didn't have much use for weaknesses; not in anyone. Like a true knight of old, he had very firm notions about right and wrong. She wondered if he'd ever seen the world in shades of gray and uncomfortably decided that he hadn't.

Despite her still-simmering annoyance over the way he'd finessed her agreement to accompany him, the trip to Helena had passed surprisingly quickly. Jed had flown them in his four-seater Cessna, and she'd been fascinated watching him handle the small plane. She'd kept him busy the entire way, asking him questions about the dials and knobs before him, and by the end of the trip, a resolve had formed in her mind.

She was going to learn to fly. She could already imagine the thrill of being in control of the small aircraft, of making the decisions about altitude, speed and velocity. She smiled smugly and reached for her lipstick. It would serve Jed right if she decided to make him teach her.

The thought was cheering. She wondered if he'd ever recovered from the trauma of teaching her to drive. He'd been a stick-in-the-mud even then, she remembered, insisting she drive around in an old four-door sedan tank until he deemed her ready for something with a little more zip. If he'd had his way, she'd still be driving that old Ford, but Harley had taken the decision out of his hands. He'd called home, flush after a gambling venture, and had acceded to Julianne's demands for a little red sports car. Despite Jed's dire warnings, she'd never once managed to wrap it around a tree or roll it into a ditch. Although she'd collected more than her share of speeding tickets, he'd been a good instructor. She'd never had an accident.

She finished with her makeup and rose to get the dress she'd chosen for this evening. Untying her robe and letting it drop to the floor, she carefully stepped into the royal blue sequined dress. She twisted her arms nearly out of their sockets trying to raise the back zipper. Slipping into her shoes, she went back to the mirror, turning this way and that to check her appearance. The strapless dress might have been a little chancy, given the hotel's penchant for icy air-conditioning, but she was counting on the crush of the crowd to keep the temperature comfortable.

A knock sounded at the door. Throwing a glance at the clock on the dresser, she smiled. If nothing else, Jed was always prompt. She opened the door and, for a moment, just stood there, staring.

"Well?" he growled, shifting uncomfortably under her silent scrutiny. "Are you going to let me in?"

She stood back silently and let him enter the room, afraid if she opened her mouth she'd trip over her tongue.

He looked...magnificent. She'd always thought denim suited him; a perfect package for rugged angles and hard muscle. She'd forgotten what an impact he made dressed up. The dark, discreetly pin-striped suit jacket seemed to stretch across acres of shoulders, and the light-colored dress shirt made his tan seem darker. She tried to remember the last time she'd seen him in a tie, and then decided it had been at her high school graduation. The one he'd attended, and then afterward held her while she cried out her disappointment over Harley missing it, despite his vows to be there.

She took a deep breath and resisted the urge to press a palm to her jittery stomach.

He was watching her intently, and being the focus of that fierce regard was doing nothing to calm her pulse. His words, when they came, were low and rough, and sent a fast skitter up her spine. "You look good, Buchanan."

His simple words sent an absurd sense of pleasure shimmering over each and every one of her nerve endings. She forced the air back through her lungs. "I've always admired your way with words, ace." Turning away, she picked up her purse and headed to the door, concentrating on walking steadily.

He followed her into the hallway, his long strides easily catching up to hers. She entered the elevator ahead of him, sidling to the corner to put some space between his large body and her own.

"You never told me what the program was for tonight. Will people come by to kiss your ring?"

"Very funny."

The tinge of irritation in his voice made her smile come a little more naturally, and her lungs eased. Maybe she wasn't suffocating, after all. "Sorry. That's the pope, isn't it? Exactly what is proper protocol for addressing the head of the Cattlemen's Association?"

He ignored her banter and said, "The hospitality hour started a few minutes ago. We'll eat at six, there will be a short presentation, and the band begins playing at eight."

The light indicating their floor winked at them, a discreet bell sounded, and the doors slid open. Jazzed by nerves, she sailed out of the car. "I suppose it would be considered poor taste to tell the waiter I prefer pork?"

He took her elbow in his grasp, his touch sending a sharp electric thrill up her arm, and steered her in the direction of the hospitality room. "Julianne," he warned in an undertone, "behave yourself tonight."

Shooting him a sideways glance, she inquired, "What fun would that be?"

As it happened, it was more fun than she'd anticipated. She'd deliberately slipped away from Jed's watchful eye soon after their arrival and wandered among the crowd doing what she loved best...mingling. The wine was a very decent chardonnay, but judiciously, she held herself to one glass. She hadn't had lunch, and she really wasn't much of a drinker, anyway. She'd spent too many years watching Andrew try to crawl into a bottle to find the solution to his unhappiness.

As she casually threaded her way through the crowd, she checked on Jed across the room and found him watching her. She raised her free hand to waggle her fingers at him, but the gesture didn't ease the slight frown he was wearing. She watched as one of the group of men surrounding him snagged his attention, and she decided that he would be fine on his own for a while. Jed had never been a big one for socializing, at least not at anything more formal than a barbecue with neighbors, but as long as he had fellow ranchers to discuss cattle with, she figured he'd be content.

A white-jacketed waiter stopped in front of her with a tray loaded with rich appetizers, and he seemed inordinately pleased to help her make her selections. Now balancing both a plate and a glass, she looked around for a place to set them.

"Just my luck to find the loveliest lady here with her hands full," a gravelly voice sounded in back of her. "I guess that means I don't get a hug."

Whirling around, Julianne smiled delightedly. "Walter! Oh, it's wonderful to see you. It's been ages." She went up on tiptoes to press a kiss to the man's leathery cheek.

Walter Larkin owned the ranch south of the H/B, and when she'd been in school she'd spent as much time at his ranch as at her own. She and his daughter, Shelby, had been inseparable while they were growing up, and partners in a great many more scrapes than they'd ever been caught at.

She eyed the man soberly. "I was sorry to hear about Laura." Annie had kept her informed about Walter's wife's losing battle with cancer. She'd died the previous winter.

The older man patted her arm. "The flowers you sent were real nice. All Laura's favorites. And your letter was a comfort."

She smiled up at him. "Do you know how many hours

she spent feeding Shelby and me? Or how often she'd help us experiment with our hair?''

His faded blue eyes twinkled. ''Or how many times she kept one of your and Shelby's escapades quiet?''

Simple sincerity laced her voice. ''She was the best.'' Her eyes went misty at the flood of memories. ''I called Shelby last month, but our visit was cut short by the demands of your new grandson.''

A broad smile settled on Walter's creased face. ''J.T. He's got a pair of lungs like a howler monkey and a temper to match. You'll get a chance to see for yourself soon enough. Shelby's bringing him for a visit next week. When she finds out that you're home, she'll be over the moon.''

''I'll call her,'' Julianne promised.

''Walter, shame on you for monopolizing our long-lost neighbor like this.''

Wincing a little at the instantly recognizable strident tones, Julianne turned around to greet another of the ranch neighbors, Eleanor Pooler. Shifting her plate and glass between them in one smooth movement, she prevented the hug the woman tried to press on her, and smiled brilliantly.

''Eleanor, how have you been? You're looking well.'' The flounced dress the woman was wearing was a rather ghastly shade of yellow and did uninspired things to her sallow complexion, but she had made efforts with her hair, which was tightly curled and colored a determined shade of dark brown.

''Oh, my dear Julianne,'' Eleanor cooed in a lowered voice. ''You can't know how I've worried about you. We all have, haven't we, Walter?''

Walter lifted first an eyebrow and then his glass. ''What are you talking about, Eleanor?''

Julianne stifled a grin. Walter's testy manner was barely

held in check. Like most of the neighbors, he genuinely liked the taciturn Jim Pooler, but only tolerated his wife.

The avid interest in Eleanor's raisinlike eyes contrasted with the oozing sympathy in her voice. "Well, my dear, we heard the most awful things about you. I, for one, just couldn't believe what people were saying."

Balancing her plate on top of her wineglass, Julianne selected a crab-stuffed mushroom. "That's always wise, Eleanor. I've found that people will say quite a bit. The trick is in not repeating it." She sampled the mushroom and swallowed approvingly. Whoever had been in charge of the appetizers deserved every cent the association paid them. She made a mental note to mention it to Jed.

"There, there, dear, no need to put up a brave front. Not with us." Her voice lowered conspiratorially. "Is it true you had to spend the night in jail with common criminals? I actually heard you were put in a cell with a ring of prostitutes, but I wouldn't believe anything so outlandish."

"Eleanor, for heaven's sake!" The outrage in Walter's voice was enough to keep the smile on Julianne's face at least partially sincere.

"What people will believe is really a measure of their gullibility, isn't it? Actually I was never arrested, so I didn't get to spend a night in jail. I can tell you that I was terribly disappointed to miss the adventure of a strip search."

"Julianne, the head table is beginning to be seated. Hello, Walter, Eleanor." Jed's voice interrupted them.

Walter returned his greeting with obvious relief, while Eleanor shifted her attention to him. "Jed, how nice to see you. I was just telling Julianne how worried we all were about her."

"We appreciate her concern, don't we, Jed?" Julianne

offered her plate to him. "Try some of these mushrooms. They're to die for."

"Oh, Jed," Eleanor gushed. "Marianne is here. I just know she's going to want to see you. You've met her husband, haven't you? Randall Craig?" In an aside to Julianne she added, "Marianne and her husband have several hundred acres in the eastern part of the state. She was horribly worried when she told me those horrible stories circulating about you. She's just so deliriously happy with her husband, she can't bear for anyone else to be miserable."

"If I remember correctly, Marianne was delirious most of the time." The weight of a size-thirteen boot pressed firmly on her toe, and Julianne winced. "Delirious about her friends, I mean."

"Are you staying for the dance?" Jed asked Eleanor. Barely waiting for the woman's nod, he continued, "Then we'll see you later. Right now Julianne and I need to find our places." Nodding to Walter, he grasped Julianne's elbow and steered her away.

"You may have to carry me," she muttered, barely restraining a limp. "I think you broke my foot."

"Don't see how, since you had it stuck in your mouth. Can't you even chat with the neighbors without causing a ruckus?"

She stopped dead in her tracks and glared at him indignantly. He had to stop as well or risk seeming to drag her in his tracks. "You have no idea what that woman said to me."

"I caught the gist of it. Can't say it surprised me any. I seem to recall some bad blood between the two of you. Something about pushing her daughter outside the school naked?"

She smirked. "My involvement was never proved, and

anyway, it wasn't outside. Somehow Marianne managed to find herself locked out of the girls' changing room and in the gym, wearing only a skimpy towel. I believe boys' soccer practice was going on at the time. And you could be right. Eleanor and Marianne both had the most unjustified suspicions about my part in that unfortunate incident."

His lips twitched. "My point exactly. So Eleanor can be forgiven a little sour grapes, can't she? Especially since she's stuck wearing that dress all night. Makes her look like one of those stuffed artichokes they're serving."

Julianne's laugh gurgled out of her. She set her plate on a nearby table and tucked her free hand through his arm. Tipping her head up at him, she said, "You know, I'd forgotten how much I like you sometimes, Jed."

He raised his brow, and together they walked toward the front table. "Lord, help me."

"Oh, I don't think divine intervention is called for. At least not yet."

Chapter 5

There were plenty of occasions throughout the rest of the evening, Jed reflected later, when a little divine intervention would have come in handy. For instance, there was the seating arrangement at dinner. What hand of fate had placed Julianne next to Percy Cunningham, the temperamental Montana senator? The man didn't even seem to like people, women in particular. He was present only to make a token effort at listening to the association's concerns about the current costs of using government land for grazing.

When Jed had tried to circumspectly change seats with her, Julianne had fixed him with a challenging look and said in a ringing voice, "Now, Jed, you just sit in your own chair. Senator Cunningham and I will get along just fine. Isn't that right, Percy?"

Predicting disaster, Jed had barely tasted the excellent fillet, and he found it difficult to concentrate on the conversation of the man seated at his other side. When he was

introduced and walked up to the podium with the short
speech he'd prepared, he snuck a look at Julianne and
barely stifled a groan. She was leaning toward the senator,
those brown eyes wide and sincere. Damned if her eye-
lashes weren't fluttering. Although he couldn't see the senator's response, his gut churned with uneasiness. He barely
had a memory of what he said when he addressed the
group; he was too worried about how much damage Julianne was doing with Percy Cunningham.

When the band started up, he leaned over and grasped
Julianne's hand tightly. "C'mon."

Her fingers twisted in his as she tried to free herself.
"Is this your charming way of asking me to dance?"

It wasn't exactly what he had in mind, but it was an
excuse to get her away from Cunningham, so he agreed.
"Yeah, sure."

She rose, and he stood, as well. She smiled sweetly up
at him. "Well, then, I'm sorry. You'll have to wait. I've
already promised the first dance to the senator." And Jed
watched, poleaxed, while Cunningham, with an almost
painful-looking stretching of lips that passed for a smile,
rose and took Julianne's hand and led her to the dance
floor.

Jed wandered to the bar set up in the corner of the room
and leaned against it. "Scotch," he ordered when the bartender looked at him quizzically. "Neat." He turned to
give himself a better view of the dance floor, but Julianne
and the senator had been swallowed up by a mass of couples and he could only catch occasional glimpses.

He picked up the glass the bartender slid in front of him
and absently dug in his pocket for a bill to give the man.
Taking a long swallow of Scotch, he waited for the fiery
explosion in the pit of his stomach. Maybe the liquor
would cure the nerves that had started jumping the instant

he'd realized who Julianne was seated by. But he figured the best cure for that was getting the unpredictable little witch away from the man, before the senator was arrested for murder. Cunningham wasn't known for being long on patience. And Jed had the experience to know that Julianne could try the patience of a saint.

"I'll have what he's having."

Jed shot a glance at the brunette in a very off-the-shoulder red dress, and straightened slowly. She took the glass from the bartender and brought it to her lips, her eyes meeting Jed's over the edge of the glass.

"Do you like Scotch?" he asked as she sipped daintily.

"It's not my normal drink," she answered. "But I try to leave myself open for…new experiences." Her direct look made no secret of her interest, and when her gaze dropped to his left hand her smile took on a slightly predatory look. "I'm going to let myself fantasize that you're not married."

Jed settled against the bar and returned her smile. Aggressive women didn't usually interest him; he preferred to do his own hunting. Right now, though, he welcomed the distraction. "Nope."

A few more people edged up to the bar, and the brunette moved closer to him. Jed could smell the slightly musky aroma of her perfume as she circled the rim of her glass with one damp fingertip. It was nothing like the gut-knotting scent Julianne wore. It trailed in her wake like a sexy signature. He could actually enter a room and be instantly aware of her presence, just by the faint fragrance in the air. Unconsciously, he frowned into his glass. It seemed everything about Julianne was designed to get a response. He counted himself lucky that the predominant one she stirred in him was an overpowering urge to throttle her.

She cocked her head. "And the blonde you're with tonight? Are the two of you seriously...involved?"

Her question had the unfortunate timing of coming just after he'd taken another swallow of Scotch. This time he choked on the liquor, and its burning path threatened to take a wrong turn. Coughing and sputtering, he attempted to bring calm to his system. The havoc in his brain was another matter.

The brunette was eying him quizzically. "You're going to have to clarify that answer, I'm afraid."

Jed shook his head a little to clear it. "We're not involved at all. She's my...she's just..."

"His psychiatrist," a voice put in smoothly. Jed's head jerked around as Julianne tucked her hand in his arm. She surveyed the other woman gravely. "You see, Jed here has a teensy little problem I've been working with him on."

"Julianne," he warned. He may as well have saved his breath. She was on a roll.

She patted his arm. "How many times do I have to reassure you, 'catlaphobia' is nothing to be ashamed of?" She shook her head and lowered her voice to the brunette confidingly. "Men. They hate to admit to a weakness."

The other woman forced a smile. Her attention was focused on Julianne now; Jed may as well have not been there at all. "Cat...laphobia?"

"Fear of cattle," Julianne fabricated. "It makes roundup a real nightmare."

The brunette sent a speculative glance toward Jed. "I'll bet."

"He's had some success with positive mental visualization, however." Julianne beamed at Jed, a proud doctor-to-patient smile. "He just pictures all the cows naked."

Setting his glass on the bar with a restrained clink, he

grasped Julianne's arm in his hand. "Excuse us," he muttered, and pushed Julianne toward the dance floor. "Not for the first time, I'm regretting your lack of discipline as a child." He wondered wistfully if it was too late to rectify that void in her upbringing.

"I didn't need much discipline as a child," she answered brightly, linking her arms around his neck and swaying to the music. "I was exceedingly well behaved."

"Only when you slept."

"No need to get nasty. I was just rescuing you from that woman's clutches."

He sent a considering glance to the brunette. She'd already attached herself to another man, who looked slightly dazed at his good fortune. "Maybe I liked being in her clutches."

"She'd only have used you for mindless sex," Julianne predicted.

He closed his eyes and wondered if a minor miracle would be too much to pray for. Apparently so. Julianne was still there when his eyes reopened.

"There are worse ways to go."

She cocked her head. "I thought about telling her you had a social disease, but she looked too determined to let a minor detail like that put her off."

His temples began to throb, a sure indication that he'd spent too much time in her company. "I just hope that's the least of the trouble you've caused tonight. Just tell me that Senator Cunningham isn't threatening to have my state citizenship revoked, and I'll get started on a little damage control." The music changed to a slow, haunting ballad, and he automatically adjusted his steps to hers.

"Oh, ye of little faith," she scoffed. "I'll have you know that Senator Cunningham is giving serious consideration to sponsoring a bill to revise the schedule of charges for grazing on public lands.''

He couldn't help it. He stopped and stared at her. "No way. We've been asking him for that for two years and haven't gotten anything more than a growl from him. What the hell did you say to him?"

With a gentle nudge, she reminded his feet to start moving again. "Oh, this and that. You know, he really is quite sweet if you take the time to get to know him. I think he's just shy."

He gaped at her, incredulous. Sweet. Percy Cunningham. He gave his head a shake to clear it. Julianne would probably refer to a snarling mountain lion as a nice kitty. An unwilling grin pulled at the corner of his mouth.

"I know I'm going to hate myself for asking, but just how did you manage that?"

Her head tilted up and her eyes met his, a self-satisfied smile on her face. "By taking the time to find out what's important to him."

His lack of comprehension must have shown on his face, because she went on to explain. "Your problem, Jed, is you've never learned the art of social conversation. Your communication skills are limited to receiving or giving only the information necessary to get from point A to point B."

He didn't pretend not to take offense. "What else is there?"

"Concern, interest. Did you know that Senator Cunningham was worried about maintaining multiple use on public lands and feared that overgrazing would limit accessibility for recreational purposes?"

His brows drew together. "The association has long worked to increase technical assistance to the ranchers about responsible conservation practices. We know darn well that our efforts at improving the land will actually benefit all users, regardless of their purpose.''

"Sounds like you're both on the same page, then. Have you actually sat down and explained that to him?"

His jaw snapped shut.

"I thought not. Try listening to his concerns before you expect him to listen to yours. Did you know that his daughter, Celia, was Montana's champion woman's equestrian for two consecutive years in the early eighties?"

He started to shrug, then stopped and looked down at her. "What's that have to do with anything?"

She smiled easily. "Nothing, I just thought it was interesting. Although, come to think of it, with his daughter's interest in horses, the senator just might be intrigued by the breeding operation you're planning at the ranch. You could mention it to him. Just as an icebreaker." She regarded him gravely. "Your lack of conversational skills don't come as a complete surprise, you know."

"Do tell."

"It's a scientifically proven fact that women invented communication. If it wasn't for us, men would still be pointing and grunting." She patted his cheek. "Be a good student and remember, most people ease into conversation with some civil pleasantries. They don't immediately go for the kill. You might give polite chitchat a try."

"Somehow I think a flirting woman might have more of an edge in that department."

It was her turn to be offended. "I do not flirt!"

Lightning should have struck her where she stood. "With those eyes, baby, you're the world's champ."

"I'm almost sorry I helped you." Her mouth moved suspiciously close to a pout. "It'd serve you right if I didn't tell you that he asked to be invited to your next

Cattlemen's Association meeting. He said something about seeking the group's input.''

''That's what we've been trying to give him for almost three years.'' He watched as her eyes slid shut and she hummed under her breath to the music. Regardless of the bizarre way it had happened, he wasn't about to look a gift senator in the mouth. Or something to that effect. The band switched to another slow song, and he tucked Julianne's hand more snugly at his shoulder. Feeling undeniably more cheerful, he said, ''Maybe bringing you along won't turn out to be the catastrophe I feared.''

She opened her eyes, and arched a brow. ''Keep talking all mushy to me and I'm liable to melt right here at your feet.''

He twirled her around a corner and grinned at her pleased smile.

''You've got some mighty unexpected moves, cowboy.''

''You haven't seen the half of them.''

''Where'd you learn to dance?'' she asked curiously.

''Maybe it's natural.''

''Or maybe you spent your teen years practicing with the posts when we thought you were riding fence.''

He regarded her gravely. ''You still have a smart mouth, Julianne. That's a mighty unattractive quality in a woman.''

As usual, his barb was ignored. ''You're just mad because I guessed your secret. Don't worry. You wouldn't be the first boy to practice his…social graces…on inanimate objects.''

He squeezed her hand more tightly and did a complex little series of steps guaranteed to impress. She kept up with him effortlessly. ''All right, Annie taught me. Are you satisfied?''

Her laugh gurgled out of her. "Annie? When?"

"When I was fourteen and lacking many of those...social graces...you mentioned. She'd banish you from the kitchen, and once we were sure you were in your room or out of the house, she'd close the door and start the music."

"She said she was helping you with your Spanish," Julianne recalled.

"*Bailar*," he said solemnly. "To dance. You were a snoop even then. I lived in constant fear you'd come in and discover us, and make my life a living hell."

She laughed again. "I could have used the ammunition."

"You've always done pretty well on your own."

The music ended, and the band members drifted away on break. Julianne turned her head, and for an instant, her hair brushed against Jed's face. It smelled of springtime and flowers. Deliberately, he dropped his arms and stepped away.

"There's the senator," she murmured, turning back to face him. "It looks like he's getting ready to leave."

His gaze followed the direction of hers. "I think I'll go talk to him before he does."

"Wise choice, Sullivan." As he moved away, he heard her voice trailing after him, filled with amusement. "And don't forget the chitchat."

As Jed looked around the room, he realized with mild surprise that it had been a couple of hours since he'd given a thought to cutting out early. It would have been a stretch to claim he'd enjoyed himself all evening, since he'd spent the majority of his time fearing Julianne was going to wreak some kind of social havoc. But the night was drawing to a close, and so far, disaster seemed to have been averted.

Although he hadn't settled anything with the senator, they had had a cordial conversation that had ended with Cunningham asking to be invited to the next Cattlemen's meeting. He figured he was a big enough person to admit when a person was right, and he scanned the crowd for Julianne.

But she wasn't dancing, as she'd spent much of the evening, nor was she in the middle of a cluster of women laughing in a way that drew men's eyes. In fact, he didn't see her in the large room at all.

Jed paused, a frown beginning to form between his brows. Admitting she'd been right was enough of a sacrifice, he figured. The least she could do was be available when he was ready to do so.

The band was midway through their final set. Although the crowd had thinned considerably, many people had stayed to take advantage of the old-time rock and roll that was saved for the end of the evening. It wasn't like Julianne to miss this music.

Turning, he noticed several sets of French doors had been opened to let in the cool night air. He sipped from the glass of Scotch in his hand and moved toward the nearest set. Maybe she'd gone outside for some fresh air.

He squeezed between two women who laughingly tried to pull him out to the dance floor. Smiling slightly, he shook his head, and continued on his way.

The early summer night air was brisk, a welcome contrast to the stuffiness inside. Small groups or couples were scattered around the large terrace. But he didn't see Julianne's glittering bright blue dress. He brought the glass to his lips and swallowed, before drifting to a shadowy corner of the terrace. He set the glass on the railing, took out a cigarette and lit it. Inhaling deeply, he took a moment to enjoy the semi-solitude. Crowds never failed to make him feel hemmed-in, both by the walls of people and the social expectations. Those expectations summoned ghosts from his childhood.

Stand up straight, Jed…Don't speak unless you're spoken to…You may have come from trash, but there's no need to act like it. His adoptive mother's strictures floated across his memory like bits of mist. Insubstantial, meaningless. Like the life they'd lived, before Kimberley had finally realized that adopting a son wasn't going to be enough to glue her crumbling marriage back together. Then she'd left Luther Templeton and dragged Jed with her. He'd often wondered how long it had taken Luther to notice they'd gone.

"Honestly, Julianne, you could have knocked me over with a feather when Mother told me you were here. I just think it's so brave of you to face all these people, after your…troubles." The voices were coming from behind some huge potted plants several feet away.

He turned. Apparently, he'd found Julianne, after all. And so had Marianne Craig. His first instinct was to intervene before there was bloodshed. Despite her casual manner, he knew what kind of effort it had taken for Julianne to face a crowd of this size.

The next moment he subsided against the railing. She'd made no secret of what she'd considered his interference. Maybe she was right. Perhaps it was time to let her fight her own battles. How bad could this get, anyway? Julianne had been halfway well behaved this evening and there were no locker rooms in sight.

Her voice sounded then, amused. "Trouble and I are old acquaintances, Marianne. Don't you remember?"

There was a high, tinkling laugh, reminiscent of breaking glass. Jed got a quick mental memory of a bubbly, airheaded redhead, whose bouncy demeanor hid a malicious streak wide enough to drive a truck through. He hadn't seen Marianne in years, but from the sound of things, she hadn't changed much.

"Well, I must say, dear, you look marvelous. Did the government actually let you keep that sweet little dress you're wearing? I always heard that with drug seizures, they could take absolutely everything you owned."

"I believe that applies to people who are convicted of criminal behavior, Marianne. Since I was never charged, it would hardly affect me."

"You were always so clever about extricating yourself from the most suspicious circumstances. So tell me. Did you have to hire a frightfully expensive lawyer to keep them from pressing charges?"

The woman was nothing if not persistent. Julianne's tone had chilled considerably when she answered, "I didn't have to hire a lawyer at all. Although I may have need of one if I'm arrested for homicide."

"Well, I never believed a *thing* people were saying about you. The media can be so ruthless, can't they? You were wise to hide out at the ranch until things die down in Florida. I'm sure some other headline will come along to catch people's interest." Marianne's voice was laced with doubt.

"I'm not hiding out, I just came home."

That high-pitched laugh came again, along with a slight noise Jed fancied was Julianne's teeth clenching together. He brought the almost-forgotten cigarette to his lips, filled his lungs with smoke and continued eavesdropping unabashedly.

"Oh, I've just been feeling so sorry for you! I said as much to my husband. I can't imagine what amusements you'll find on the ranch. I'm sure you're used to much racier pastimes. Though I was…free-spirited…in high school, I'm afraid I just never could get used to that jaded life-style you've been leading.''

"Free-spirited?''

Jed straightened abruptly. He recognized the danger in Julianne's lethal purr. Flicking his cigarette aside, he decided it was time to make his presence known.

"All this time I just thought you were cheap,'' Julianne continued. "Obviously that hasn't changed. Although I must say, that tacky little dress you're wearing does slightly more for you than the skimpy towel you were wrapped in when we locked you out of the girls changing room in high school.''

There was a shriek, and Jed walked faster.

"That was you! I knew it all along. Your bitchy friend Shelby was probably in on it, too.''

"She provided some of the muscle, but it was my idea.'' Jed winced at the satisfaction in Julianne's voice. "I understand the soccer team still has nightmares about it.''

"You…'' He heard the sound of a slap, followed by another shriek. As he rounded the potted plant, he could already imagine the lawsuit to follow. When he caught sight of the two women, Marianne was frantically wiping liquid from the front of her dress, and Julianne was setting her empty glass on a nearby table.

"Ladies.'' He forced a falsely genial tone in his voice, and purposely stepped between them. "Marianne Craig. What a nice surprise. Your mother said you were here.'' He reached in his pocket and withdrew his handkerchief, offering it to her. She snatched it from him and dabbed at her dress.

With his free hand he reached for Julianne's arm and gripped it tightly. "I hope you'll excuse us, Marianne. I need to steal Julianne for a moment." He turned and, ignoring the resistance in her body, propelled her away.

"You can pitch her over the side of the balcony for all I care. Oh, my dress is ruined!" Marianne's voice ended on a wail, which followed them around the corner.

Jed didn't stop until they were on the opposite side of the terrace, isolated from any interested observers. Then, because he couldn't be sure of his temper, he forced himself to let go of Julianne.

"God almighty, Buchanan, can't you behave for five minutes? Another few minutes and they'd have had to call in a SWAT team."

She strolled away from him and relaxed against the balcony railing. "Another five minutes and they'd have had to scrape her remains off the tiles. I was never too good at tolerating Marianne Pooler, and age and marriage hasn't cured her bitchiness."

"Just tell me if I'm going to have to bail you out of jail for assault charges."

Her shrug had the sequins in her dress shimmering in the darkness. "She took the swing at me, which naturally upset my hand carrying the full glass." He heard, rather than saw, the pout. "A waste of good chardonnay, too."

Irritation still riding him, he snapped, "Well, you're just going to have to develop some tolerance. Dammit, Julianne, you're not a kid anymore. You can't act on every impulse you have."

"So tell me what you would have done after another guy belted you? Turned the other cheek?"

He ignored the question. They weren't talking about him, at any rate. "You know what she's like. It's not like you to let someone like Marianne make you lose your temper."

She turned away from him to lean over the balcony. She

was silent for a long time. When she did speak, it was so quietly he had to move closer in order to make out her words. "She didn't say anything you haven't said. But regardless of what you both think, I didn't come back to the ranch to lick my wounds."

He lifted a shoulder. "Whatever happened in Florida is history. You deserve a chance to get on with your life. It's nobody's business where you choose to do it."

She didn't look at him. Her gaze was trained on something in the darkness. "Tell me something, Jed. Did you go charging to my rescue in Florida because you thought I was too brainless to smooth things out myself?"

The pensive wistfulness that traced through her words elicited an answering, unfamiliar emotion. Julianne could move something inside him at the most unexpected times. Something he was unwilling to identify. He drank from his glass, welcomed the scalding slide of liquor as he swallowed.

"I've never thought you were brainless," he said finally.

Impulsive, certainly. Given to wild whims and high spirits that he'd never really understood. She had a tendency to lead with her heart, and it had taken a battering more than once. He wondered if the divorce had done some permanent damage to it, and the notion caused a quick, savage twist in his gut.

She looked at him, unwilling to let the subject die. "But you didn't think I could handle the situation on my own?"

He gave an uncomfortable shrug. With more care than the act required, he set his empty glass on the railing. He hadn't spent a great deal of time examining the rage that had filled him when he'd found out just how much trouble she'd been in. Rage that stemmed from the knowledge that she was alone, immersed in what was easily the toughest situation of her life. "What does it matter how the issue was resolved? The important thing is that the press and the authorities quit bothering you."

"Oh, it matters," she said softly. She turned away again, and her voice trailed off. He had to strain to hear it. "You can't know how much." A strand of blond hair that had worked loose from the knot she wore framed her profile softly. Because he had a sudden, uncustomary urge to push it away, he jammed his hands into his pockets.

"You've never failed at anything, have you, Jed?" The question hung suspended in the air between them. Shrouded by the darkness, the voices and music seemed a very long way off. It was easy to blank those sounds out; to pretend that they were alone together. To pretend that Julianne hadn't just asked a question he had no interest in answering. The trouble with poking at old ghosts, he'd found, was that they had a way of rising up to haunt at the oddest times. Better to let them be.

She seemed to take his silence for agreement. "Well, I'm here to tell you, it sucks. Not to mention the bite it takes out of your self-esteem. It makes me wonder if I can ever trust my own judgment again."

Assuming she was talking about that loser she'd married, he'd have to agree about the error in judgment. But he didn't like to see her like this, pensive and depressed. Julianne was normally too vibrant, too full of life for him not to be concerned with this current mood of hers. In an uncharacteristic effort to soothe, he said gruffly, "Put it behind you. We all make mistakes. The trick is not making the same one twice."

"In this case I think I can agree that once was certainly enough."

Because he was uncomfortable lingering over old regrets, he strove to lighten the mood. "You made another one tonight, you know."

She sent him a quizzical glance, and he explained, "Marianne. I'll bet you never figured she'd attack you like that."

Her lips curved. He was close enough to make out the disdain on her face, even before he heard it reflected in her voice. "That little tap? Marianne was always a wimp. That's not why I doused her with wine, you know."

He leaned his weight against the railing, facing her. "It isn't?"

She shook her head. "Heck, no. It was having her say she felt sorry for me that had me seeing red. I was obliged to soak her for the insult."

"So it's only expressions of sympathy that release your savage impulses." He nodded soberly. "I'll keep that in mind."

"False sympathy," she corrected him. "And I can't think of a reason for you to worry about that. You're about the least empathetic person I know."

He cocked an eyebrow. "What do you want me to do? Kiss your boo-boo and make it all better?"

Impudently, she offered her cheek. "Would you? It does sting a little."

Maybe it was the hint of dare in her voice, layered over the humor. Maybe it was the need to shake some of that certainty of hers; she was so sure she had him pegged. He had no desire to bare his soul to her, but that didn't mean he was comfortable with the niche in which she'd placed him. Whatever it was had him leaning forward and brushing his lips over the softness of her cheek, inhaling the fragrance that was uniquely Julianne.

It was only for an instant, but he heard the catch in her breath at the contact, saw her eyes widen. For a moment he felt cool amusement that he'd managed to surprise her, and then his gaze fell to her mouth, slightly parted in surprise. Need razored into him, jagged and edgy. He'd seen those lips countless times, laughing, pouting, snarling. He'd never before experienced this fierce urge to cover them with his own. He'd never allowed himself to feel it. Without stopping to think, he did the very thing he'd been warning her against.

He gave in to impulse.

His hand came up to cup around her throat and he lowered his mouth to hers. Her taste was fresh, sweetly intoxicating. His lips pressed hers apart, and her flavor fired through his system. His mind went blank in a brilliant explosion of light, and then sensation crowded in, slapping at heightened nerve endings.

Closer. He was aware of the demand, if not the action that followed it. He wrapped his arms around her waist and pulled her against him. He wasn't so far gone that he didn't feel her arms slide around his neck, her fingers twist in his hair.

Deeper now. Faster, hotter, more urgent. Her sigh only intensified his greed. He should have known that she'd be pure energy in his arms, lightning and heat flashing and strobing around him. His mouth ate at hers, savagely hungry, as if this moment had been a promise long denied. She returned his kiss with all the inner fire that burned so brightly in her, all but singeing him.

He buried his face at the smooth skin of her neck and fought for reason. He'd never known need to be so quick, so violent. He was a man who prized control above all else. And yet it wasn't control he thought of when his hand went to her breast. It wasn't control he fought for when she pressed against his palm in an unspoken plea for more. His lips streaked back to seal her mouth with his, as if he could get his fill with just one more taste, desperately certain that he could never get enough.

Laughter sounded nearby, close enough to intrude. He lifted his mouth a fraction from hers and looked down into her face. Her eyelids lifted slowly, and she gazed at him, stunned bewilderment giving way to shock. They drew apart with a haste that would have been amusing under other circumstances. Right now, though, the situation seemed serious as hell.

"God," Julianne said shakily, one hand pressed to her stomach. She moistened her lips, and Jed gritted his teeth against the sudden, vicious ache that bloomed low in his belly at her action. She took a stumbling step backward from him, and then another.

"God," she said again, and shuddered out a breath. "Maybe you were right. Some impulses can be downright dangerous."

Chapter 6

It didn't rank right up there as the biggest mistake in her life, but there was no denying that kissing Jed Sullivan wasn't one of her wiser decisions.

Julianne pressed her knees into the mare's sides, urging her to a faster pace. It was enough encouragement for the horse to break into a gallop. She'd been bred for speed and loved to run. That's what Gabe had told her when she'd asked for a mount. And that had sounded exactly like what she'd been looking for.

She ignored the shouted greetings of the men working fence as she passed by them, and leaned low over the mare's neck, letting her jump the stream in a powerful forward movement. She tried to focus on the lush green pastureland she was riding over, the majesty of the mountains in the distance, the sound of the stream thrashing and humming as it wound its way from the Missouri River in a path across the H/B Ranch. Her concentration, however, was shot. She was more than willing to blame Jed for that, as well.

When it became apparent that the horse was tiring, Julianne reluctantly straightened in the saddle, a gentle pressure on the reins signaling the mare to slow. She'd missed this, for so long. When she'd lived at the ranch, she'd ridden every day, but there had been very little opportunity in Florida. And after the first disastrous visit to the ranch during her marriage, she'd never attempted another. So many pleasures she'd denied herself.

So many years wasted.

The horse slowed to a walk, and her mind crowded again with the troublesome thoughts that had only been swept away momentarily. The uppermost being Jed Sullivan.

Just the thought of him made her wince, and a flush warmed her cheeks. There was no use questioning why that kiss had ever been allowed to happen. She'd asked herself the question a thousand times already and had come up with no logical answer. Oh, it was easy enough to explain away the quick explosion of pleasure she'd experienced at his kiss. She would have to be dead not to respond to him. A few moments in Jed's arms had proved that her pulse was, indeed, thumping right along.

Julianne swung off the horse's back and let the mare graze. Dropping down in the new summer grass, she stretched out on her back and contemplated the clouds skudding across the sky.

Admittedly, there had been a brief period as a schoolgirl when she'd harbored secret, guilty dreams about Jed. Those dreams had withered under the reality of living day-in and day-out with the man. It was hard to maintain fantasies about someone who hadn't thought twice about publicly humiliating her when he'd disapproved of her actions.

She'd been about sixteen the time he'd seen her in town and hauled her back to the house to change out of the tube top and miniskirt she'd been wearing. Her lip curled as she remembered her mortification. She'd been ready to kill him that night. And he'd been less than tactful with his opinions, as well. Her stinging assessment of his high-handed actions hadn't discouraged him. Later that same summer he'd bloodied Davy Stoner's lip for bringing her home two hours past curfew.

Her eyes closed and she folded her arms over her face to block the sun. How could she have kissed Jed? Jed, who had been ordering her around since the first day he stepped foot on the ranch, who had taught her to drive and bought her her first car. Jed, who had sneered at her crushes on teen stars and rock singers, then bought her tickets to the concert of the year. Jed, who'd always been there in the background, sometimes hassling her to the brink of madness. And other times stepping in to soothe the hurts her father's broken promises had caused.

It should have been like kissing someone familiar. They were almost family, for heaven's sake. But there had been nothing in the least bit sisterly in the feelings his kiss had elicited. His lips had been hard, insistent, and she imagined she could still feel the shock waves of pleasure that had eddied inside her. She'd heard the rumors when she was growing up; had, in fact, taken great pleasure in taunting him about his reputation. Finding out for herself that for once the gossip had been understated had been a fascinating revelation.

Absently, she let one arm drop to her side and plucked at the blades of grass with her fingers. The trip home from Helena had been the most awkward in her life. The only words Jed had spoken had been to snap out orders. She could have understood embarrassment; she ping-ponged between that and total amazement herself. But Jed hadn't seemed embarrassed. He'd seemed…angry. No doubt he was beating himself up for not being in control for once in his life. She couldn't deny that she'd been grateful for the silence, even if it had made the trip seem interminable.

She wasn't up to being casual about the kiss. An insect hovered, and she waved it away with a languid lift of her hand. Maybe later, after her memory stopped supplying her with instant replays of the sudden firestorm that had raged through her system. Then they could go on as usual.

To give them some necessary distance, she'd made sure she hadn't come downstairs until long after the usual time Jed began his day. Avoiding him might be considered cowardly. She preferred to think of it as cautious.

After all, it wasn't as if she didn't have other things to occupy her mind. The mess in Florida no longer seemed like a dark cloud of doom hovering overhead, but she did have some thinking to do. She was twenty-eight years old, and divorced from a very wealthy man who had every available asset tied up by the drug enforcement agencies, the IRS or a trust. It was a tiny sliver of irony that Marianne Craig had been correct about one thing; Julianne had come home with little more than her clothes, some jewelry and a few other personal belongings.

She hadn't planned very far ahead while she'd been in Florida. She'd spent years reacting to each new crisis of Andrew's. But now she was home, and the details of the scandal were beginning to seem very far away. It was time to decide what she was going to do with the rest of her life. The one thing she was certain about at this point was that Jed wasn't going to factor into those plans.

She took a deep breath and released it, a little of her tension easing away. She hadn't gotten a great deal of sleep last night. And the rest she had gotten had been filled with hard gray eyes, a clever mouth and strong arms. But here she felt more at peace than in the strange hotel room. The air was filled with a bounty of freshness that couldn't be found anywhere else. The sweet smell of the new grass and the lazy, droning sounds of the insects mingled with the sense of security she always had on the ranch. She let herself drift. Her last coherent thought was that she absolutely refused to dream of Jed Sullivan.

The pickup jolted over a hidden rut in the field with bone-jarring force. The bumpy journey did little to improve Jed's disposition. When he'd checked on the men, they'd laughingly mentioned that Julianne had bolted by on the back of a horse. The mere mention of her name had been enough to signal the return of the dull headache that had been riding him for the past twenty-four hours. Common sense dictated that he turn around and head in exactly the opposite direction from the one she'd taken.

Common sense had been in short supply recently. Certainly it had been completely absent a couple of nights ago. There had been no logic present when he'd covered her lips with his and discovered for himself the intoxicating flavor of that sweet, sassy mouth. And there had certainly been no sense in the desire that had knifed through him once he'd had her in his arms. The feel of that soft body pressed against his had ignited a fire in him that had yet to subside. Which was making sleep elusive, and his temper uncertain.

Knowing her as he did, he could imagine too easily the speed with which she was riding. Jumping the stream, for God's sake. She wouldn't consider the fact that she hadn't ridden in years. His mouth flattened. No, she was acting in typical Julianne fashion. Spoiled, reckless, headstrong. There was a time when he'd tried to save her from those

kinds of behaviors. Had tried to convince her to think before she acted. The way he remembered it, she'd never
thanked him for his efforts. Deliberately he drove east, to
check on several other hands who were working fence. He
did his best to push her from his mind. She'd been lodged
there for far too long already.

The sun read close to two o'clock when he headed back
toward the buildings. He hadn't gone more than a mile
when he caught sight of a mare, contentedly cropping at
grass. His gaze swept the area, and when he caught sight
of Julianne's body sprawled out on the ground, the blood
in his veins congealed. He threw the pickup into park with
a speed that had the transmission grinding, and was out of
the truck and by her side in one swift movement.

"Julianne!" In contrast to the urgency in his voice, the
hand on her shoulder was a bare whisper of movement.
Already his gaze was sweeping her form, trying to detect
any injuries.

Then her eyes were flickering open, and the dazed,
drugged look in them was so similar to the way she'd
looked after their kiss that his stomach drew up in a tight,
painful knot.

"I thought I told you to stay out of my dreams." Her
voice was slightly slurred, a little petulant.

"Are you hurt?"

She blinked a couple of times, then rubbed both hands
over her face and sat up. "No, why would I be?"

Relief fired through his system and unleashed his temper.

"Maybe because fate decided to pay you back for
tempting it all your life. When I saw you lying here, I
figured you'd finally taken the fall you've always been
begging for and broke something."

She yawned and worked her shoulders lazily. "I think

fate intervening with another nasty surprise at this point would be a little redundant, don't you?''

''Why, because you've had a few disappointments lately?'' He knew his tone was hard but made no effort to soften it. Recent experience had taught him what to expect when he allowed himself to soften toward Julianne. ''Grow up and deal with it.''

She was wide awake now, and spitting mad. ''You're going to lecture me about life? That's rich. It's easy to be an expert when you rarely leave the confines of the ranch. When your biggest challenge is having to get up in front of a bunch of ranchers and make a two-minute speech.''

He simply stared at her, grateful that she'd never know about the biggest challenge he'd ever faced. And just how horribly he'd failed. ''We're not talking about me. It's time you grew up, Jules. If it took some bad things in Florida to convince you of that, maybe they were worth it.''

Her lips tightened and she looked away. ''You don't know what you're talking about.''

''I know you. I figure that at least some of the trouble you found yourself in was due to your own recklessness. You don't seem to have a hint of self-preservation. You dive in to save people without thinking about what the cost to you might be. At the very least, people like your ex will only end up draining you. At the worst they'll drag you down with them. Like Andrew almost did.''

She didn't turn around, but he could see the muscles in her back go tense. ''Fascinating analysis. Unfortunately, I've heard it all before, ad nauseam, from you.''

He frowned and reached for a cigarette. Lighting it, he blew a stream of smoke in her direction and narrowed his eyes. ''Too bad you never listened. But you'll listen now.''

She turned and shot him a look sharp enough to draw blood.

Imperturbably he continued. "You're impulsive. You always have been. And not thinking things through can land you in a mess of trouble. Hitching up with Andrew Richfield is a prime example."

"You'll have to excuse me if I find marital advice from you to be a little hard to swallow," she said caustically. "What's your definition of a long-term relationship, three weeks?"

He'd had plenty of practice over the years ignoring her barbs. He did so now. "You're also spoiled, willful and careless." He drew in a deep breath of smoke consideringly. "I guess that's natural, given the way you were raised, always trying to get Harley's attention. But you're not a kid anymore, Jules. It's time you used your better qualities and made some changes in your life."

The look on her face was deadly enough to make him glad there was nothing nearby she could throw at him. "Better qualities? Don't tell me you think I have some."

He gazed at her through the narrow haze of smoke trailing from his cigarette and wondered with a sense of unease when he had started letting her twist up his insides. "You've got a few. Your heart's as big as all Montana, even though it's too soft sometimes. You're loyal and determined to a fault. When you set your mind to something, there's no stopping you." He brought the cigarette to his lips and drew in thoughtfully. "You've got a good mind, use it. So life jumped up and slapped you in the face. Slap back."

"Don't tempt me," she muttered meaningfully.

"You returned to the ranch to regroup. Use that time to make a mature decision about what you want. Make sure you have a plan before you take off again."

She cocked her head challengingly. "What makes you think I plan to leave?"

He said nothing for a moment, just brought the cigarette to his lips and watched her. Of course she'd leave. He ignored the quick churn in his gut at the certainty. Everybody did, eventually. Just as Kimberley had left. His birth mother hadn't exactly left him, she'd just given him away, when he'd been little more than a mass of burnt flesh and sullen bruises. Life had taught him it was infinitely easier to be the one to do the leaving. Since that wasn't always possible, the next best thing was not to give a damn.

He dropped the stub of the cigarette and ground it out carefully. "You'll leave," he said with certainty. "But this time you'll be wiser, more careful. Think before you act. That's all I'm telling you."

She raised her chin. "You don't know me half as well as you think you do. I'm a hell of a lot more than a half-brained idiot chasing after my impulses."

"Good. I'm glad you realize that."

"You know something, Jed?" she said, taking a step toward him. "I'm not ashamed of marrying Andrew. I may not have been the best judge of character, but I tried to do the right thing. I don't have to apologize to anyone for that. Maybe it wasn't the right choice to stay with him as long as I did, hoping he'd change. Maybe it wasn't the safe one. But at least I tried. I took a risk. Haven't you ever gambled on anything? Haven't you ever played the odds, taken a risk that just maybe wasn't the smartest, the safest?"

He watched her unblinkingly. "Sure. The most recent time was the other night on the terrace."

He had the satisfaction of seeing the response on her face, her eyes widening slightly, her cheeks blooming with a fascinating shade of pink. And then she brushed carefully at the blades of grass clinging to her jeans. The act seemed to require an inordinate amount of concentration.

"Oh, that. Well, as risks go, a kiss isn't exactly daredevil material. Especially with someone who's almost your sister."

"You're not my sister," he said flatly, and studied the renewed burst of color in her face with intense interest. "I'm not lying to myself about it. Why should you? I kissed you because I wanted to, even though I knew it was a bad idea. The worst."

His words had her eyes shooting sparks, and he paused for a moment, prepared to see her get a great deal more irritated. "I'm used to regarding you as a pest, a worry and a sometimes major pain in the butt. Wanting you was a shock. And it's not a habit I'm going to allow myself to get into."

Her mouth opened, then closed again. He could see the confusion, amazement and fury work over her face. If the emotions hadn't mirrored so closely the ones he'd experienced in the hours since he'd followed that particular impulse, he would have been amused. But he was dead serious.

Her voice, when she found it, was lethally dangerous. "Kissing you didn't exactly make the top ten of my personal billboard chart of smart moves, either."

The statement almost made him smile. Julianne in a snit could do that. "I just don't want you reading more into it than was there."

She sighed gustily. "How will I ever get over the disappointment of not bearing your children?"

"I don't want you getting sidetracked while you're here. You've got a lot of thinking to do, and that's where you need to focus your concentration. To keep a clear mind you need to avoid complications."

"All those profundities, and still no bubble gum," she

marveled. "You want to be careful, Jed. It's starting to sound an awful lot like you can't wait for me to leave."

Pulling out his pack of cigarettes again had less to do with a craving than for a sudden need to keep his hands busy. "I'm not pushing you on your way, if that's what you mean."

She surveyed him thoughtfully. "I wonder how I can make you understand. Remember when you changed your name from Templeton to Sullivan? How old were you then, eighteen?"

He lit the cigarette he'd placed between his lips and puffed. "Nineteen. So what?"

"I couldn't understand why you felt you needed to take your birth name back, and you told me…"

"Because it was mine," he confirmed flatly. "I wasn't adopted as a baby, you know."

She nodded. "I remember. You were…what? Three?"

"I was four when I was taken away from my mother, six when I was adopted." He lifted a shoulder negligibly. "When I was eighteen I asked Kimberley for a copy of the adoption papers. After a few months of putting me off, she finally sent them. I don't remember much about my life before I went to live with the Templetons." The statement was not quite a lie. He spent more time than he cared to think about locking away the few memories he had. But that didn't change the fact that when he'd taken his birth name back he'd taken back a piece of that life. A piece that belonged to him.

"It was yours," she said, satisfaction lacing her voice, as if she'd just discovered some deep, dark secret. "You wanted it because it represented a part of yourself."

Because she was reading his motives a little more clearly than was comfortable, he feigned disinterest. "So?"

"So the way you felt about your name is the way I feel about the ranch. I wanted to return to it because it's mine." She waved a dismissive hand, as if she noticed a protest on his lips. "Oh, I know it still has Harley's name on the papers, but my soul is here. I don't know whether I'll ever leave it again."

Her words struck both gladness and terror in his heart. The last thing he wanted to do was to let her see either of the emotions. "That will be your decision," he said, not looking at her. "Take your time."

It wasn't until she'd remounted and ridden off that he lifted his eyes. He didn't deny himself the pleasure of watching her ride away. Her hair flowed like gold behind her where the wind caught it, and she moved as though she were one with the horse she was riding.

She'd be sore tomorrow. There was nothing like horseback riding to awaken muscles that had been unused for years. He made a mental note to have Annie put some liniment out for her. An image of him rubbing lotion warmed from his palms into Julianne's taut, screaming muscles flitted across his mind and refused to be banished.

She'd been right when she'd said he wasn't a risk-taker. Life had been too full of events over which he'd had no control for him to enjoy giving up that control easily, to situations or to people. And wanting Julianne constituted the biggest risk he'd ever faced.

By the time she was a speck in the distance, the cigarette had burned down in his fingers. He ground it out absently. The feeling in her voice when she spoke of the ranch still rang in his ears. It shouldn't have surprised him. He'd always known what the ranch meant to her. It represented just as strong a pull for him, if for different reasons.

He gazed into the distance and wondered miserably how he'd forgive himself if he was responsible for driving Julianne off the ranch for good.

Chapter 7

Julianne braced one foot against the rim of the tub and soaped it indolently. The water was as hot as she could stand it, frothing with bubbles, and deep enough to reach her chin when she slid down in it. She'd piled her hair haphazardly on top of her head to keep it dry, but already strands had loosened from the careless knot and were trailing in the water. She didn't care. It felt too darn good to soak like this. She had every intention of staying in the tub until dinnertime.

She held the washcloth over her leg and dribbled water over it. After a week, her muscles were slowly becoming accustomed to riding again, but they still protested at the end of the day, and loudly. She'd never mentioned it to Annie, but a bottle of liniment had magically appeared on her dresser the first day she'd gone riding, and Julianne had been using it ever since.

Lowering her leg, she slipped down in the water, resting her head against the back of the tub. The water lapping above her shoulders, she closed her eyes and tried to recall the last time she'd felt this contented, this peaceful.

She'd been right to return to the ranch, right about the healing effect of being home with people who loved her. She'd divided her time almost equally between Annie and Gabe. For the first time in her life she was actually taking an interest in learning to cook; an interest, that is, aside from the obvious end result. Annie was teaching her, and their lessons ranged from hair-raising to hysterical.

For a couple of hours a day she followed Gabe around, taking a simultaneous joy and sadness in their time together. Jed had been right. The older man was slowing down. He appeared healthy enough, aside from the arthritis he stubbornly refused to admit to. But Julianne was struck by an awareness of how many years had passed since she'd dogged his tracks as a child. She'd learned a lot since those days, and wasn't taking for granted one minute of the time she had with him.

She shifted positions in the tub to ease her aching posterior. Her relationship with Jed was a little more complicated, but surely with both of them working at it, they could return to their old familiar footing. She looked forward to the time when they could once again be in the same room without that tension simmering and sparking between them. A shiver ran down her wet spine, and she sank lower in the water. The unexpected awareness between the two of them was the only thing that marred the days. But even with it, she was more content than she'd been in years.

Certainly life with Andrew hadn't fostered a similar sense of security. Even at the beginning, when their love had seemed fresh and strong, she had worried about his happiness, his reactions to life's disappointments.

Lazily, she reached out with her toe and pushed up the

lever, allowing some water to drain. Seconds later she pushed it down again and, with the same surefooted dexterity, turned on more hot water. When the bathwater was returned to a steaming temperature, she settled back again to soak.

"Might be someone else in the house who will need some hot water tonight," a voice called through the bathroom door. "You'd best be leaving some."

Julianne smiled without opening her eyes. "I will, Annie."

"You've got a phone call. You want to return it when you're done in another few hours?"

Her smile grew wider. "Just bring it in here, will you?"

Annie pushed open the door and walked in the room, clucking her tongue and muttering dire warnings when Julianne dried off one hand and took the phone from her.

"You wouldn't want me to waste this hot water, would you?"

The housekeeper shook her head reprovingly. "I heard tell once about a woman in Butte who dropped the phone in a bath full of water and electrocuted herself. Took a week for someone to find her."

"I'll bet her bath was cold by then."

"You just keep smartin' off, girl. Someday maybe you'll learn to listen to your elders." With that pronouncement Annie turned and exited the room. "Don't say I didn't warn you." The words trailed in her wake.

"I could never say that," Julianne murmured in amusement. She brought the phone to her ear. "Hello?"

"Julianne. Darling."

For an instant it felt as if every organ in her system failed. Breathing stopped, veins clogged. And then, as comprehension registered, they resumed their functions with a violent rush that left her weak.

"Andrew." She sat up straight in the water, which only a minute ago had been the temperature of a Jacuzzi. Now it seemed as icy as a snow-fed stream. She moistened her lips, strove to keep her voice steady. "Why are you calling me?"

"I've missed you, darling."

Oh, God, she could almost picture his face as he formed the words. The too-sensitive mouth with its determined quiver, that little-boy vulnerability that could be so tempting to nurture. So destructive to live with.

"We don't have anything to say to each other."

"Don't be like that, sweetheart." There was just enough shake in his voice to make the demand sound persuasive. "Surely you'll want to know when the trial is starting. Don't you care enough to wonder whether my release on bail is going to be my last taste of freedom for the next decade?"

An unnatural calm settled over her then. In the months since she'd left him, the reasons had never seemed clearer than they were right now. "You made your choices, Andrew. I made mine. We both have to live with them."

She heard the faint rattle of ice against crystal and knew intuitively that he was drinking. She closed her eyes for an instant as pain twisted through her. It had taken her too many years to realize that the only kind of strength Andrew had was what he could draw from her or from the bottle. Even before she'd moved out, before the scandal, she'd had the sensation of drowning in her ex-husband's excesses.

"You're the one who always seemed to know what was right, Julianne. You had all the answers."

If only that had been true, she thought, she wouldn't be having this conversation. "Hardly."

There was a long pause, and when he spoke again, his

voice was slightly steadier. "I didn't call to argue. I need your help, darling. I know I can count on you. You were always there for me."

Bitterness welled, from a pocket buried so deeply she was surprised at its explosive appearance. "Would that have been when you tried to crawl into the bottle to solve your problems, Andrew? Or when you'd disappear for weeks at a time and come home a few hundred thousand dollars poorer? Maybe you're thinking of those other women you were with, or perhaps it's all been a hallucination caused by the current drug of choice."

"I know I've disappointed you. I've disappointed myself." His voice held a fine tremble. "But I've hit rock bottom here. My lawyers say there's no way I can avoid jail time unless I give up the name of the man I was running the drugs for."

"So do it," she said flatly. "For once in your life, do the right thing."

She heard his breath hitch over the line. "I can't, he's too powerful. He'll kill me. I owe him money, and he's not going to stop until he gets it. Please, you've got to help me. I have to pay him off so he'll leave me alone. I won't even be safe in prison."

"I don't have any money." She was suddenly, fiercely glad that it was true. "Every liquid asset of ours you either lost or is tied up. I couldn't help you if I wanted to. And I don't."

"I was desperate after you left me, don't you see? I never would have gotten in so deep if I had been thinking clearly. Your leaving drove me over the edge." In the silence that followed, the only noise was the quiet crackling of the bath bubbles popping.

"I'm not going to let you lay this on me, Andrew." The process of getting air to her lungs had never seemed more difficult. "For once, just admit you made the wrong choice. No one forced you, no one is responsible but *you.*"

How familiar this conversation seemed, she thought wildly. Like an unwelcome episode of déjà vu. So many scenes had played out just like this one. Andrew pleading, her demanding that he take responsibility. And this awful sense of guilt for not being able to be strong enough for both of them.

"I miss you, Julianne. You know how much I love you."

"Don't say that!" Water splashed dangerously close to the edge of the tub as she stood up and snatched at the towel nearby. "Don't ever say that. My mistake at one time was in thinking that your sick need for me constituted love. It never did. I was your crutch, but that's over. I don't have any money, and I can't help you get out of this mess you've made."

"You have the ranch."

For a moment the room seemed to circle and spin, before his next words righted it, and set the final spark to her temper.

"Call your father. He promised the ranch to you. All you have to do is have him sign over the papers. I'm not asking you to sell the whole thing, but there's so much land, Julianne." The words didn't quite manage to avoid a whine. "All I need is five hundred thousand. The ranch must be worth millions. I'm just asking for a piece of it."

At that instant, her head had never been clearer, her resolve stronger. "Never. I'm not surprised you'd ask, Andrew. But I am surprised if you thought it would work. Don't call me again."

She cut his protest short with one touch of her finger. With more care than the acts required, she put the phone down and used the towel to dry off. She caught her re-

flection in the glass. Her face was pale, set. For just a
moment it reminded her of other times over the past few
years, other reflections: After she'd spent the day finding
and pouring all the liquor stashed in the house down the
drain, only to have Andrew stagger in after an afternoon
at one of his clubs. Or when she'd accompanied him to
Gamblers Anonymous meetings for a month, and then discovered that he'd taken off again, this time for Atlantic
City.

She slipped her robe on and walked into her bedroom.
And then, of course, there was that final time when she'd
followed him to their place in Key West, hoping to keep
him from the booze and the high stakes card games. Instead she'd found him entertaining a redhead in their bed.

Life with Andrew, she reflected, had been no life at all.
She'd had little opportunity to do more than react to his
choices. It had taken her too many years to recognize the
vicious circle that she'd been drawn into, the cycle of abet-
ting and enabling his weaknesses. She wondered how long
it would take for her to stop feeling as though walking
away from him constituted a personal failure.

She crossed to the dresser and took out underwear. She
was just slipping on a fresh pair of jeans when the phone
she'd left in the other room rang. She started for an instant,
and then ignored it. No doubt it was for Jed. Annie often
took messages for him, which he returned after supper
when he went to his den.

She stood in front of her closet, tapping a finger against
her lips. The large space was filled to overflowing, making
it difficult to find anything easily. She resolved to spend
some time the next day hauling some of her clothes to a
closet in one of the extra bedrooms.

Making a decision, she took a pale yellow short-sleeved

silk blouse from its hanger and put it on. She was button-
ing it when Annie knocked at her bedroom door.

"Phone's for you again, Julianne."

Her gaze flew to the door, her body going still. It was
a long moment before she found her voice. "Tell him...I
can't come to the phone." Her words were greeted with
silence. Annie had returned downstairs.

Immediately castigating herself for her cowardice, Julianne strode into the bathroom, picked up the phone and
turned it on. "I don't want you calling me again. I gave
you my answer and it was final."

There was a long silence, and then a familiar voice
drawled, "I hadn't expected a rousing rendition of 'Auld
Lang Syne,' but I think you can do better than that."

Relief and delight rushed through her. "Shelby! Oh, it's
great to hear from you. Tell me that you're at your dad's
place."

"We just got in this morning. J.T. has been a tyrant.
The plane ride wore him out, poor little thing."

"How long are you staying?"

"A week." Julianne could picture the other woman as
she answered, pacing through the house. Shelby could
serve as evidence for the theory of perpetual motion.
"We're having supper with Dad tonight, but he mentioned
wanting to invite a few neighbors over for a get-together
tomorrow evening. We can catch up then, and make plans
for the rest of my stay."

"Sounds great."

"Invite Annie and Jed, will you? And don't let Annie
bring too much. Tell her she doesn't have to worry about
the food. I've actually become pretty domesticated over
the last few years."

"Now, that's hard to believe," Julianne teased.

"Believe. I didn't mind endless suppers of Ramin noodles for myself, but Steve requires a bit more nourishment. I take pity on the man occasionally and provide him with a real meal.''

It was nice that some things didn't change, Julianne reflected after hanging up the phone. Catching up with Shelby had taken the better part of a half hour, and only the interruption of J.T.'s howling had cut their chat short. It didn't matter how much time passed between their talks or visits. Their friendship remained constant.

She hadn't admitted how shaken she'd been by Andrew's call until she realized how much the conversation with Shelby had soothed her. She'd found peace here, finally. That wasn't going to change. She wouldn't let it.

Annie's brows rose when Julianne entered the kitchen a couple of minutes after six.

''Fall asleep in the bathtub? You know what time we eat around here.''

Circling the table, she snatched a piece of still-warm homemade bread off Jed's plate and barely dodged the fork he stabbed in her direction. She took a bite and closed her eyes in ecstasy. ''Oh, God, Annie, this is so great.'' She slipped into her chair and countered Jed's glower with a smug grin. ''Way too much butter on this, though, big guy. You better start watching your cholesterol. Can't have those arteries hardening up on you.''

He reached for another piece of bread and took great pleasure in smothering it in even more butter than he'd put on the one she'd swiped. Taking a deliberate bite, he chewed, swallowed and said, ''I'm not worried. But I suppose you have to watch those calories pretty close. What with your weight problem, and all.''

Her eyes narrowed and he settled in to enjoy his meal.

''What weight problem?''

The fact that Julianne's figure had always bordered on the slender didn't enter into the situation. The verbal warfare was reminiscent of times past and helped mask the uncomfortable awareness of her that he couldn't seem to shake. He helped himself to two thick slices of roast beef, then passed her the plate. When she didn't immediately take it, he set it down beside her. Going to work cutting his meat, he lied, "Well, I overheard Gabe say the mare you've been riding has been coming back each day exhausted. Seems she's getting a little swaybacked, too. He thinks she's been carrying too heavy a load." He laid down his silverware and winked at Annie as he took the bowl of mashed potatoes she was passing to him. "So I reckon Annie will understand if you don't want a helping of these."

Julianne was toying with the knife next to her plate, looking as if she was contemplating throwing it. "Gabe never said that. Big liar. And I've never had to watch my weight a day in my life."

"For goodness' sake, Jed, quit ribbing the girl. She's no bigger than a minute. If she ate any less she'd blow away."

"Or roll," he murmured, just loud enough to be audible. Deliberately, he set the bowl just out of her reach.

"I seem to recall that Jed's taste in women ran more toward the meaty." Julianne got out of her chair and rounded the table, picking up the bowl of potatoes with one hand and deliberately jostling him with her elbow. He barely managed to right the glass of milk he was reaching for before he spilled its contents across the table.

Smirking, she slipped back into her chair and dished up a huge helping of mashed potatoes that she couldn't possibly eat in three sittings. "Remember Amanda Lassiter, Jed's lady love in high school?"

"Amanda," he said, while pouring generous amounts

of gravy over his meat and potatoes, "was a gal with many hidden charms."

"Hidden, my eye," Julianne snorted. "With those low-cut tops, she had no secrets. And her jeans were so tight you could read the number of her MasterCard in her back pocket."

He grinned. Her description was on the money, as usual. He hadn't thought of Amanda Lassiter in years. Despite Julianne's opinion, his taste had grown more subtle since his high school days.

"Honestly." Annie got up from the table and fetched another carton of milk. "Listening to the two of you, a person would think you were a couple of kids, the way you squabble. And the gal Jed's dating now is a real nice woman. She's new to town. Carrie Fredericks is her name. Does the prettiest cross-stitch you've ever seen, too. Took a blue ribbon at the county fair last summer." Her eyes twinkled as she sedately went about her meal. "So apparently he's learned something since high school."

If he hadn't been looking at Julianne, he might have missed her reaction to Annie's words. Shock, certainly, followed by a fascinating flicker in her eyes, one that vanished when she caught him looking at her.

"Well, they say it's never to late to acquire taste," she drawled, her voice dripping with doubt.

"Thought maybe you might have made a date yourself," Annie said to Julianne, her voice teasing. "Who was that man who called earlier?"

Taking an inordinate amount of interest in her food, Julianne concentrated on cutting her meat into tiny pieces. "It was only Andrew. But the second call was from Shelby. Did you know she was home? She'll be at her dad's the rest of the week. Wanted to have a get-together tomorrow night for some of the neighbors. You and Jed are invited.''

She chattered on to Annie, the conversation centering on what food to take, and Shelby's son, J.T., whose crying had brought the reunion to a quick close. Their words didn't register. Jed had stopped listening after she'd answered Annie's first question.

''What'd he want?''

Julianne looked at him with guileless brown eyes. ''J.T.? His dinner probably. Shelby says he's growing like a weed and eats all the time. I can't wait to see him.''

His mouth tightened, and his voice went low and smooth, revealing none of the dangerous emotion trapped inside. ''Andrew. What'd he want?''

Reaching for her glass, she took a drink before answering. ''He wanted help.''

The defiance in her tone was reflected on her face. It lit the fuse of his temper as surely as a gasoline-soaked match. ''You're not giving him any.''

Julianne's fork dropped to her plate. All semblance of eating was discarded. ''I don't take orders from you, cowboy.''

Annie's gaze went from Jed to Julianne and back again. ''Now, Jed. This is Julianne's business. You mind to your own and so will she.''

He gave a tight grin at the obvious untruth. ''That would be the day. And I meant what I said. You're not helping your rich ex-husband out of this jam of his.''

She brought her napkin to her mouth and wiped her lips. ''Ex-rich, actually. It appears he's a little short of cash.''

''It's not too hard to figure how he thought you could get your hands on some. The only time he was here all he could talk about was the value of this place.'' She remained silent, and his gaze narrowed. "Is that it? He actually suggested you get the money from the ranch?"

"Can I interest anyone in pie?"

Annie's words went unanswered. Jed's gaze was fixed on Julianne, and he saw he'd guessed accurately. He rose. "We'll discuss this in the study." He half expected to get a fight from her, but her gaze flicked to the housekeeper, and then she stood.

"I'll be back for pie later, Annie," she promised, and preceded Jed out of the room.

"Let's hope you're both in a condition to eat it by then," the older woman muttered.

Jed closed the door behind him. Julianne remained standing in the middle of the room, facing him. "I didn't figure we needed to do this in front of Annie and upset her."

"I agree." Julianne stalked toward him. "That's the only reason I'm here."

"You're not going to get a chance to bankrupt this place to bail out Richfield," he said tersely. His body was tense, all his instincts on attack. No one threatened the ranch's security. Not ever. "So if you made him any promises, you'd better call him back and tell him he's on his own."

"I didn't."

Her words failed to register. The need to move did. He strode to his desk and absently picked up a book there, slamming it down in the next moment and whirling around. "Dammit, Jules, what the hell are you thinking, anyway? You wouldn't seriously consider putting the ranch in jeopardy for that wimp you married."

Her head was cocked, and she was watching him warily. "No, I wouldn't."

It was hard to think when his whole body was rigid with reaction. "I won't allow it. I stopped Harley when he was intent on doing the same thing, and if you think you're going to threaten my home..." He stopped abruptly and stared at her. "What'd you say?"

"I said, no I'm not considering helping Andrew. But I'm more concerned with what *you* said. What was that about Harley draining the ranch?"

He ignored the question. "But you said you were..."

She shook her head. "There you go again, Sullivan, not listening. Have I taught you nothing? I said Andrew asked." Her next words were simple and laced with sincerity. "I told him no."

An emotion he couldn't identify as relief flowed through him. "You told me you felt sorry for him."

The look she gave him was incredulous. "So I did, but that doesn't mean I'm willing to sell off part of the ranch for him. Assuming Harley is even ready to sign it over to me."

He couldn't look at her. He picked up a glass paperweight in the shape of a horse that he kept on the corner of his desk. Julianne had given it to her father one Christmas years ago. Jed remembered how she'd saved for months to buy it. When Harley had taken off, he'd left it behind. Just as he had his daughter.

Because he was tempted to hurl it at the wall, he set it down deliberately. It wouldn't satisfy his destructive mood, at any rate.

"What did he want the money for?"

There was a pause, long enough to draw his gaze to her. Julianne lifted a shoulder. "Like I said, he's broke. Why don't you tell me what you meant about Harley?"

"You know how your father is. He gets in deep sometimes and looks for a quick source of cash. The ranch starts looking mighty inviting then."

Her face went sober, her eyes hard. "He wanted to raid the ranch's finances."

Feeling the need to move again, he circled the desk, trailing an absent hand over its surface, the oak bookcase behind it, the leather chair in front of the desk. Their touch comforted him. They felt solid and permanent, the way the ranch did. In a way that little else in his life ever had.

"He took as much as he could, while still leaving the ranch to limp along. It was in dire straits for a couple of years. We needed a transfusion of cash, fast."

The distress on her face was easy to read. So was the guilt. "I didn't know about any of this."

"You weren't here." The words hung in the air between them. They were simple enough. They shouldn't have had the power to cause her to flinch and turn away.

"What's to stop him from doing it again? Sure, Harley's flush now, but you know as well as I how quickly that can change."

"It won't happen again." His voice was certain.

"But how can we be sure?"

"Jules." He waited until she turned, looked at him. "I made sure." When her mouth opened, he raised a hand to stem her words. "If you want to know more, take it up with Harley."

"You bet I will," she said grimly. "But right now you're here and I have something to take up with you. Why didn't you let me know about the problems with the ranch?"

He stared at her, a part of him noticing how the yellow shirt she wore clung and skimmed in all the right places, how it mirrored the brightness of her hair. He couldn't help noticing, couldn't help responding, but he could prevent it from touching him on any deeper level. "You weren't here, remember? You left." And then, because the words seemed too much like an accusation, felt too much like one, he added, "Besides, what could you have done that I couldn't?"

"I could have talked to Harley!" she exclaimed, eyes blazing. "I could have reminded him of his promise and maybe made him see what he was doing with this endless gambling...."

"The way you did with your husband?"

She looked as though he'd slapped her, and he felt an instant jolt of remorse. He wasn't accustomed to dealing deliberate hurt. But experience had taught him that hurt delivered casually could wound just as deeply.

She raised her chin, but her voice was shaky. "Sometimes you are really a bastard."

He acknowledged her words silently. They were no less than the truth, both figuratively and literally. But it didn't stop him from starting toward her, the need to comfort an irrepressible urge.

He caught her before she got to the door, and stopped her with a touch on her shoulder. "Julianne." It was all he could manage, but it was enough to keep her there, rooted to the floor.

Tucking his chin on top of that shiny gold head, he slipped an arm around her waist and applied just enough pressure to coax her to lean against him. It was the apology he couldn't voice, and had her legs been steadier it wouldn't have been effective.

For an instant, just an instant, he felt her weight against him, as if for once in her life the fight had streamed out of her and left her limp. It was a whisper of time, but it was long enough to stir memories of when he'd last held her, and of all the reasons he'd told himself it couldn't happen again.

As if she'd read his mind, she stiffened and turned to

face him. "I understand, you know. You don't think I can, but I do."

"What's that?"

There was a faint tilt at the corners of her mouth, but her eyes were serious. "You. I know what it means to want to reach out and hang on tight to the one thing in your life that's stable. You love the ranch as much as I do. You always have."

Because her words were too close to an echo in his mind, he lifted a shoulder casually. "I did what needed to be done. And I did it alone."

His words put a distance between them that had nothing to do with the physical. Her gaze searched his, looking for answers that he couldn't, wouldn't give.

"I'd better go assure Annie that neither of us killed the other."

He nodded and watched her turn and walk away from him.

As certain as if he could see grains of sand draining through an hourglass, he could feel time slipping away from him. He wondered how much longer he had before she walked away for good. Away from the ranch.

And away from him.

Chapter 8

"Girl, you're looking so good I'd hate you if I didn't love you so darn much."

Julianne grinned at Shelby's wry tone and finished her barbecued rib with relish. "Nice try. To sound properly envious, of course, it would help to actually work some real jealousy into your voice. And if you could manage to wipe that smug expression off your face every time you look at Steve or J.T., I just might believe that you'd willingly trade places with me."

Shelby laughed and tossed a chip at her friend. "Witch. I'm just glad that I never managed to convince Dad to put in a pool. If I had to watch all the men here ogle you in a bikini while I'm still struggling with the last ten pounds I gained with J.T., I might be driven to murder." She waggled her brows in mock menace. "Hormones are uncertain in postpartum moms, you know."

Blandly Julianne observed, "Really? Your hormones

sure seemed in working order when I surprised you and Steve in the kitchen earlier.''

To her amusement, Shelby colored. "Well, J.T. is several weeks old now, and Steve and I have been waiting…that is, I saw the doctor before we flew out here, and he said…''

"He gave you permission to wrestle Steve to the floor and have your wicked way with him?'' Julianne suggested helpfully.

Shelby's eyes gleamed. "Which I plan to do at the earliest possible opportunity.''

Julianne laughed. She'd liked big blond Steve Carrington the first time she'd met him at Shelby's wedding four years ago. The man seemed to have settled into marriage and fatherhood with an ease she found at once enchanting and baffling. In her narrow field of acquaintants, she'd observed no other men who handled the responsibility of a family with such equanimity. Her friend was the lucky one, and she was certain the other woman knew it.

"So, how are you really?'' Shelby asked. "How much damage did Andrew manage to inflict before you dumped him?''

Julianne released a breath. Shelby was never less than direct. "You didn't like him.''

"No,'' she admitted without remorse. "Oh, he was exciting, I'll give you that. Living in the spotlight, skydiving, mountain climbing, squiring around rock stars and Hollywood beauties. I never doubted that you'd be good for him. I just didn't think he'd be good for you. I never understood why you married him.''

Julianne dropped her gaze. "I'm still working on that one myself.''

Shelby patted her leg. "Well, you've got time to figure it out. That's why you're home, isn't it?'' Seamlessly she shifted to a less sensitive subject. "I was a little surprised to be snubbed by Eleanor when the Poolers arrived. She was so frosty I could have scraped ice off her greeting."

Julianne reached for her glass of lemonade. "That might be my fault. I attended the Cattlemen's bash in Helena with Jed a week ago and ran into Marianne."

"Literally, I hope."

She took a long drink, delighting in the simple pleasures of icy lemonade and her best friend's company. "I'm ashamed to admit that the mystery of how Marianne happened to find herself in the gym half naked has been put to rest."

Shelby clapped her hands in delight. "Oh, you fiend. I suppose you took all the credit yourself."

"I'll have you know I gave you your due." Julianne ran a finger down the cheek that had been slapped. And then kissed by Jed, just minutes later. "I believe I owe you half a slap, in Marianne's name."

"Damn!" Shelby exclaimed. "The pièce de résistance with Marianne Craig, and I missed it. You always get to have all the fun."

"It was...an experience," Julianne allowed. "Jed intervened before I could redo that nose job her parents bought for her, so there was no real damage done." A slow smile crossed her face. "Except to her dress."

"Jed." Shelby cocked her head and fixed Julianne with an intent stare. "What exactly did you say you were doing with him in Helena?"

Julianne set her empty plate on the patio beside her lounger, then leaned her weight back and crossed her legs at the ankles. "With Jed?" She waved a hand carelessly. "Oh, nothing. He just thought I'd find it amusing."

Her friend still had that eagle-eyed look about her, and her gaze hadn't wavered from Julianne's face. "Uh-huh."

"Actually, it was entertaining, up to and including the scene with Marianne. And of course, I spoke to your dad there." Growing increasingly uncomfortable under Shelby's scrutiny, she tapped a rapid tattoo on the side of her glass with the nail on her index finger. "He told you we talked, didn't he? He's looking really good. How's he been doing since your mom died?"

"Okay, I think. He's been to see us several times, and you still can't lie to me, so don't even try."

Julianne raised a brow and willed her nerves away. "What are you talking about?"

A satisfied smile pulled at Shelby's mouth. "There. That casual pose, the nervous tapping, the geyser of words. I could always tell when you were hiding something. I was the one who thought up most of our alibis, remember?"

"Most of which lacked imagination."

"Yours were too creative to be entirely believable. So," she purred, leaning forward to scoot her chair closer to her friend's. "What exactly has been happening between you and Jed? Tell Auntie Shelby all about it."

Despite herself, Julianne felt a glimmer of amusement. "There's nothing to tell. He thought I needed to get away from the ranch and offered to take me along. I went and enjoyed myself."

"Oh, I'll bet you did. But what, exactly, did you enjoy? Or should I say, whom?"

Her scandalized tone not totally feigned, Julianne said, "Shelby! We're talking about Jed here."

"Yes, we most certainly are." Her gaze slid to the man in question, who was leaning against the edge of a picnic table, eating and talking to a group of neighboring ranchers.

Julianne's eyes followed the path of her friend's. She wondered if there was a color that didn't suit the man. The red T-shirt was snugged into a pair of black jeans, providing a perfect foil for his dark looks. He looked relaxed, or as relaxed as he ever seemed to get. His teeth flashed then as he grinned at something one of the other men said, and her heart stuttered a beat.

Deliberately she dragged her gaze from Jed, only to meet Shelby's knowing smile.

"I've said it before, I'll say it again. It's too bad about that man's body."

"What man?" Julianne asked blandly.

Her friend only laughed. "The one who has kept you in his sights the entire time you've been here."

"Shel, get a grip. There're only a couple dozen people around. *Everyone's* in his sight."

"Maybe so, but he doesn't keep shooting those little glances at everyone else. See? There he goes again."

Julianne kept her eyes trained on her friend. "He's just checking to make sure I don't do something inappropriate, like dance naked on one of the picnic tables."

"Why, has he caught you at that before? Or was it a private exhibition?"

Teeth grinding at her friend's good-natured persistence, Julianne replied, "Jed doesn't tolerate mistakes easily, and he's made no bones about what he thinks of my debacle in Florida. I'm surprised he didn't suggest using a leash on me when I leave the ranch."

Shelby watched her concernedly. "Oh, Jules, are you sure? I know Jed could come down heavy when he didn't approve of something, but we were kids then."

"Believe it. He catalogued my faults for me not a week ago. I didn't even start on his because there wasn't enough daylight left to do the job justice."

Disappointment colored Shelby's tone. "You mean you two have been fighting the whole time you've been back?"

"Not the whole time." Without invitation, the scene that had taken place on the balcony in Helena drifted across her mind like smoke curling under a door. There hadn't been disapproval in his kiss, she remembered. It had been hard, fierce and hungry. His hunger had torched hers, and despite her best efforts, the memory was still shimmering through her system, refusing to be exiled.

Realizing her friend was looking at her with renewed hope, she tucked that particular memory away and added, "Sometimes I manage to avoid him completely. Don't go fabricating happy endings for us, Shelby. I'm pretty leery of any relationship at this point, and Jed…well, I understand he has interests elsewhere."

"You mean Carrie Fredericks?" Shelby waved a dismissive hand. "That's not serious."

Unable to help herself, Julianne looked hard at her friend. "How on earth would you know that?"

Shelby grinned, smug. "Susan Gray at the post office. You remember Susan, don't you? Two years ahead of us in school? Anyway, I stopped in there yesterday and she filled me in on just about everyone around here. I have it on good authority that Jed and Carrie are only dating casually." She winked. "He still has quite a reputation, but apparently has learned some discretion over the years."

"You got all that from stopping in the post office?" Julianne didn't know whether to be amused or annoyed. The small town of Lisbon was twenty miles from the ranch. In Montana, that was considered no distance at all.

"Heck no, there's lots more. Bill Larkin and his wife in Arizona just had twins, the Barnetts are on the verge of bankruptcy, and if Mr. Finley at the general store raises his prices one more time he's going to put himself right out of business." This was delivered in a tone so like Susan Gray's that Julianne couldn't prevent a laugh.

"You're a fountain of information, Shel."

"I do what I can." Shelby brushed crumbs from her lap and smiled a greeting to her approaching husband and son. "There are my two favorite guys. How was the nap, tiger?" This was addressed to J.T., who was blinking owlishly.

"*Tiger* is a pretty apt description for the way he woke up," Steve said. "What do you think, Julianne? He's got his father's good looks and his mother's charming personality, right?"

Julianne held out her arms. "I can only answer that question upon closer examination." Steve put the baby in her arms, and he was surprisingly heavy.

"He's a moose, isn't he? He's already in the ninety-fifth percentile for his weight."

"Has his father's appetite, too," Shelby remarked.

Julianne wrapped the baby closer in her arms and dipped her head. He felt soft and warm and smelled of the uniquely baby scents of powder and sweet infant skin. She ran a gentle finger over J.T.'s downy cheek. She'd considered starting a family early in her marriage but had put it off, perhaps even then realizing that her husband was too much of a child himself to ever be a good father. She didn't regret that decision now, but the dream of a real family of her own lingered.

"He's a sweetheart," she murmured.

"He can be," Shelby said cheerfully. She raised a hand to her husband, who took it and helped her from the lounger. "But if I don't feed him pretty quickly you'll change your opinion in a hurry." She bent down and took the baby from her friend, shifting him expertly in her arms. Glancing at her husband, she said, "You can come along, too, Daddy. You're on diaper detail today, remember?"

Steve groaned good-naturedly but didn't seem reluctant

to follow his wife and son into the house. Julianne watched them go with a slight smile on her face and a wistful feeling in her heart. When the couple was out of sight, she looked away and met Jed's gaze. A tendril of heat traced up her spine. Despite Shelby's prodding, despite her own confusion, she knew better than to get involved with Jed Sullivan. Andrew had been so needy, he'd almost managed to drain her emotionally. Jed was exactly his opposite, and much more dangerous.

Her index finger traced a line down the condensation of her glass. Jed would never be clinging and needy. He was the most self-contained man she'd ever met. Jed Sullivan didn't need anybody.

"Jed? What in heaven's name are you still doing up?"

He raised his gaze from the breeding magazine he was reading to see Annie highlighted in the doorway of his study, wrapped up in a robe.

"My lands, it's after two. Doesn't anyone go to bed around here?"

He looked at the clock on the wall, as if to prove her words. After the party had broken up around midnight, he'd been too wired to even consider sleep. He'd settled in the study for some paperwork and reading.

"I guess it is getting pretty late, at that," he said finally.

"I should say so. I got up to get myself a glass of milk and noticed that Julianne's jacket wasn't there. Where on earth do you think that girl has gotten off to?"

Rather than tell the woman that he put quite a bit of effort into *not* thinking about Julianne, he gave a shrug. "Maybe she took it up to her room with her."

Annie crossed her arms and began to tap her foot, a sign of her dwindling patience. "Now, don't you think I checked, once I saw her coat was missing? Her bed hasn't been slept in and she's nowhere in the house. I looked on the porch and patio, too.''

He scrubbed his hands over his face, suddenly weary. ''Well, she must be around somewhere. She came home with us, and if she'd left the ranch I would have heard an engine.'' The silence stretched between them. He dropped his hands and noted the determined look on the house-keeper's face. He recognized that look from years ago. Rising, he muttered, ''But I'll sure as hell go out and find her for you.''

''Thanks, Jed. I'm sure she must be around, but I wouldn't be able to sleep not knowing for sure.''

He paused in the mudroom to tug on his boots, his mood grim. Chasing after Julianne wasn't his idea of a perfect ending to an evening. There was no telling where she'd gone off to; he hadn't heard her go out. He slipped out the side door and headed toward the outbuildings. If her horse was missing, at least he'd know that she'd gone out for a midnight ride. More than likely she just went for a walk.

He tried the horse barn first. Julianne's favorite mount was accounted for. He stood still for a moment, thinking. The baby foals and calves were all pastured with their mothers, or he wouldn't have had to think twice about where to find her. She'd always loved to spend time with the young animals.

The memory sparked another, from earlier this evening. He'd looked up and seen her holding J.T., and the sight had impacted him like a brick to the chest. Her hair had curtained her face as she'd looked down at the infant, but there had been no missing the tenderness with which she'd held him, touched him. He'd been struck by how natural she'd looked, how gut-wrenchingly intimate it had seemed to watch her with the baby. He knew better than most that maternal instincts weren't guaranteed in all females. His mother and adoptive mother had been prime examples of that.

He exited the building and went to the truck parked nearby. The edginess that had ridden him all evening had grown teeth. There was no telling how long his search would take him, and damned if he was willing to tromp all over the ranch looking for the woman.

The truck roared to life and he headed toward the cattle barn. Noticing lights winking in the distance, he let up on the accelerator. There was still someone up in the bunkhouse, and he paused, considering. Years ago he'd had a cluster of small homes built nearby for some of the hands with families, and the more senior men, like Gabe. Most of the other hands still resided in the bunkhouse, though.

Giving a mental shrug, he turned the wheel and headed toward the bunkhouse. Maybe someone there had seen her. If not, he'd go back to the house and see if she had turned up there yet. A tinge of concern traced through him. Wandering around a ranch in the wilds of Montana wasn't a bright move at any time. In the middle of the night it could be downright dangerous. He just hoped he wasn't going to have to rouse the men to form a search party before the night was over.

He pulled up to the bunkhouse and walked rapidly to the door. Giving a cursory knock he pushed it open. He heard Julianne before he saw her, and relief quickly gave way to the irritation she caused so effortlessly.

"Watch and learn, gentlemen. The game's five card draw, nothing wild but your fantasies."

Jed pushed the door closed and leaned against it. Julianne was seated at the round dining table surrounded by—he counted automatically—eight men. Even as he watched, she finished dealing the cards and set the deck in front of her. She picked up her hand in one smooth motion and fanned the cards out. Even from this distance, he could read them and tell that she didn't have a jack.

"Dealer starts the bidding at twenty."

"Dammit, Julianne, either you have the devil's own luck or you're bluffing again." Zeke, a hand who'd worked for them since Julianne was a teen, spoke. He flicked a glance at Jed. "If you came to get in on the game, Jed, you can take my place." He threw his cards down in disgust. "Lady Luck has been ignoring me all night."

"Now, if you were Lady Luck, who would you rather smile down on, a grizzled old coot or the prettiest woman in the county?" asked Blair Ramsey, aiming his famed lady-killer smile in Julianne's direction. "I'm in for twenty, darlin', and I'll be taking two cards."

Jed's eyes narrowed and he sauntered to the table. Ramsey had been with them for two years and had quickly established a reputation for having a soft touch with horses and smooth moves with women. Jed had never held the latter against him. He didn't care what a man did in his free time if it didn't affect his work or reflect poorly on the ranch. But he was suddenly reconsidering his open-mindedness.

Drawing even with the table, he could see the bottle of tequila sitting in front of Julianne, right next to a wad of cash. She had a wicked-looking cigar clenched between her teeth. Shooting him a sideways look, she grinned, reaching up to take the stogie out of her mouth. "Deal you in, cowboy?"

He leaned on the back of Gabe's chair and shook his head. "No, I think I'll just stand here and take bets on how long it will take you to puke tonight." The men chuckled.

Julianne raised a brow. Around the cigar she'd replaced

in her mouth, she said, "It'll be the first time you've ever taken the long odds." Laughter broke out again.

She turned her attention back to the game and finished dealing the cards, taking no hits for herself. "No guts, no glory, guys. I'm betting fifty. Put up or shut up."

"I've lost my limit, Julianne." Tyler, the youngest hand there, folded his cards and pushed back his chair. "But I sure did appreciate the chance to make your acquaintance."

Jed watched as she took the cigar from her mouth and beamed at the boy, reducing the kid to a quaking mass of hormones. "I enjoyed meeting you, Tyler. And I'll be taking you up on that offer to teach me the latest line dances, too."

Tyler clenched the brim of his hat in both hands as a look of stunned pride crossed his face. "I surely do look forward to that, ma'am." He backed away from the table slowly, turning only after he tripped over a chair. Then he met Jed's gaze, flushed and hurried from the room.

"We used to have us friendly games," one of the men mumbled, tossing his cards in.

Another jeered, "Yeah, right. This is the first one in a month that didn't end in a fistfight."

"The night's young," Julianne observed blandly, and the men broke up again.

Jed sat back to watch her in action. Ramsey was the only one who held out until the end. The bidding and counterbidding finally depleted the store of cash before him.

"C'mon, Gabe, loan me a hundred until payday," he wheedled. "I've got me a sure thing here."

The older man shook his head. "Can't do that, Blair. I make it a point never to bet against Julianne unless I have a clear view of her cards."

Ramsey appealed to all the other men at the table and, when each refused, threw his cards down faceup. "A full house! I had to waste my best hand all night." He cocked a wry grin at Julianne, who was busily scooping up her winnings. "Let's see what you had, sweetheart."

She aimed an easy smile back at him. "You didn't pay to see my cards, Blair."

His grin disappeared and his voice turned hard. "Hell, sweet thing, you cleaned me out. The least you owe me is a look at the hand I lost to." He reached out for the cards she'd laid facedown on the table beside her.

Jed's hand snaked to the man's wrist, holding it immobile. "You heard the lady. Game's over, Ramsey." He exchanged a hard stare with the hired man, and the room went silent.

Blair tugged at his wrist. It wasn't until he muttered, "Sure thing, boss," that it was freed. His gaze cut back to Julianne. "Another time, sweet thing. You can show me…whatever you want."

Chairs scraped as the men pushed back from the table. Some headed for their homes, and the others ambled to their beds. Julianne folded her stack of cash and stood up, tucking it in the pocket of her jeans. Her gaze clashed with Jed's.

"Have I told you recently how tedious your knight-in-shining-armor routine is?" she inquired.

"Have I told you recently what a pain in the ass you are?" he returned caustically. "Next time you feel like a night out with the boys, leave a note or something. Annie woke up and missed you. She was worried."

Her eyes flickered. Gabe rose laboriously and put her jacket over her shoulders. "You'd better go on in with Jed, Julie girl. But I had a real fine time tonight. Just like the old days."

She gave the older man a quick hug. ''I'll come back after payday,'' she teased, and he chuckled.

''You do that.''

Jed reached over and ground the cigar out in the ashtray. He caught Julianne's gaze on him and asked, ''You didn't want to save this for later, did you?'' She stalked toward the door.

Gabe clapped him on the shoulder. ''Now, son, don't be too hard on the girl. She let them fellas win most of the night.''

''Trying to soften them up?'' He watched, unwillingly captivated by the gentle sway of rounded hips encased in soft, worn denim.

''You ask her why she threw away three ladies earlier and let Tommy Milford have the pot,'' the man advised. Shuffling away, he shook his head at the memory. ''Never seen the likes of that girl. Nope, I never have.''

Neither, Jed thought sourly as he walked toward the truck where Julianne was waiting, had he.

He climbed into the truck silently and started it, driving the short distance to the house.

''You know, I'm not sixteen anymore.'' Julianne's voice came in the darkness, smooth and coolly amused. ''You're going to have to get used to that fact.''

''And you're going to have to get used to the fact that you've got folks who worry about you,'' he countered. And then, because the question wouldn't quit nagging at him, he said, ''Why'd you throw away a perfectly good hand tonight for Tommy Milford?''

''Maybe I was just priming him for the next time.''

''The truth, Jules.'' He parked the truck several yards from the house and turned it off but made no move to open the door.

After a long moment she answered. "I met his son a couple of days ago. Do you know Ricky?"

"Bright red hair, freckles and the orneriest little s—cuss on the ranch," he amended. "Yeah, I know him. So what?"

"Well, he said it's his birthday next week, and the thing he wants more than anything else in the world is the black bike in the window of Wilson's hardware store." He could hear the satisfaction in her voice when she added, "That was a sizable pot I lost. Tommy ought to be able to afford that bike for Ricky for sure." She laughed softly. "Now the kid will really be hell on wheels."

Her words struck him hard in the chest, and he stared at her in the darkness. She looked smug and sleepy-eyed, and so damn pleased with herself. There had always been that softness in Julianne, that genuine goodness that was so at odds with her smart mouth and careless manner. It never failed to sneak up on him unaware, uncurling something inside him that he didn't even recognize. Didn't want to identify.

His hand shot out without his conscious permission and caught her hair, dragged her laughing mouth to his. He swallowed her gasp and claimed her lips for his own.

Dark flavors swirled, banked, unleashed by a rising fury of emotion. She slid closer and fisted her fingers tightly in his hair to bring him nearer. He complied willingly, turning her and pulling her onto his lap in one smooth movement. He felt her start of surprise but never released her mouth. He couldn't. The energy crackling between them was that strong. That hot.

He let the sharp-edged wave of desire wash over him, swallow him whole. Her tongue touched his, a long velvet glide and need burst quickly, fanned by her answering hunger. He'd thought he'd imagined it. The dim thought shifted across his mind. Surely no woman could taste that sweet, feel that devastating. Logic couldn't fade that quickly, control disappear that fast. But he was being proved wrong all over again.

He changed the angle of the kiss, wanting more of her, demanding it. She caught his bottom lip between her teeth and scored it lightly, then soothed it with her tongue. Tearing his mouth from hers, he pressed his lips to her throat in a desperate quest for her scent. He satisfied his need for the taste of her flesh at the same time his hand found her breast.

Her gasp was a faint sound in the air, and her fingers curled tightly into his shoulders. He could feel her nails biting lightly through his shirt and wanted more. Her nipple stabbed at his palm through the layers of her clothing, and he wanted to close his mouth over it, tease it with his teeth and tongue. He wanted to lay her down on the seat and unwrap her clothes until she was gleaming naked in the moonlight. And then he wanted to taste all her sweet hidden secrets and make them his.

His mouth returned to twist across hers, desperation pummeling from the inside with wicked, jagged fists. He squeezed her breast lightly, felt the firm flesh shape to his touch and wanted to howl. He'd wondered how she could topple his control so easily, dominate his senses so completely. He was no closer to the answer but damn close to giving in to every sensation she caused in him.

He kissed her once more, hard, then pulled away. It was maddening to recognize the whipping of his pulse, the sawing of his breath. And because frustration wasn't his favorite sport, his voice when he spoke was little more than a snarl.

"For someone who doesn't need complications in her life, baby, you're working on a whale of one."

There was just enough moonlight slanting into the truck to see her eyes flutter open, dazed and drugged. Then comprehension followed, and she sat up suddenly. Her swift movement brought her into jarring contact with his masculinity, and he winced.

"Me? I'm not the one doing a caveman imitation of Fred Flintstone." She scrambled off his lap, sending her elbow into his ribs in what was surely no accident. Safely ensconced once again on the other side of the truck, she pushed her hair back with one hand and glared at him. "And I thought you were the one who said you had no intentions of following up on this…this…thing between us."

He leaned forward and went in search of a cigarette, finding half a pack in the ashtray. He lit it with the lighter on the dash and drew in a desperately needed puff. "That was what I said, and I meant it. Then." He narrowed his eyes at her through the stream of smoke drifting between them. "But I'm changing my mind. Fast."

"You ass. Like I don't have a say in this?" The words came fast and furious, and curiously, lightened his mood. "I might have a little more taste than to get involved with an insufferable baboon."

"I'm giving you a say. I'm also giving you a hell of a lot of responsibility. I'm about through fighting this attraction between us. If you don't want the two of us to end up in bed, you'd better stay a good distance away from me."

It was one of the few times he'd ever seen her speechless. Her voice was strangled when she finally managed to say, "Believe me, it won't require much sacrifice." She threw open the door and jumped to the ground, slamming the door with enough force to take it off its hinges.

He made no attempt to follow her. He sat in the truck

and finished his cigarette, reflecting over the last few minutes. He'd given her fair warning, and some damn good advice. He hoped to hell that she'd take it.

For both their sakes.

Chapter 9

Julianne was sulking. Oh, she could pretty up the word, but there was no denying that an uncertain temper, a bout of self-pity and a curled lip all added up to one thing. She slammed the pots and pans together with a satisfying clash. The din provided slight relief for her nasty mood.

She'd said goodbye to Shelby yesterday, and her friend's exit had left a hole in Julianne's days that had yet to be filled. Then today when the mail had been delivered she'd received the bill from her divorce attorney and discovered that every lawyer joke she'd ever heard was true. How the heck could it cost that much to extricate her from a marriage when she was asking for nothing but her freedom? Paying him was going to take a sizable chunk out of the pitiful amount she had in her savings. There was no longer any refuting it. She was broke.

As if that wasn't enough, Annie had chosen today to visit her niece in Butte. She wouldn't be back until sometime tomorrow evening. Last night at the supper table she had dismayed both Julianne and Jed by announcing that Julianne could do the cooking tonight, since she'd been giving her lessons.

If Jed hadn't looked so wary, Julianne would have refused on the spot, but her pride had been on the line. Then he had offered to eat at the diner in town, and pride had become something more. She wasn't too eager to make supper for a man whom she would give away her diamond earrings to see choke on a chicken bone. But when it had been clear that he'd thought she couldn't do it, she'd had to prove him wrong, for integrity's sake.

Right now, though, integrity seemed a miserable excuse. She stared balefully at the mound of ground chuck in the bowl in front of her and tried to remember what all Annie put in meat loaf. It had seemed a relatively innocuous selection for tonight's menu. What could be more simple, really, than a pile of meat shaped into a pan?

Because she knew Jed hated it, she'd made a big bowl of spinach salad. With some of Annie's homemade dressing, it was really all she needed to fill her up this evening. There was something about cooking, she'd observed, that killed the appetite. For appearance's sake, of course, she'd have to taste everything, so regardless of how tempting it was, she should probably curb her urge to poison him.

She used a generous hand with the salt and pepper and then remembered onions. She was certain that Annie put onions in meat loaf. Her search through the refrigerator yielded three. She peeled them and then threw all three into the food processor. It made a heck of a racket, but it was better than dicing them up herself and ruining her makeup with watery eyes. She'd agreed to make supper for the big oaf, but she'd be darned if she'd sacrifice her looks for him. Remembering their parting words in the pickup, she scowled. Or anything else, for that matter.

The bread she'd prepared earlier that day was rising nicely. She recovered it and left it on the counter. It should be ready to go in the oven shortly, and she couldn't wait to see Jed's face when he bit into it and realized that she'd learned Annie's baking secrets. It might be petty, but she was game for anything that proved she wasn't as useless as he seemed to think she was. The big jerk.

Dinner was always promptly at six, and though she wasn't exactly certain how long meat loaf should cook, she figured an hour would be plenty of time. She mixed the onions with the meat loaf, pressed the whole concoction into a pan and smeared it with ketchup. She turned the oven on and placed the meat in to cook.

Wiping her hands down the front of her jeans, she gave a satisfied sigh. A firm believer in the restorative nature of bubble baths, she decided to treat herself to a leisurely soak. Halfway up the stairs, she backtracked and poured herself a glass of wine to take with her. A job well done, she thought smugly, should always be rewarded.

Whether it was the bath or the wine, she was feeling decidedly more mellow when she reentered the kitchen forty-five minutes later. She set two places at the table and put in a couple of potatoes to bake. The microwave oven was perfect for someone with her cooking inexperience. It even had a setting specifically for potatoes. She heard the door open and close, and Jed's footsteps on the stairs. He always showered before dinner. She started the microwave, set the salad on the table and poured herself another glass of wine.

She sat down and propped her feet up on another chair, feeling very Martha Stewart. She was midway through her wine when two loud explosions, one right after the other, jolted her upright. Her first thought was that someone was firing a gun right outside the kitchen. But as she ran to the door she passed the microwave, and her eyes widened with dismay. Reaching out with one hand, she opened the door to the appliance and surveyed its interior with amazement. How the heck had Annie managed to buy exploding potatoes?

She heard Jed come into the kitchen then, and she shut the door quickly and whirled around. "You're late," she snapped.

He slid into his seat and cocked an eyebrow. "It's only six-fifteen. Ramsey ran into some trouble with the fence line. Found the place where the cattle have been getting out and…" He stopped and sniffed. "Is something burning?"

She jerked around and lunged for the oven. Opening the door, she waved away the smoke, reached for a hot pad and removed the meat loaf. It didn't look that bad, she consoled herself, and it was really only burned around the edges. She threw a hot pad on the table, slammed the meat loaf down in front of Jed and silently dared him to say a word.

Eyes gleaming suspiciously, he surveyed the blackened meat loaf, then raised his gaze to her. His tone polite, he inquired, "Are we having any potatoes?"

"Only if you feel like scraping them off the inside of the microwave." She fetched the wine bottle and tipped some more wine in her glass. On a second thought, she went to the refrigerator and got a gallon of milk and set it down next to him with a bang. Then she dropped into her chair, took a big gulp from her glass and dished up a large helping of salad on her plate. It appeared to be the only edible thing on the menu tonight, and the fact that Jed hated it was just a bonus.

She kept her knife within reach just on the off chance that he would dare say anything. But when she shot him a sideways glance, he was gallantly sawing at the meat loaf, lifting out a generous portion for himself. The inside, she was relieved to note, looked normal.

She wasn't watching him; she really wasn't. She just happened to look up as he was chewing the first bite, just happened to catch the arrested look on his face as he paused. She eyed him warily.

"Onions." He resumed chewing and then swallowed, reaching for the milk.

"So? Annie always puts onions in the meat loaf." At least she thought so. "Doesn't she?"

He eyed her above the rim of his glass and nodded. Lowering the glass to the table, he picked up his fork again, this time looking resolute. "She sure does. She just never—" he hesitated, looked at her again, then finished "—just never puts enough in to suit me. This is just about perfect."

Partially mollified, she watched him take another bite. He held her gaze, chewing and swallowing with a look as stoic as any plaster of paris saint.

"What's that?" He nodded at the counter. "Did you leave your laundry up there?"

Julianne's head swiveled, and then she let out a small shriek. "The bread!" Jumping up, she hurried over and whisked off the towel she'd had covering it. Her eyes went round. How could flour, water and yeast balloon up to that size? Jed came to join her and they both stared incredulously. "It's the thing that ate Montana," she murmured in awe. She pressed the back of her hand to her mouth to stifle an unexpected snicker. "News at eleven."

Jed reached out and punched it with his fist, and air hissed as the mass of bread dough deflated. They both stared at the flat substance for a long moment.

"I think you killed it." She tried, valiantly she thought,

to battle laughter, but it bubbled up, anyway. "My hero." Grasping the counter for support, she struggled for composure.

His mouth quirked. "Shucks, little lady," he said in a passable John Wayne imitation, "t'weren't nuthin'."

Delighted with him, she gave into the mirth that was shaking her and howled. He joined in with a chuckle so low and rich and deep that it threatened her insides with nuclear meltdown.

"Only your quick thinking saved us," she gasped helplessly. "So glad you could *rise* to the occasion."

He put a gentle hand on her face and gave a friendly shove. "Puns are the lowest form of humor." After waiting a beat, he drawled, "At yeast, that's what I've heard."

She turned to the table, still snickering. With the exception of the wine, the offerings on the table looked decidedly unappealing.

"Well, the whole meal wasn't a bust. The meat loaf turned out okay."

Absurdly touched, she said, "Bucking to be fit with a halo, Sullivan?"

He lifted a shoulder. "Believe me, I've had worse. Actually tried my hand at cooking once or twice before I almost burned the kitchen down. After that Annie started leaving meals that could be warmed up."

For some reason, hearing him admit to a very human flaw softened her enough to offer, "Well, I can always look in the refrigerator and see if there's enough ham left over for some sandwiches."

The hopeful look on his face made her smile. In another moment she discovered that there was, indeed, enough ham left over for several sandwiches. She knew it would require a plateful to fill up Jed.

"Tell you what," she said, her head still in the fridge,

"we'll have a picnic in your study. You get things ready in there and I'll make the sandwiches."

"Why aren't we going to eat in the kitchen?"

She balanced the leftover ham, mustard, butter and mayo in a wobbly tower in her arms and headed toward the table. "I don't know about you," she said, her voice muffled by the mountain of ingredients, "but I don't think I could eat staring at the corpse of meat loaf past over here."

"You've got a point. After supper we can give it a decent burial, with a shrine to burned offerings."

"You've already admitted your deficiencies in the homemaking department, so drop the superior act, Sullivan."

"It isn't an act." He ducked out of the kitchen in time to avoid any missile she would have thrown in response and missed the smirk his words brought to her lips.

She may not have achieved gold-star status in cooking, but she could put slabs of ham between pieces of bread. In no time she had fixed a mound of sandwiches, taken out some chips and loaded cookies onto a plate. Carrying the sandwiches to the den, she nodded approvingly at the afghan and pillows Jed had spread out on the floor.

He gave a shrug when their gazes met. "Everybody knows that food tastes better when eaten on a blanket. It's some kind of picnic law, or something."

"I hope you didn't deplete your store of macho strength when you laid out that blanket, ace, because there's still food to be brought in from the kitchen."

He followed her obediently to the door and asked blandly, "Didn't you ever hear that you catch more flies with honey than with vinegar?"

She seized the opportunity to return to their old relationship with the easy bantering. "If I was a frog, I'm sure I'd treasure that bit of wisdom."

In the kitchen she gave him the chips and cookies, then picked up her glass and the wine bottle. "Get me a couple of beers," he ordered.

Raising her eyebrows, she did as he requested and trailed after him to the den. "Beer at dinner? My, my, Jed. Whatever will Annie say?"

"Let's leave that burned carcass of a meal on the table until tomorrow night and then hear what Annie has to say."

Any discomfort that had lingered from their encounter from a few nights ago dissipated over flavorful ham, salty chips and sweet cookies. It was simply impossible, Julianne reflected, to nurse a good grudge over Snickerdoodles. Actually, it had always been difficult for her to stay mad. She figured that she was basically too lazy to sustain that level of emotional intensity for long. Her temper tended to be the kind that exploded easily, spectacularly, then faded as quickly as it had ignited.

Stretched out on the floor with some pillows at her back and the wine at her side, she contemplated the man opposite her. Jed's blood, on the other hand, tended to run hot, as did his temper. He had a fuse that could sputter and spark, and his temperament could be a bit unreliable. But it wasn't the explosion at the end of that fuse that was to be feared. When infuriated, he maintained an icy calm that was all the more frightening for its control. It was then he was the most deadly.

Involuntarily, she gave a quick shudder. At least, so she'd always thought, until those occasions when she'd been in his arms. Now she knew for certain that the one time Jed Sullivan was the most dangerous to her was when he was aroused. It was a basic biological reaction to all that testosterone, she assured herself. Nothing to be worried about. After all, this was Jed she was thinking of. The man who, if she exerted herself just a bit, she could almost remember as a thin, gangly preteen with a wary disposition and an appetite that rivaled a small army's.

She nudged his stocking foot with one of her own. "You've got to admit, Sullivan, this was a great idea I had."

"*We* had," he corrected her.

Her eyebrows skimmed upward. "We? Let's be realistic. If we're dealing out credit here, your share is pretty paltry. I made the sandwiches—"

"Burned the dinner—"

She ignored his interruption. "Gathered the chips, cookies and beverages. You, on the other hand...spread a blanket. In the grand scheme of things, I'd hardly call our parts equal."

"You forget, I did bring my appetite."

He had a point, and the appetite he'd brought was truly awesome to witness. He'd just finished off his third sandwich and was making a serious dent in the plate of Snickerdoodles. She gave a brief thought to battling him for the last cookie, then gave up the idea as too arduous. She was feeling entirely too mellow. The wine had done its job— well enough, in fact, that she was on her final glass. A slight buzz was pleasant, but she never allowed herself to get tipsy. Just the thought inspired too many unpleasant memories from her marriage.

All in all, the evening was turning out much better than she'd had any right to expect, and merely strengthened the conclusion she'd drawn. Anything between them but friendship and a certain quirky connection should be avoided at all costs.

She raised her glass in a toast. "To us. And to a return to the sometimes strained and ever-amusing relationship that passes for normal between us." She sipped daintily, then noticed that he'd failed to do the same. "What's the matter, Sullivan, not big enough to admit when you're wrong?"

"Not usually," he said with an indefinable glint in his eye. "But you're going to have to help me out here. Just what was it that I was wrong about?"

"Do you want the short list? Specifically, about you and me, and that…flicker of passion we indulged in." Ignoring the quick rising heat at the memory, she shook her head. "Frankly, neither of us wants, or needs a diversion at this point in our lives. Am I right?"

Seeming bemused, he nodded slowly and tipped his beer to his lips.

She looked at him with approval. He was going to manage to be civil about this, after all. It was more than she'd dared hope for. "It would be ridiculous for us to risk what we have together for a temporary flight from our senses."

He contemplated the label on his bottle. "And just what is it that we have?"

Waving a hand casually, she said, "Oh, you know. Familiarity, some degree of affection and a certain grudging respect."

His gaze rose from the bottle to fix on hers. "We have all that?"

Because it suited her to do so, she ignored the hint of irony in his words. There was a higher purpose to be achieved here, at any rate. "Even more than that. Too much to throw away on some momentarily clashing hormones." She was almost certain she saw him choke slightly at her words. "I think we can rise above our libidos to salvage what's really important, can't we?"

He took another long swallow, and his answer was slow in coming. "I guess I can if you can."

"Good. Good for you." She beamed a smile meant to

charm. "Our relationship might not be the easiest, but I don't think it's wise to mutate it into some shortsighted orgasmic mistake, do you?"

This time he did choke. "You're a poet, you know that? Julianne Dickinson."

She set her wine aside and clasped her hands over her pleasantly full stomach. "You're just being sarcastic because you know I'm right." Lazily she stretched to jostle his foot with hers. "Would you mind bringing me a bottled water while you're up?"

"I'm not up," he pointed out.

"But you should be. Eating the way you did with no follow-up exercise is a terrific way to start a paunch. Middle-age spread begins in the thirties, you know."

Doing her bidding was easier than listening to her lame gibes, and that was the only reason he got up and brought the water she requested from the kitchen. As a silent comeback, he also grabbed a couple more cookies. Unconsciously, he ran a hand over his washboard-flat stomach. The woman's tongue could rival that of a demented mynah bird.

He sat back down, finished off the cookies and washed them down with a long drink of beer. Crossing his legs at the ankle, he decided that there were worse ways to spend an evening. He'd always liked this room, had felt an immediate connection the first time he'd entered it. Although filled with valuable western paintings and the occasional work of art, it was then, and had always remained, a man's room. There was a quiet elegance to the entire house that missed fussiness and targeted on relaxing. It was a house meant to be lived in.

It couldn't have been further from the spacious penthouse where he'd lived so briefly with Kimberley and Luther Templeton. He imagined that the home they'd brought him to had been just as expensive. Certainly it had been jammed with priceless objects. Objects meant to be observed and appreciated. Objects that broke too easily in a young boy's hand. Kimberley's displeasure had been swift and sharp.

You clumsy child. Learn to be more careful, Jed. You're not living in a back alley slum anymore.

Although memories of that back alley slum were dim, they were still there, seeping into his unconscious when he least expected them. Mostly he remembered the smells, the sharp pangs of hunger, the incessant noise. He couldn't summon a memory of his birth mother's face, but he remembered a short temper and quick hands. And in the darkest part of his dreams lingered the memory of another child in that squalid apartment, the smell of smoke, the stench of burning flesh and a sizzling agony that had seemed endless.

Before the memories could completely bloom, Jed switched off his mind, concentrating on the cool beverage in his hand and the simple indulgence of doing nothing at all. Not that looking at Julianne constituted nothing. She was easy on the eyes, explosive to the senses. He frowned into his beer as he remembered how casually she'd dismissed the idea of something more intimate between them. She hadn't said anything he hadn't thought himself, although admittedly never in such colorful terms. But he was male enough to be annoyed at how easily she'd managed to dismiss the whole idea. Moodily, he surveyed the woman stretched out across from him.

He should have been relieved at her words. With the two of them working to stomp out the sparks they'd been striking off each other, they ought to be able to avoid a mistake that could be disastrous. He'd spent a lifetime keeping most people at a distance, and didn't especially appreciate the sensation of being dragged into something by his glands. Julianne wouldn't be content with the little he was willing to offer to a woman. No, she'd push and prod until she held a man's heart in her hand. His heart was perfectly healthy behind the shield he'd constructed around it, and he planned on keeping it that way.

Still, there was no denying the purely masculine disappointment he was feeling, which only pointed out the vast distance between logic and libido.

He ignored her nagging to put on some music, and eventually she roused herself enough to slip a CD into the stereo before plopping back down. In the next moment he reconsidered his stubbornness as the familiar crooning of a popular rock star filled the air. Her taste in music hadn't improved since she was a teen, a fact he felt obliged to point out.

She didn't bother to open her eyes. "The insult would have more sting if it didn't come from a guy who regularly listened to grown men wailing about their dogs, their pickup trucks and their women, in that order."

"The term you're searching for is *country-western,* and to bad-mouth it is almost unpatriotic. I think you can get jail time for that these days."

"For what, failing to salute a gun rack?" Her lip curled. "I'll take my chances."

She hummed along with the music, the smoky drift of sound just loud enough to curl through his system and tangle in the heat that was inexplicably blooming there.

"This is nice," she murmured lazily, propping her head on one of the pillows he'd set out and leaning back. "I've always loved this time of day. I used to imagine that if my mother had lived, we'd have been a real family. One who would gather after dinner to play games, put puzzles together...." Her voice trailed off. She opened one eye to consider him. "Did you ever have that? I mean, before Kimberley and your father divorced?"

What they'd had, he recalled, were long, icy silences, punctuated by the sound of crystal shattering during some of Kimberley's more violent tantrums. A growing sense of defeat, as he began to understand that the purpose of his adoption, to make the couple a family, was doomed to failure.

He sent her a long look meant to silence. "Yeah, I really miss Ward and June." He should have known that she wouldn't be put off. If anything, she was intrigued, both eyes open now and head cocked to survey him consideringly.

"She wasn't much of a mother even then, was she?" He remained silent, but she continued to muse aloud. "I mean, Kimberley never struck me as the maternal type, but then, I was only a kid when the two of you came here. Even though we didn't have much to do with each other, I sort of tolerated her because I thought maybe she could make Harley happy." A note of wistfulness entered her voice. "She must have loved him once to marry him and move the two of you out here."

What she'd loved, Jed suspected, was the way Harley had spent money when she'd met him in the casinos, and the prospect of plenty more of it. Love was one emotion he doubted Kimberley was well versed in.

"Do you see her much?"

That, at least, he could answer honestly. "No. We exchange birthday and Christmas cards, all very civilized. Maybe a couple times a year, a phone call." Usually when her finances were in a mess and she needed someone to untangle them. He didn't mind helping her out occasionally, but he did think it odd that what he felt for Annie was ten times stronger than any emotion Kimberley had ever inspired in him. He'd never spent a lot of time worrying about what that said about his family. He was certain he already knew.

Julianne was in a contemplative mood. "My mother died before I could know her, but I did miss having one. I always thought that if she'd lived things might have been different."

"What things?"

She lifted a shoulder self-consciously. "I don't know. Maybe she would have been enough for Harley. Maybe he would have been satisfied to stay here, instead of chasing the excitement of a big win." Shaking her head, she settled back against the pillow. "I'll never know. Don't you ever wonder about things like that?"

He could have told her that he didn't waste his time on things he couldn't change. Instead, he focused on making sure he didn't lose any more than he already had. He tipped the bottle to his lips and drank. "What's the point?"

"The point is figuring out who we are and why we do the things we do. Haven't you ever considered tracing your roots, trying to find your birth mother?"

His answer was immediate and heartfelt. "No."

"But why not?" she pressed. "Kimberley and your adoptive father might have failed you, but you may have blood relatives out there. Don't you wonder about them?"

"My birth mother signed over her legal rights to me when I was four," he said tersely. His relaxed mood was fast dissipating. "When you talk about failure, it doesn't get more definite than that."

He had her interest now. He recognized it in the way she leaned forward, her pretty face serious and her wide eyes sincere. "She might have had no other options. It doesn't necessarily make her a monster."

"Doesn't it?" His lips quirked humorlessly. She liked to push and poke at a person until she could peer inside them, dissect their thoughts and feelings. Wanting to shock her, he took a slice of the truth and slammed it down between them like a gauntlet. "I don't remember much about her, but after bugging Kimberley for months, she finally told me what she knew. My birth mother was charged with neglect. She'd gone off for the evening and the apartment caught fire."

Horrified fascination sounded in her words. "Did she come back in time to rescue you?"

His palms began to itch and he wished for a cigarette. He folded his arms across his chest. "I never saw her again." There was no emotion in his voice. He was practiced at keeping it trapped deep inside. "When she returned two days later, I was in a hospital and the cops were waiting for her." And the other child he could remember only faintly, his younger brother, was never seen again.

"Your shoulder," she murmured in understanding. The scars on his right shoulder blade had been a part of him so long he no longer questioned them. When she was a kid, she'd pestered him about their origin until Annie had caught her at it and put an end to her torment.

"What with skin grafts and endless infections, I'm told I was in and out of hospitals for almost two years." Dredging up the past never brought him any measure of comfort, but his words had finally managed to silence her. Her eyes were sober and soft with sympathy, a sympathy he didn't want.

"You're going to have to harden that soft heart of yours if you don't want it splashing all over the ground in front of you, Julianne. There aren't always happy endings. You, better than most, should understand that."

But if he thought to quiet her he should have known better. Her chin angled up and she met his cynicism head-on. "I don't blame you for not wanting to find your birth mother, I guess. But what if you have brothers or sisters out there somewhere? Aunts or uncles? You might be denying yourself the chance for a real family."

He ignored the dart of pain that pierced him then. He'd never seen his brother again after the fire, and he was certain he knew the reason why. "I'm not like you, Jules." He drank from the beer in his hand and wished for something stronger. "You might need someone to hang on to. I don't."

He uttered the words, and believed them with every fiber of his being. "I don't need anyone."

Chapter Ten

Julianne rode out the next day, her hands unsteady on the reins, her heart in her throat. Gabe had said that Jed was checking on the cattle in the south pasture. The men had spotted elk nearby, always a worry because of the disease they could spread to the herd. She urged her mare to a faster pace and silently cursed the man for choosing this day to fail to carry his two-way radio with him.

She spotted his truck and some horses ahead, and breathed a silent prayer of relief. She stopped her mare, slid off and gestured him over. He took one long look at her face and started toward her, his long strides eating up the ground.

"You've about got poor Casey worked into a lather. What's up?"

She wet her lips and forced her voice to remain steady. "It's Annie." Her voice deserted her then and she paused to fight down the unreasonable panic. One of her hands was wrapped tightly around the fence post and he covered it, his larger, rougher hand engulfing hers and providing an immediate, soothing comfort.

She took a deep breath. "Her niece just called. Annie took a tumble down the front steps yesterday and spent the night in the hospital."

His fingers tightened around hers and his voice became urgent. "How badly is she hurt?"

Julianne shook her head and took a breath, trying to force her drumming pulse to a more sedate pace. "Betsy, her niece, said it wasn't too bad, but they held her for X rays and observation. That's all she knew. The doctor hadn't been in to talk to them yet. I don't want to wait, Jed. I have to go see her now."

"We'll take the plane," he said simply, and she turned her fingers under his and squeezed as a wave of silent relief washed over her. She was overreacting; she knew that. But in this battle of reason and emotion, emotion was clearly the victor. Annie had always seemed somehow indestructible. Julianne couldn't imagine life without the woman.

Refusing to let the tormenting fears take root and bloom, Julianne focused instead on the terse orders Jed was giving the men. At his suggestion, she left her mare for one of the hands to take home and climbed into the truck with him. It occurred to her on the way back to the ranch that the knot in her throat had eased a bit, and she knew it was because Jed was at her side. For the first time in her life, she welcomed having his strength to lean on. She was too worried about Annie to contemplate the ramifications of that.

Julianne paused outside Annie's bedroom door and took a deep breath, trying to force aside her bone-deep exhaustion. The woman had always had her own room and bath just off the kitchen, a fact that had saved Julianne many steps these last few days. Pasting a determined smile on her face, she knocked lightly, then pushed open the door. Annie looked up.

"Good heavens, girl, you don't need to be bringing me fresh lemonade. You're gonna run yourself ragged the way you wait on me hand and foot."

"Well, since you've got two bum feet, I'm loaning you mine for a while." Julianne set the tray on the table Jed had placed next to Annie's bed and poured the woman a glass.

Annie took the lemonade from her and sipped. Setting it down on the table, she patted the bed. "Come sit down for a few minutes. You look ready to drop where you stand."

Julianne smiled wryly. There had never been any fooling this woman. She saw way too much. She pulled up a chair rather than chance jostling Annie's ankle.

"How's the pain? Any better?" As Julianne spoke the words, she carefully searched the woman's face. Although the doctor had diagnosed her right ankle with a nasty sprain, and a deep bone bruise on the other, Annie still resisted taking the pain medication he'd prescribed.

"Oh, it's not so bad." The words would have been more convincing if the pain lines etched near Annie's mouth weren't so apparent.

"Liar." Julianne reached for the bottle of medication, shook out a pill and offered it to the woman. "Take it. And I don't want to hear any back talk."

Annie looked mutinous. "I hate the way those darn things make me feel, all woozy and light-headed. Why, thirty minutes after taking it I'll be falling asleep."

"And did you have any more pressing plans for the evening?" Julianne inquired. "Busting a few broncs, running a marathon, dancing till dawn?"

"Go on, rub it in." Annie sighed, but she took the pill and washed it down with a swallow of lemonade. "I've never felt more helpless in my life." Glowering, she added, "I hate it."

Julianne smiled sympathetically. "Well, it won't be forever. If I know you, you'll be back on your feet soon enough to qualify as a medical miracle. Why, they'll be asking you to fly to medical conferences all around the world to spill your recuperative secrets. Once you're there, I'm counting on you to give me the credit I deserve."

The woman smiled reluctantly. "You and your foolishness. You're the one who looks like she could use some rest." Sharp eyes examined Julianne's face. "You're trying to do too much. The house, the cooking, waiting on me. You need to slow down."

Working her tired shoulders, Julianne countered, "It's not too much. It's no more than you do every day." A fact that was filling her with more awe by the hour. "I guess I've been living too soft if I can't handle a little dusting and baking."

Annie leaned back against her pillow. "You've never been soft, and that's a fact. It's just a different kind of activity, one you're not used to."

Refusing to give in to the urge to rub her aching back, Julianne smiled faintly. "Don't worry. Once you're up and about again I'll gratefully resign your position. Is there anything I can get you?"

"You might fetch me some writing paper and a pen from the study. I think I'll try to stay awake a bit longer and catch up on some letter writing I've been puttin' off."

"You've got it." Julianne got up and went after the items Annie had requested. The study was empty, which was unusual at this time of night. Jed generally worked for several hours after dinner. His computer was on, though.

She went over and studied the screen curiously. Listed were the current market prices for crops and cattle. She knew very little about this kind of technology, but she'd heard that through the Internet a person could access just about any kind of information they wanted. She supposed some found that wonderfully helpful. She couldn't help thinking it was a bit creepy. A friend had once told her that he could type in a name on the Web and often come up with the address of the person he was searching for, sometimes with a map to the house. She skirted the machine distrustfully and went to rummage through some of the drawers in the desk. There was something to be said for a person's right to privacy, technology or no.

She found some pink stationery, which certainly couldn't belong to Jed, and a pen. She started to rejoin Annie, and then stopped and eyed the computer thoughtfully.

Just about any kind of information. The Web was accessed by people all over the globe. She wondered if it could be used to elicit information about finding birth relatives. If Jed changed his mind, it seemed as good a place as any to start.

That possibility seemed unlikely. He'd been adamant about his lack of interest in family. She still found it difficult to fathom the reasons for his refusal. There was no denying that he'd suffered some terrible hurts as a child. It seemed as though he'd spent much of his life insulating himself from any further ones. Maybe she could understand his reaction, but that didn't mean she agreed with it. Ghosts from the past had a way of rising to haunt long after they should have been banished. Jed's ghosts may be dormant much of the time, but they were there. She'd sensed them the other night when he'd offered the little he had about his childhood.

She quietly left the study and returned to Annie's room beyond the kitchen. She wished she could tell him how to lay those ghosts to rest for good but knew that he'd have to work that out on his own. Personal ghost-busting was a very private matter.

Annie was already looking a little sleepy-eyed when Julianne returned with the paper and pen. "Told you that darn pill would knock me out," she grumbled. Determinedly, she took the writing materials from Julianne. "But I'm staying awake until nine tonight if it kills me."

Julianne smiled, doubting the woman's success. Her own exhaustion seemed to have dissipated. Restless now, she got up and paced to the window, pulled the lace curtain back and looked out. From the window, Annie could view her prize roses during the short Montana summer. She doted on those roses, tended them as carefully as a baby. With a guilty pang, Julianne realized that even though she'd snuck some of the long-stemmed beauties to hoard in her room this morning, she'd completely forgotten to water the garden once since Annie's fall.

But the roses didn't look neglected. They were, as usual, dripping with blooms. And in the next instant she knew why. It was only a glimpse, but she'd swear she saw Jed just rounding the corner of the house. She let the curtain drop, a slight smile playing over her lips. He had the same view from his office as Annie did from her room. He must have looked out and been struck with the same thought Julianne had had. He'd just been quicker at acting on it.

The bit of thoughtfulness shouldn't have surprised her. Jed cared for Annie as deeply as Julianne did herself. He'd taken to stopping in her room after dinner, bringing her the mail and magazines he'd sent a man to town for. While she'd cleaned up the kitchen, she could hear the low rumble of his voice as he filled the woman in on the daily events of the ranch. She even occasionally heard a rare masculine chuckle.

No, his thoughtfulness shouldn't surprise her, and it certainly shouldn't soften something deep inside, unleashing feelings that were best left unexamined.

She turned away from the window. "Annie, what do you know about Jed's childhood?"

The woman didn't raise her gaze from the letter she was beginning. "I know he was quiet as a priest, determined to a fault and, at times, rivaled only by you for sheer orneriness."

Julianne slipped her hands into the pockets of her gauzy summer dress and shook her head. "No, I don't mean after he came here. I mean before."

The other woman did raise her gaze then, and it was quizzical. "You mean before Kimberley divorced his father? Or before the adoption?"

When she lifted a shoulder, one thin strap slipped and Julianne reached up to move it back into place. Strolling aimlessly around the room, her fingers trailed over the odds and ends Annie had set about on every available surface. There were numerous framed pictures, both of her and Jed, taken at various ages. She paused, picking up a plaster imprint of her hand that she'd made when she'd been in kindergarten. Harley hadn't been interested in the endless collection of personal keepsakes from his daughter's childhood, but Annie had tried her best to fill the voids he'd left in Julianne's life. With a surge of gratitude, it occurred to her that the woman had had remarkable success.

Replacing the piece of plaster, she moved on to the woman's collection of whimsical frogs. Belatedly, she answered Annie's question. "What do you know about his real mother?"

The woman was slow to answer. "I have my suspicions, but I don't really know anything for fact. Enough to figure that he was well rid of her. Even though Kimberley and her first husband weren't much at parenting, Jed was taken care of after the adoption, physically at least." Her gaze sharpening, she added, "Why do you ask?"

Unable to maintain eye contact, Julianne's attention drifted to the frogs arranged in a variety of silly poses. The pieces ranged from dime-store quality to carved pieces of jade and molded brass. Picking one in polished ebony, she ran a fingertip over its sleek lines. "Just a conversation we had. I wondered why he wasn't interested in opening his birth records. He could have other family somewhere. I would think he'd want to know."

Annie sighed. "I can just imagine how he reacted to that suggestion. Julianne, sometimes you can't pick things apart and examine why they are the way they are. Sometimes you just have to accept and go on. Whatever came in Jed's childhood before we knew him had a hand in shaping the man he is today. He can't go back and change that, and he's not the type of man who would want to."

"I'm not suggesting he could change anything," Julianne protested, "I just thought…"

"Jed's a private sort," Annie said firmly. "He didn't have much to hang on to when he was young. I can't see him stirring up what he's found here while he reaches out for what-might-have-beens." She struggled to fight a yawn and failed.

Certain that the woman would be asleep in only a few more minutes, Julianne crossed to the bed and dropped a light kiss on her hair. "I'll see you in the morning. I'm going to finish up in the kitchen and probably make an early night of it myself."

"Hah. I know what you're up to, girl." The woman

waggled her pen at her. "But I said I'm staying awake until nine, and that's exactly what I'm going to do."

Julianne cocked a grin. "Care to make a little wager on that?"

Annie sniffed. "Certainly not. Way I hear it, there's been more than enough wagering going on around here." Her voice was stern, but she couldn't disguise the twinkle in her eye. "Don't know what those men were thinking, sitting down with you over a deck of cards. The fools are just lucky you left them with their shirts."

Julianne didn't bother to inquire where the woman had gotten her information. "I had to leave them something for the next time, didn't I?" She moved to the door. "I'll see you in the morning. You let that medication do its work, now, you hear?"

Smiling at the woman's mutterings, Julianne stepped into the kitchen and was met by the sight of Jed standing at the kitchen sink running water over his bloody hand.

"How'd you manage to hurt yourself watering the flowers?"

He grunted and continued to hold his hand under the faucet. "I sliced my hand on one of those blasted little shovels she uses to dig out the weeds."

"A trowel did that?"

"Damn thing is all rough edges and rust." His voice was little more than an embarrassed mutter. "I don't see how Annie manages not to cut herself to pieces."

He pulled his hand out of the stream of water to examine it. The wound oozed sullenly. Julianne could feel nausea roll through her stomach. She didn't do well around blood.

"It needs stitches," she said faintly. The cut wasn't particularly long, but it was wickedly deep, with ragged edges.

"It's not that bad. I just need a couple of Band-Aids."

He cocked an eyebrow at her. "Think you can manage to stay on your feet long enough to help with that?"

She swallowed hard. "Me? No problem."

"I seem to recall you have a little trouble around blood."

Taking a deep breath, she willed the pounding in her ears to subside. "Not as long as it's only yours."

He turned off the water with his uninjured hand and carelessly wadded a wet paper towel against the wound. "Then you're in luck. Go get those bandages, will you?"

Julianne eyed him doubtfully. "I still think you should let me take you into town and have Doc Brierly stitch you up. When's the last time you had a tetanus shot?"

He spun on his booted heel and headed to the bathroom. "You're stalling. I'll do it myself."

She trailed after him. "How are you going to do that? Grow a third hand?"

He was already opening the bathroom cabinets and rummaging through them. She gave a mental sigh and gave in. She could do this, she assured herself. It was simply a case of mind over matter. She hoped.

"Wait, let me." She snatched the box of Band-Aids from him and turned back to the cabinet. "You should at least treat it first with a disinfectant. We don't want your hand to turn green and fall off, do we?" She set the box down and turned to him with a bottle of first-aid spray, keeping her gaze scrupulously away from his injured hand.

He eyed the bottle in her hand warily. "That's not going to sting, is it?"

She rolled her eyes. "Try to be brave, champ." She had to force herself then to look at the wound, and although the bloodstained paper towel had the nausea rising in her throat again, she pulled it away from his hand and squirted a healthy dose of disinfectant on the injury.

"Dammit to hell!" He yanked his hand away and blew on it, glaring at her. "Not exactly Florence Nightingale's cosmic twin, are you?"

Reaching for the Band-Aids, she grinned unsympathetically. "Don't be such a baby. I remember the time that bull caught you in the chest with its horn. Where's your tight-lipped tough guy routine now?" She finished wrapping the bandages over his wound and took a breath. She had to be at least as grateful as he that it was over.

He examined her handiwork carefully. "I seriously doubt you caught much of my tough guy routine, since you were busy keeling over at the sight of all the blood."

"I definitely did not keel. It was more of a ladylike swoon." She was almost certain of it. Tossing her hair back, she looked at him, conscious that the room seemed to have shrunk since they'd entered it. His shoulders were broad enough to block her view of the doorway. Strange that she hadn't noticed until now how close they were standing. With effort, she tore her gaze away from Jed and focused blindly on a point beyond his left shoulder.

"If you say so." The amusement in his voice didn't surprise her. The finger he stroked down her cheek did. Her head jerked at the touch, and she stared at him, shocked. "Thanks for the first aid. I'm willing to make an exchange to show my gratitude."

She swallowed hard, her gaze trained on his lips as he formed the words. "An exchange?"

His mouth quirked. "Sure. I won't tell Annie that you've been sneaking some of her yellow roses for your room."

"How'd you..." She stopped when he raised an eyebrow. Of course, he'd noticed when he'd done the watering. "Well, as crimes go, it's not going to get me five to ten." The casual conversation gave her time to let out the air that had unexpectedly backed up in her lungs. That crazy shaft of awareness that had pierced her earlier was fading. It *was,* she assured herself. The need to put some distance between them no longer seemed urgent, just wise.

"Why don't you let me clean up in here?" she suggested, turning to the mess she'd left in the sink.

"Sure. I'd like to talk to you about Annie when you're done, though. Can you stop in the den?"

Her agreement earned her some breathing room as Jed turned and left the small space. Immediately, the air expanded. Julianne attended to the task at hand automatically. She threw the wet paper towels in the trash and put the first-aid supplies back in the cupboard. How nice and neat it would be, she thought wryly, if she could shut away her emotions as easily.

When she walked into the den a few minutes later, Jed was nursing a Scotch and frowning at the computer screen. She strolled around the desk to peer over his shoulder.

"Cattle prices went down again today," he muttered, scrolling down the market listings.

"It's a good time to buy, then."

"It would be. I just wish that the damn barn was done."

"You can make do with the old barn for now, can't you?"

He turned his head as he replied. "Sure, but..." His words stopped abruptly, his lips close enough to her face to brush against the skin of her cheek.

Self-consciously, Julianne drew back. She would have moved away if she hadn't found herself suddenly fascinated by the way his evening beard darkened his chin, giving him a faintly disreputable look.

His frown deepened, and a muscle in his jaw went tight. She straightened and rounded the desk, dropping safely into a chair.

Embarrassment balled in her throat, making her voice sound thick. "What were you saying about the barn?"

"The barn?"

In the time it took him to answer, she carefully smoothed the gauzy material of her dress over her legs and crossed one knee over the other. Only then did she risk looking at him again. His gaze was dark and feral, and an unexpected shiver slid down her spine.

"You said you wished the new cattle barn was done. I said you could use the existing one. You said…"

"Yeah." The word sounded rusty. He cleared his throat. "I'm not just talking about getting the new barn up. We don't really need it until the snow flies. But I wanted to get that expense out of the way, and make a few more changes around here before I dip into the cash flow again."

Julianne welcomed the distraction the conversation provided. And she was well versed enough with ranch matters to speak about them knowledgeably. "You mean you're weighing the advantage of the lower prices against a fear of overextending your capital?" At his nod, she asked something that had been bothering her for days. "Aren't you worried about mixing your money with Harley's in the ranch?" At the stillness that came over him then, she hurriedly added, "You know how he is when he hits a rocky patch. I'd hate to see you lose anything that you've invested here."

"That won't happen," he said with finality. He moved his chair away from the laptop open on his desk and reached to take the glass he had resting beside it. Swirling the amber eddies of liquor in his glass, he forestalled her next question. "I won't let it."

She was unconvinced. From what she'd seen of the ranch, the only improvements that had been made in her absence had taken place very recently. Which meant, of course, that Harley hadn't put a penny into the place. When she'd been a teenager, they'd kept as many cattle as the ranch could support. Jed's talk of adding to the herd could only mean that her father had sold hundreds of head off, to support himself during one of his losing streaks.

A sudden thought struck her then, and her gaze flew to the man before her. "He never…he didn't sell any of the land, did he?"

Jed's voice was cool and smooth, but his calm was belied by the way his fingers suddenly clenched the glass in his hand. "About a hundred acres to Jim Pooler, a couple of years ago."

Although his answer wasn't unexpected, the words still stole her breath, weakened her knees. She was grateful she was already sitting.

"He…he must have been desperate." She couldn't keep the bitterness from her voice, from her heart. It didn't take much to fuel desperation in Harley. The thought of missing out on the next big stakes game would be enough. He'd brought the ranch to the verge of bankruptcy more than once, mortgaging it so heavily that at times it had seemed as if her childhood home would become a distant memory. Each time, his luck had taken an upswing. And on each occasion, she'd been left wondering how long before it happened again.

"You're taking a chance here, more than I thought. You could lose your entire investment if Harley…" She couldn't even manage to finish the sentence, but her meaning hung in the air between them.

"I don't take chances, you told me that yourself." His voice was flat. "Harley is never going to threaten this ranch again."

Julianne ran her hands up and down arms that were suddenly chilled. She didn't want to consider this anymore, didn't want to remember the times she'd lived in fear as a child that she wouldn't have a home the next day, the next month, the next year. That everything she valued could be gone at the blink of an eye.

She sprang from her chair, driven to move. She stopped before the windows. The sun had exploded with spectacular brilliance and was rapidly sinking behind the mountains. Darkness fell quickly in their part of the state.

The sound of ice clinking in a glass sounded behind her, and without even trying she could visualize Jed as he watched her. And he was watching. She didn't question her certainty of that. A warm river of heat streamed down her spine, as if jettisoned by his gray gaze. She shoved a hand through her hair and shuddered a breath. Her reaction to him was becoming too unpredictable, too uncontrollable.

"You said you had something to discuss," she said, not turning around.

"Hmm?"

She glanced over her shoulder at him and was immediately pinned by that enigmatic gray gaze. "About Annie?"

He set his glass down then, with more care than the act required. "It's really not so much about Annie. It's about you."

"Me?"

He nodded. "I know you've had to shoulder all of Annie's duties while she's laid up. Not to mention looking after her, as well. I just wanted to let you know that I've arranged to get some help out here starting next week."

"What kind of help?"

"Someone to do the cleaning, take care of the house. All you'll have to do is check up on Annie occasionally."

Her emotions, which had ping-ponged all evening, settled abruptly into anger. "Unarrange it."

He blinked. "What?"

Her voice went dangerous, which suited the sudden shift
in her mood. "I thought I was clear enough. Whoever you
hired, unhire them. If I had wanted help, I would have
asked for it."

"Don't be stubborn, Jules. Of course you need help."

"Of course? Why 'of course'? Because I couldn't possibly be counted on to handle things?"

He eyed her warily. "I only meant that you could use
a hand at it. The house keeps Annie busy all day, and
you've got her to watch over, too. Admit it. You're wearing yourself out trying to keep up with it all. Hell, you're
exhausted right now."

The fact that his words were true didn't lessen their
sting. "I'm not brainless, or useless. I don't need help, I
don't want it, and if I did I could damn well arrange for
it myself."

Now he looked completely mystified, with more than a
little mad mixed in. "Where did that come from? I've
never thought you were useless or...what's gotten into
you?"

She reached him in three quick steps, pushing her face
down to his to snarl, "You. You always have to step in
and take care of things yourself. Did it ever occur to you,
Jed, that when you take over you make me feel like you
think I'm too helpless to cope? It was the same way when
you went to Florida. You just assumed I couldn't handle
things on my own. You've been doing it my whole life,
and I want it to stop now."

His eyes narrowed and his words were measured. "You
don't want to be throwing my help up in my face, Julianne."

She slapped both hands on the arms of his chair and leaned closer, close enough so their noses almost touched. "Yes, I do. I'm telling you for the last time to back off."

She glared at him and he glared back. She was near enough to see that his gray eyes had gone molten. Belatedly she realized their proximity and straightened. But when she would have moved away, his hand snagged her wrist.

"Yeah, maybe you're right." His tone had no detectable note of agreement in it. Instead, it was hard and ruthless. "As a matter of fact, I know you are. You may be a pain in the ass, but you're not weak and you're not useless. I've told you before you're one of the strongest women I know. I'm just trying to protect you."

"Why?" Her voice held a genuine note of amazement.

He flung her wrist away. His voice, when it came, was baffled and brusque. "Maybe I don't know why, okay? Maybe I've never understood where this need to protect you comes from. I don't like to think of you hurt, or tired or scared. It twists something up inside me, something I wish I could turn off. Believe me, it'd be a hell of a lot easier if I could."

Chapter 11

She stared at him as if he'd become a stranger. And perhaps he had. It had always been easier to assume Jed acted from some deep-seated belief in her incompetence than from any deeper level. Had always been safer to assume so.

He reached up and brushed a knuckle beneath her eye. She knew her mirror would tell her his touch traced a shadow that lingered there. "You've been running yourself ragged. Did you expect me not to notice? Not to care?"

Her breath clogged in her throat. Jed simply observed everything. She'd always known that. But caring...no. That was unexpected. And achingly touching.

"You don't have to prove anything to me. It's not a weakness to ask for help, to accept it."

"Maybe..." The words were difficult to summon, more difficult to force out of her throat. "Maybe I have to prove something to myself."

She searched his gaze, wondered if he could understand

what it was like to be buffeted by self-doubt, until virtually paralyzed with overanalysis. She doubted he could comprehend even if she could find the words to explain. He'd never seemed to suffer any second thoughts.

Except for a moment ago. His voice had been harsh, bewildered, as if he truly couldn't understand the tricks his instincts played on him. He wasn't alone. Right now she'd give a great deal to understand what was behind his need to protect her, as well.

He slowly stood, his body brushing against hers as he rose. Her pulse throbbed, and thoughts scattered. It was difficult to think when that piercing gaze was fixed on hers. Hard to remember caution with his thumb tracing her jawline with a touch that trailed heat.

When his hand dropped away she should have stepped back, should have made a casual remark and an easy escape. But this didn't seem casual and it didn't seem easy. She blinked in wonder when he reached for her hand and smoothed his thumb over the blisters she'd gotten from mopping the acres of floors in the house. Her breath caught as his eyes went smoky. He brought her hand to his lips and touched his mouth to her injuries. And her heart quite simply turned over.

Perhaps she could have fought the fire and hunger that he unleashed in her so easily. But tenderness from this man was impossible to resist, devastating to the senses. He released her hand, tipped her chin up and fanned his fingers across her cheek. And in the seconds before his descending mouth met hers, she could have sworn she saw a flicker of uncertainty on his face.

His kiss, when it came, wasn't uncertain. It was the softest of touches, with an underlying hint of possession. She took a breath, drew in his scent. The aroma was a mingling of tobacco, Scotch, and something uniquely Jed, something a little hot and wild. Their lips met, clung and didn't quite part. Then Julianne heard his breath rasp, felt the quick clench and quiver of nerves jumping in his fingertips, and the bottom dropped out of her stomach. She leaned closer and sank into the kiss.

This wasn't the free fall into pleasure she'd come to expect, but a slow, almost gentle glide. The softness of it weakened her knees, the sweetness melted her defenses. His taste was almost familiar now, but different, too, flavored with a hint of hesitation, a dash of expectancy. Surrounded by the still, rigid air of a man used to control.

She stepped blindly forward, deepening the kiss, welcoming the immediate answering pressure of his mouth on hers. The solid warmth of his body was close. Her hands came up to rest on his chest, smoothed upward to clutch those muscled shoulders. She was in need of something to steady herself, to counteract the dizzying spiral of need that could consume so quickly.

He put his arms around her and splayed one hand on the skin bared by the backless sundress. Reaction shuddered through her at the stroke of that calloused palm, the fingers that caressed and claimed. Her mouth twisted beneath his, and too late she considered the danger. Slow, lazy sips of him were no less shattering to her senses than taking him in great greedy gulps. The journey was different, but the impact was the same.

His mouth left hers, cruised to her throat, found a pulse hammering beneath the skin and laved it with his tongue. Her blood immediately thickened, began chugging moltenly through her veins.

One hand slipped, braced against his chest, and she was once again reminded of his strength, his endurance. He had always seemed so strong, so indestructible. She was captivated to discover that his strength was tempered by taut muscles and skin that was—her fingers slipped between two buttons of his shirt—smooth and hot to the touch.

He caught her hand in one of his and held it captive, and his words when they came were ragged and harsh. "I'm not fighting it this time, Julianne." Her eyes fluttered open, and her head continued spinning at the primitive promise etched on his tightly drawn features. "Stay or go, it's your decision. But you need to make it." His fingers tightened convulsively on her back and then relaxed. "Now."

She studied him through eyes that struggled to close again, wanting to shut in that picture of him: muscles coiled tightly, jaw clenched, and a whisper of dampness glossing his five o'clock shadow. She wondered how long ago her decision had been made. Swaying forward a little, she whispered against his lips, "Stay." And felt the utter stillness that came over him, a whisper of a moment before his arms yanked her closer and that rigid control sprang free.

His mouth claimed hers again, and this time there was nothing gentle about the pleasure that rammed through her. The floor abruptly tilted beneath her feet, and she hooked an arm around his neck to anchor herself. His lips were hungry, almost bruising, and there was primitive satisfaction in the moist tangle of tongues, the scrape of teeth.

Her head fell back, a gesture of surrender she would have denied had she been aware of it. He took immediate advantage, switching his attention to the long line of her throat, the exquisitely sensitive spot behind her ear. With fingers inclined to tremble, she began to release the buttons on his shirt, guided only by an overpowering need to feel his heated flesh.

He shuddered when she touched him, and the evidence of her effect on him was heady. He was heavily muscled, his tight skin smooth, and a mat of crisp hair angled down his chest. She pressed her mouth against his skin in a shocking need to taste him, and was rewarded by his ragged groan.

The sound fueled her edgy need, sparked an equally fierce desire for more. Much more. In the next instant that desire was answered by the slide of his hand beneath her dress, along the bare expanse of thigh. She gasped and shivered at the touch.

"I've wondered all night what you had on under here," he murmured. And then he found the answer to his question, discovered the lacy wisp of panties beneath.

Desperate need, fierce and urgent, gushed forth with the force of a geyser. He soothed the tremors rippling through her with long, sure strokes, molding, petting, possessing. But there was no calming the chaos to her senses when his fingers slipped inside the elastic and cupped warm, damp flesh.

She quivered against him, feeling like she was poised on the edge of a frightening discovery, but without the will to turn back. His touch was light, his fingertips barely grazing the sensitive folds of flesh, and she could feel herself growing soft and moist.

He leaned forward and took her mouth, his tongue stabbing deep even as his fingers slipped inside her. His thumb found and circled the taut bundle of nerve endings, and he took her to the first climax with fingertips alone.

She cried out as the fast hard orgasm crashed over her, her knees buckling in the aftermath, driving him deeper. He held her to him for a moment, the touch intact, waiting for her rioting nerve endings to calm. "Jed," she whispered achingly against his mouth.

The sound of his name on her lips seemed to unleash a wave of violent emotion. "Yes." His voice was thick, barely recognizable.

"Jed." He drove her up again with one firm movement, and the heated excitement flared anew.

Twisting against him helplessly, Julianne felt the edges of relief, so recently attained, spiral away. He could cause that so easily, so effortlessly. But not again. Not without him. Even as the colors fragmented behind her eyelids with each bold stroke of his fingers, she reached for his belt buckle, fumbled for his zipper. He hissed in a breath and crowded her against the desk, arching into her touch.

And cursed. Roundly.

Her eyes fluttered open and a smile tugged at her lips as he released her to struggle with half-undone clothes and a desktop littered with papers and the laptop. Their gazes caught, and he leaned over her, an answering smile on his hard mouth, his gaze hot. With a tug he pulled her to him and engaged her mouth in a voracious battle of lashing tongues and deep, hot kisses.

Julianne was dimly aware of being moved, guided backward, but she kept her eyes closed, too involved in the bombardment of dark tastes, desperate flavors. Something bumped up behind her hips and her weighted eyelids half opened. He'd moved her against a marble-topped table and bunched her skirt up in one fist.

His shirt was only halfway unbuttoned, and she rectified that oversight now, tugging it from his waistband. His free hand slipped inside her panties for a moment, briefly cupped and squeezed her buttocks, before he pulled the undergarment down her legs.

"Step out of them," he rasped, and mindlessly she did so, while at the same time pushing his shirt off his heavy shoulders. He moved between her legs and pulled first one strap down her shoulder, over her arm, and then the other.

Julianne's breath jammed in her throat. She watched

him, feeling vulnerable and exposed, as he dragged the bodice of her dress down, revealing her bare breasts. The air was cool on her nipples, already drawn into tight, painful knots. His eyes narrowed and he swallowed hard, his breathing harsh in the silence of the room. And then he filled his hands with her, lowered his head and took a nipple in his teeth, and sensation exploded into tearing need.

A ball of heat formed, low in her belly, and each flex of his mouth sent a fiery streamer of sparks flashing through her, burning her from the inside out. Her hands were restless, smoothing over his broad chest, clutching tight muscles in his shoulders, lingering over the smooth, puckered flesh on his back. The legacy from his childhood. Her touch slowed, became caressing, but he wouldn't let her calm, wouldn't let the pace slow. He moved closer, feasting on her, shoving the dress further down until the material was bunched around her waist.

She stroked her hands down his sides in a sensuous slide, then moved to cup his heavy masculinity in both hands. He started, shuddered mightily, then thrust into her touch. She freed him from his clothes and caressed him with hands that trembled with a touch of awe. He was hard, huge, pulsing. And she wanted.

They were the only two in the room, in the state, in the universe. At that moment, with his mouth on her, his tongue pressing her nipple to the roof of his mouth to pleasure it, she believed it. Was certain of it. Thoughts dimmed, sensation crowded in until there was space for nothing but the feelings he was creating in her, the brutal needs that even now were spiked to a fever pitch. Again.

Her touch grew more desperate, and he understood her demand. He reached into his pocket and withdrew a foil package, brushing her hands aside when they would have tried to help. Then he stepped closer, close enough for his manhood to tease the tender flesh between her legs, and stopped.

"Open your eyes, Julianne." The words were harsh, guttural. And he waited until she obeyed. He brought her forward until her breasts pressed against his chest, arranged her legs around his hips. And still he waited.

"I want to watch you." The words seemed dragged from him, from a place deep inside that he usually kept well hidden. A place that simmered with dark, primitive desires. Her gaze was helplessly entrapped by his. Just as she was trapped by the promise of ferocious pleasure shimmering just out of reach. His face worked, and she couldn't have looked away if she'd tried. He was a man in the throes of a violent emotion. "I want to see your eyes when we…"

He moved then and her cry mingled with his ragged groan. His fingers went to her hips and he held her still as he drove deeply inside her. She clenched her legs tightly around his waist and wrapped her arms around his shoulders. They were linked, in the most intimate way a man and woman could be, and still it wasn't enough. "Jed." His name was a cry, a plea. It was answered with a powerful thrust, deeper still, followed by a pounding rhythm that bound them both. Tighter. Harder. Higher.

Her nails scored his shoulders, mindless now, urging him on. Her body shook with each powerful lunge of his hips. She arched, offered more, and he took it. She could feel the climax shimmering, just out of reach, and she held back, suddenly desperate that he join her before going over the next jagged brink.

He felt her hesitation and reacted immediately. One hand moved between her legs. "Let go," he urged, de-

manded. His face was damp, his dark hair clinging damply
to his forehead.

"Not without you," she panted. She locked her ankles
behind his back as his hips thrust with increasing intensity
against hers. "Now, Jed. Now." Their gazes met, held,
until his image began to blur as her vision grayed.

Abruptly she crested, the release slamming into her with
a violence that left her breathless. Dimly she was aware
of her name on his lips, his body drawing tight and his
last powerful lunge before he joined her in a free fall into
pleasure.

Rocking to the Boss's lyrics blasting through the head-
phones, Julianne's hips bumped and circled as she
hummed an enthusiastic accompaniment to "Born in the
U.S.A." The vegetables she was chopping by an enthusi-
astically wielded butcher knife lay in a dizzying array of
color that owed more to exuberance than to accuracy. She
couldn't remember a time she'd felt so loose, so carefree.
Every muscle in her body felt vibrantly alive, crackling
with health and energy. And she would cheerfully credit
the night she'd spent wrapped around Jed Sullivan as the
cause.

It had taken long moments for their breathing to steady,
longer still for their limbs to follow suit. Finally, he'd carried her to her room, and there the night had eddied into
infinite spinning waves of passion, some long and slow
and others crashingly violent. There wasn't a square inch
of her body that had gone untouched, undiscovered. Secrets had been laid bare as sensation had layered over sensation, their hands doing battle to discover what elicited a
groan, a gasp, a plea. The hours had been spent in sensual
assault, with each of them battling to bring the other to the
pinnacle of barbed, edgy need, cresting in shattering, mind-

reeling pleasure. With a smugness that went bone-deep, she was willing to call it a tie.

It had been tempting to give in to Jed's urgings to go back to sleep when he'd begun to move that morning. It was barely dawn, and neither had given the other much rest the night before. But she'd risen when he did. The days started early on a ranch, especially now that she was taking Annie's place. A place she'd informed him unequivocally that she wasn't going to share. With anyone.

He hadn't liked it, but he'd grudgingly agreed to her plan to cancel the help he'd arranged for her. She might have been taking unfair advantage by broaching the subject when she'd just sat up in bed, the sheets rumpled around her waist, one hand pushing back her morning-tousled hair. His answer had seemed almost absent as he'd painted her with a look that had been pure liquid fire.

She put the knife down and began scooping up the vegetables and dropping them in the stew she was preparing. Yes, that might have qualified as taking advantage, but she needed every advantage she could get with Jed. There had been no room last night for doubts or planning or regrets. Nor did she have use for them now.

I can't help caring. There was a quick stutter in her heart when his admission echoed in her mind. He'd looked uncomfortable, as if he hadn't known what to do with the emotion. He wasn't alone. She didn't know what to do with it, either. One thing was certain, though. Their relationship had taken an inevitable turn last night. And though she had plenty of questions about the wisdom of the change, she couldn't seem to summon one regret about the course it had taken.

She reached for the lid to cover the pot of simmering ingredients. Although she wasn't anywhere close to Annie's league in the kitchen, she had come to the conclusion that the simplest meals could be the most filling. Beef stew and plenty of fresh baked bread would go a long way in taking the edge off Jed's appetite tonight. With a burst of warmth to her cheeks, she strove to push away the memory of his other appetites, cravings that were dark and deep and intensely tempting to explore, to satiate.

Taking a quick breath, Julianne considered what to do next. Annie had been sleeping the last time she'd checked, and she had plenty of time to complete another chore before the woman would awaken. Slipping off the earphones resignedly, she turned off the disc player and went in search of the cleaning supplies for the bathrooms. She hadn't been lying when she'd told Jed there was satisfaction to be had knowing she was running the house, if not as capably as Annie, at least competently.

But, she thought, as she trudged to the downstairs bathroom, her nose would have grown a foot if she'd actually claimed to *enjoy* every aspect of her chores.

The ringing phone was a welcome respite from the dreaded task. Julianne sprinted to answer it, afraid the sound would awaken Annie. She was slightly out of breath by the time she'd picked up the receiver.

"I'm trying to reach Jed Sullivan." The voice in her ear was unfamiliar. Low and roughly masculine, there was a hint of the South in the accent.

"He's not available right now, but I'd be glad to take a message." She walked to a drawer and rummaged through it, searching for a paper and pencil. Jed was never bothered during the day with calls. He normally returned them after supper.

The voice hesitated a moment. "He does live there, then." Although not posed as a question, an answer seemed expected. Julianne cocked her head, her curiosity piqued.

"That's right. May I ask who's calling?"

She waited for the voice to continue, but when his words came, she was rocked with disbelief.

"Hell." The word was softly explosive, rife with frustration. "I don't know how to do this, so I'll just say it right out. I think...I think I may be his brother."

Julianne had been unusually silent during dinner. They'd brought the meal into Annie's room and eaten together for the first time since the woman's accident. Jed had thought the change was due to Annie's growing strength, but over the course of the meal he'd slowly changed his opinion. She'd done little more than stir at her stew while he'd talked about the day and teased Annie about malingering. Their words had drifted around Julianne, but she hadn't joined in.

It could have just been tiredness, as she'd told Annie. God knew he hadn't given her much of a chance to sleep last night. But he'd been watching her, without seeming to, and he didn't think so. She didn't look tired, at least, no more than she'd been since she started trying to prove she was superwoman around the house. But she did look nervous.

He gave her some time after dinner. While she was cleaning up, he stayed in with Annie, acting duly impressed with her newly gained prowess with a walker. But all the time, he wondered what could have rendered Julianne quiet, not to mention so uncharacteristically anxious around him. Knots began to form in his belly. As soon as he could, he made an excuse to Annie and went to the kitchen.

Julianne was bent over the dishwasher adding the soap, so he just leaned against the counter and watched her. That mouthwateringly curvy bottom strained against the denim shorts encasing it. Her hips gave a little twitch and roll as she straightened, and his tongue grew thick in response. He shifted position and scowled. His reaction was too immediate, too involuntary for him to be entirely comfortable with it.

She closed the dishwasher, locked it and turned it on. He watched the surprise, followed closely by wariness, flit across her face when she caught sight of him. Those knots in his gut tightened. "You're quiet tonight," he observed. "Something bothering you?"

She started to shake her head and then stopped. "Yes," she answered. "We need to talk." Her gaze slid to Annie's door. "But not here."

With effort, he kept his face blank. "The den," he said tersely, and turned away, leaving her to follow. She entered the room and closed the door behind her. Still avoiding his gaze, she began to move. She rounded the chairs, running an absent hand over the butter-soft leather while nerves took control of her tongue. "Annie's getting better, don't you think? With that walker of hers, it's all I can do to keep her confined. She'd be all over the house if I let her, probably trying to push the vacuum in front of her."

His palms itched at her chatter. It wasn't too hard to figure what had her anxious and babbling around him. He should have been expecting it. Had been, in fact. But that didn't explain why those knots in his belly took a sudden violent twist, why his throat abruptly went dust dry.

He watched through narrowed eyes as she rubbed a finger over a smudge on a gleaming tabletop. "The doctor should be pleased. I just hope when her appointment comes that she doesn't convince him she's recovered more than she has. There's always a danger of her overdoing and I…"

"Why don't you tell me what's really on your mind,

Jules?'' Her gaze jerked to his, and something in his sternly controlled face must have alerted her, because her eyes went wide and she swallowed hard.

When she didn't speak he smiled humorlessly. "Nothing to say? That's unusual. Maybe I can help. It sure isn't hard to guess what has you stumbling over your words." With a quick, almost violent movement, he reached for the cigarette he suddenly needed.

She let out a shaky laugh. "Somehow I don't think you could possibly guess what I'm going to say."

"No?" He made sure none of the savage emotion swirling and colliding inside him was present in his voice. Surveying her impassively through the smoke curling from the glowing end of the cigarette, he said, "I don't think it's so difficult. You're having second thoughts about last night."

He took her silence for agreement. Despite his best efforts, his voice grew a harder edge. "I suppose it was to be expected. After all the time we spent fighting it, last night came as a shock." He inhaled, let the smoke curl between them. "You're having regrets."

Now it was she who seemed unable to do anything but stare, while he was driven to move. He strode toward the desk, around it, to the bookcase, and beyond. "Well, you're entitled to regrets, I guess. But damned if I'm going to apologize." His voice was harsh, and slightly fierce. "You wanted me last night, and you can't deny it."

She finally found her voice. "I'm not denying it."

He put the cigarette to his mouth, sucked in savagely. He could handle the anger that was welling inside him. That was a simple matter of control. He'd rather not acknowledge the tiny spears of pain that jabbed with each word she spoke. Maybe they'd be easier to ignore if they weren't identified. "Well, you're honest, at least."

A few minutes ago she couldn't seem to bear to look at him. Now she was staring, hard, that wide brown gaze assessing. It did nothing to relieve the feeling that his skin had suddenly grown two sizes too small.

"Yes. Honest enough to admit that I don't have regrets about last night. Not one."

His attention snapped to her like a whip. Because he wanted, badly, to touch her, he shoved his free hand in his pocket. "What are you saying?"

Her laugh was shaky. "I thought I was pretty clear. I do have something to tell you, but it's not about us."

His hand reached out then, quick and sneaky, and pulled her to him. She came willingly, leaning back against the hard arm he had encircling her back, and watched him from beneath lowered lids. "If I didn't know better, I'd say you look relieved."

He stubbed the cigarette out against the paperweight on his desk and flicked the stub into the waste basket. Then his free arm joined his other one and pressed her against him. He wasn't familiar with the giddy rush of relief coursing through him, but it was an improvement over what he'd been feeling a few moments ago. "Lucky for both of us that you know better, then."

He brought her to him for a quick, hard kiss, then lingered when the first failed to satisfy. When he raised his head again, her mouth was soft and her eyes were dreamy. And he wanted. An emotion that fierce, that sudden, surely could be controlled. But he wasn't interested in control. Lifting a hand, he threaded it through her bright hair, felt the silky strands caress his knuckles.

"Jed?" Her voice had a satisfactory breathiness to it. He brought her hand to his lips and nipped at the knuckles.

"Hmm?" Her scent was as much a part of her as her

personality. He followed it up the inside of her arm, pausing to investigate the crease of her elbow with his mouth.

Her free hand slapped against his chest, and she strained away. "Before this goes any further..."

"This is going to go a lot further," he assured her. "Miles. And miles."

She strained to take a breath. He watched, fascinated at the rise of her chest. "We really do need to talk."

"Okay," he said agreeably, lifting her wrist to his lips and pressing a kiss against the pulse there. "Talk."

"I mean—" she hissed in her breath and her pulse scrambled beneath his lips "—both of us."

"My mouth is busy," he murmured, trailing a chain of kisses up the side of her throat. "You'll have to do all the talking for us."

"You're going to have to stop that." She shuddered once, hard, and then leaned away from him. "I mean it. This is serious."

He looked down in her eyes. "I'm plenty serious."

He eyed the couch behind her and mentally sized it up. It would do in an emergency. And, if he wasn't mistaken, that's exactly what this was developing into. Slowly, carefully, he began to walk her backward toward it.

"You got a phone call today," she blurted out.

"I'll return it tomorrow."

"I hope you will." The words were fervent. "I really hope you will."

Something in her voice alerted him, and he paused. "Who was on the phone?"

Her gaze locked with his, and she seemed to be holding her breath.

"It was a man. He said...he's your brother."

Chapter 12

A deadly stillness came over him, creeping cold, a centimeter at a time. For one infinitesimal second, a name blew desolately across his memory. *Cage.* An emotion that had nothing to do with logic leaped, only to be reined in by a cooler more rational part of his mind. The brother he barely remembered had never had a chance to grow to adulthood. Dead men didn't make phone calls.

"You're wrong." Turning away abruptly, he went to stare out the window, as if by doing so, he could keep her from seeing those black ragged edges that still lingered within him. The tattered remains of a wrecked childhood and the constant insidious sense of guilt.

The matches had been in plain sight, an overwhelming temptation for four-year-old fingers. He'd been delighted the first time he'd gotten one to light, watching the flame dance with the fascination of the innocent. And so began the horror that revisited him in his dreams to this day.

"I'm sure this is a shock," Julianne said quietly. "But

he seemed very certain. He said he's been working on finding you for months.'' An apologetic note entered her voice. ''I'm afraid I didn't get many details. I was too surprised.''

He swung from the window to look at her. ''I don't have a brother. Whoever called here is mistaken.'' He paused for a moment, then for the first time in his life made himself say the words. ''My brother is dead.''

Detachedly, he noted the welter of emotions cross her beautiful face. Shock, confusion and…most difficult to contemplate…hope. Because it hurt to see that emotion there, hurt more to feel it, he moved past her to the desk and leaned against its corner.

''I didn't know. You never said…'' She stopped before completing the sentence, as if aware of its absurdity. There were many things he'd never spoken of. More than she could possibly realize.

He closed his eyes for an instant and rubbed the heel of his palm over the knot of pain rapidly forming in the center of his forehead. ''He died.'' The words were stated baldly, without decoration. He'd never found a way to pretty up what had happened to his brother and him in that locked apartment almost three decades ago. Never found a way to forgive himself for his part in it.

When he opened his eyes again, it was Julianne he saw, her eyes that held his. The compassion in her gaze calmed something inside him; made it possible to tuck those rarely unharnessed feelings back into a pocket in his mind. ''I had a brother. Once.'' He sensed the question poised on her lips and shook his head. ''Before I was adopted. He was younger than me. I don't remember by how much. Funny.'' His tone said it was anything but. ''I can't remember what my mother looked like, but I remember my little brother being in that god-forsaken apartment with me.'' Remembered how often the two of them had huddled in the closet together, afraid to make a sound. Terrified of the wrath of the woman who'd called herself their parent.

He went to the decanter of Scotch that sat on a portable bar against the wall. Pouring two fingers into a glass, he tossed back half of the drink and then stood, contemplating the amber eddies of the remaining liquor. ''I told you about the fire,'' he continued inflectionlessly. ''My brother didn't survive it. It was months before I was out of the hospital the first time. When I asked about him, all they'd tell me was that he was gone.''

''So you thought he died.''

He turned and pinned her with a stare. ''It's logical. My burns were severe enough to bounce me in and out hospitals for the better part of two years. Skin grafts, infections… Cage would never have survived that. He was too young. Too small.''

''Cage?'' Confusion shaded her voice. ''Jed, the man who called today said his name was John Sullivan.''

He brought the glass to his lips and took a healthy swallow, unwilling to identify the mass of emotions still twisting in his gut. ''Well, there you go. He's mistaken me for someone else.''

''I don't think so. He said you shared the same mother.''

He clenched the glass tightly and gave a bitter smile. Of course it would be the same mother. God knew, there had never been a man in those shabby apartments. At least not one who had stayed for more than a few hours at a time.

''My birth mother wasn't exactly a candidate for mother of the year.'' He reached for the decanter, poured more liquor into his glass. ''After Cage died and I was taken away from her, I kind of doubt she was so anxious to replace us that she ran out and had another kid. Most likely this guy is mistaken.''

"He seemed sure. He said he found proof of it last year—" she hesitated, as if uncertain whether to deliver the next blow "—when your mother died."

What was he supposed to feel at those words? he wondered as he stared at the alcohol in his glass. Certainly not sadness, not for a mother whom he could only remember fearing. Numbness was his uppermost sensation, and it had its advantages. Scraping up the past was like pulling scabs off old wounds. The years didn't lessen the strength with which they could still throb.

Feeling suddenly old, he strode to the desk, dropped into the chair behind it. He tipped the glass to his lips, welcomed the liquor's burning slide down his throat.

"I have his number."

His gaze slowly lifted. Julianne moistened her lips, then plowed on. "He said you should call. If you were interested in meeting."

"I'm not." He watched the surprise widen her eyes, the protest form on her lips. It was too easy to predict her reaction to his terse words. Much easier than it was to analyze his own.

When he said nothing further, she sprang from the couch to approach him. "At least take some time to think about it."

His gaze drifted back to his glass. He passed it from hand to hand. "I don't have to."

"Don't you have the teeniest bit of curiosity about meeting a man who may turn out to be your brother?" Impatience was edging into her voice. Impatience and disbelief.

He brought the glass to his lips and took a long swallow. "Nope."

"I don't believe you."

The hint of challenge in her voice had his eyes narrow-

ing in response. "You a mind reader now, Jules?" The
words were encased in ice.

She slapped both hands on the surface of the desk and
leaned forward, undaunted by his response. "If you're asking whether I think I know you, the answer is yes. At least
better than you'd like to think. You're taking the easy way
out. No risks for Jed Sullivan. No sirree. He doesn't spin
the wheel and he doesn't play the odds." Her lip curled.
"You like things nice and safe, so you don't have to feel."

What he was feeling right now was an overwhelming
urge to reach for her, so he tightened his fingers around
his glass. "And what is it, exactly, that you want me to
feel?"

She looked at him incredulously. "My God, Jed, we're
talking about *family*. The kind you've missed out on all
your life. How can you turn your back on that? Isn't it
worth reaching for? Risking for?"

"The kind of family you had, Jules? Blood doesn't
make people a family. You'd be better off if you realized
that. Maybe you wouldn't have run off and married the
first loser you met if your own family hadn't been so
messed up."

The look on her face made remorse stab deep, punctur-
ing the glacial numbness. Seeing the pain in her eyes,
knowing he'd put it there, was the worst kind of punish-
ment.

But then her chin angled with that ballsy resiliency of
hers, and she matched her temper to his. "You're right. I
lived all my life with a man to whom I was a distant fourth
or fifth. I came after my father's cards, casinos, horses....
And yes, when Andrew started gambling, it was like a
horrifying replay of my childhood. It was a mistake to
think that if I just loved him enough—" her words cracked

here, and with it, his heart "—just tried hard enough…maybe he could change."

He heard the throb in her voice and hated knowing he was responsible for it. "That's my point."

But she shook her head vehemently, holding up a hand as if to ward off his argument. "But despite all the hurt, all the disappointment, I still believe there are things worth fighting for. Sometime in your life you're going to have to take a chance on another person. Sometime you're going to realize that not doing so makes you the worst kind of coward."

She turned then and strode to the door. He wanted to call her back, wanted desperately to keep her near. Instead, he watched her walk through that door. Watched it close behind her. He knew she could never comprehend a man who considered trust the riskiest gamble of all. A man who would rather be alone than to chance the kind of pain that came from caring for someone, and having that person walk away.

He lifted the glass to his lips and drained the remaining Scotch. Setting it down, he surveyed it fixedly, watching the drops that clung to the inside trickle back to the bottom. She acted as if being alone was the worst kind of fate imaginable. What she didn't understand was that he didn't deserve to have it any other way.

Once Annie had retired for the night, Julianne went to her room, purposefully avoiding the closed door of the den. It was too early to try to lure sleep, despite her lack of it the night before. Instead, she took a bubble bath that failed to relax her, dressed for bed and puttered around the room.

There was absolutely no reason for her to have this churning in her stomach, she thought, standing at the mir-

ror and running the brush through her hair. It should come
as no surprise that Jed chose to cut himself off from all
normal human emotion. The catch in her heart gave lie to
the thought. Because it did matter. It mattered terribly.

She'd always known Jed preferred to play it safe, emotionally, at least. His refusal to even consider meeting with
the man claiming to be his brother only meant he was
running true to form. Funny how she hadn't considered
that guarded trait of his before making love with him. She
wondered what it would take to make a dent in that blasted
shield he'd built around his emotions. And the churning in
her stomach only increased when she realized that she
didn't have a clue.

She caught sight of a movement in the room behind her
and watched in the mirror as her door pushed slowly open
and Jed's reflection joined hers in the glass.

It was ridiculous to feel modest about being dressed in
nothing but the taupe-colored camisole and tap pants. Ridiculous after he'd seen her wearing much, much less last
night. She pushed the weakness aside and whirled to meet
him, bracing herself for a fight.

"In the interest of world peace I think we should wait
until tomorrow to continue our discussion." Julianne was
proud of the cool, steady tone she managed. It masked the
nerves that had her fingers tightly gripping the dresser top
behind her.

"I'm sorry."

His terse words caught her in the midsection with the
force of a blow. She drew in a breath, watching him carefully.

He stood in the doorway, looking as if every muscle in
his body was pierced with tension. "What I said to you
downstairs...you didn't deserve it." His fingers curled into
his palms, squeezed reflexively. "I have reasons for not

wanting to meet this guy, this John Sullivan. But I shouldn't have taken it out on you.'' Sincerity leaked into his next words. ''The last thing I want to do is hurt you, Jules.''

She pressed a hand to her stomach to still the fluttering there. It wasn't fair, she thought achingly, that a few simple words from him should hit so hard, mean so much. Just as it wasn't fair that his earlier careless words could wound so deeply. When had she given him this power over her? she wondered, in a sudden burst of panic. Because she was very much afraid that it was a power that wasn't reciprocated.

A wiser woman wouldn't have pushed. Knowing when to retreat was the mark of a seasoned strategist. But she didn't consider wisdom and she didn't think about strategy. Instead, she thought about the bleakness of his gaze, the flatness of his tone, and she did what it was in her nature to do.

''Tell me,'' she invited softly. She saw the instant denial flare in his eyes, watched his face close, and could have wept. ''Make me understand.''

He shifted, leaning his weight against the doorjamb, but it wasn't a pose of relaxation. ''It won't change anything.''

''Is it changing anything by keeping it inside to twist and torment you?''

He was silent long enough to make her believe he wouldn't answer. His gaze drifted down, and she knew he wasn't seeing the forest green carpet beneath their feet. He was looking inward.

His voice when he spoke was devoid of expression. ''I told you my brother died.'' He raised his gaze to meet hers then, and her throat closed up. Because in the depths of his eyes lurked brutal demons she'd never suspected existed. ''What you don't know is that I killed him.''

Shock arrowed into her, followed closely by denial. Her hair brushed against her jaw as she shook her head. "No."

"I never knew what was worse as a kid, when my mother was there with us in the apartment or when she'd leave us alone." Each word sounded as though he were pulling it from somewhere deep inside him. And perhaps he was. A place where he swept all the painful parts of his past, to rot and fester. "When she was there she was low on patience. Men would come over, and Cage and I were to wait in a closet. We never knew what we were waiting for. We just knew it was small and dark." He stopped abruptly and his eyes met hers. She knew suddenly, intuitively that they were both thinking of his love for the boundless open skies of Montana.

His fingers searched absently for a cigarette, then paused, as if remembering where he was. "She'd leave us alone. Sometimes there would be food to eat, sometimes not. That last night she left her matches on the kitchen table."

Understanding began to dawn, and with it, a terrible premonition. An image was taking shape in her mind, one too horrible to contemplate. Two boys, toddlers probably, uncared for, untended. Left to get into the kind of tragedy that most parents went to great lengths to protect their children from.

Her voice was a whisper trapped in her throat. "Oh, Jed."

"I still remember the thrill of finally getting one to light. When it burned down to my fingers, I dropped it." The words were dragged from him with a horrible lack of passion. The passion and guilt were all locked on the inside.

"That's how the apartment caught fire."

He gave a slow nod. "I remember being afraid of what my mother would do when she found out. We hid in the bedroom closet at first. When the smoke got too bad we opened the door and went for the window. The fire spread before help arrived.''

She closed her eyes, but the picture he was painting was branded on her mind. The screams of the frightened children, the smell of smoke and the agony Jed must have suffered, caught in the flames. He had the scars to remind him of his nightmare. But it was the scars on the inside that worried her most. The massive load of guilt he'd carried with him most of his life would have leveled a weaker man.

''It wasn't your fault. Surely you know that?''

He gave her a terrible parody of a smile. ''Wasn't it?''

Driven to move, she went to touch him. She laid her hand on his arm and slid it up and back in a gentle glide. ''You were a child. Lay the blame where it belongs—with your mother. She was to blame, not you.''

His tone was final. ''I lit the matches.''

Her grip tightened on his arm and she gave it a slight shake. ''You were four! It was a horrible, horrible situation, but you weren't responsible.'' Her voice softened, became imploring. ''Forgive yourself, Jed. It wasn't your fault.''

''It's all tangled up inside,'' he murmured wearily. ''Everything I do, everything I want, comes from some pathetic piece of my childhood. You said you understand me. How could you? I've never told this to anybody before.'' His mouth twisted. ''There's lots you don't know.'' In a gesture of frustrated weariness, he scrubbed both hands over his face. ''Maybe it's time you were told.''

She didn't doubt that there was more. But the fortress around his emotions had been breached and she didn't know if he could withstand another assault. Not so soon. ''Shh.'' She went up on tiptoe to kiss his throat. ''It's enough. It's enough for now.'' Her arms went around him, his suffering eliciting an instinctive offer of solace.

He cupped her elbows with his hands and bent his head. His lips were hard and more than a little desperate. She tasted his desperation and tempered it with compassion. Jed wouldn't accept sympathy, would be offended by pity. What she wanted to give him was so much more than that. Tracing his lips with the tip of her tongue, she poured her heart into the kiss.

She could feel the tense muscles under her hands, and her fingers went immediately to soothe. His primal male flavor surged through her body, and she leaned into him in a wholly female reaction.

He stiffened under her hands. ''Julianne.'' His voice was a velvet caress.

''I know,'' she whispered. He'd come to apologize for hurting her, but the pain he'd just relived for her was the worst kind of torment she could imagine. Perhaps he even believed that he didn't need to reach out to another person right now, but he was wrong. Her fingertips trailed down his shirtfront. She didn't want to think of him alone tonight with only his torturous memories for company. He should be with someone who cared about him. As she did. She pressed her lips to the hollow in his throat.

His body remained unyielding, but his face was set with the expression of a man waging a mighty war with himself. She was going to do her best to make sure it was a battle he would lose.

Her gaze locked with his, she undid each button on his shirt with smooth, graceful movements. His eyes hooded, he watched her, still motionless. When she had his chest bared, she went up on tiptoe, brushing her silk-clad body against his skin. A shudder worked through him and his arms went around her with a fierceness that should have shocked but only thrilled.

He buried his face in her hair for a moment, then stepped back and swept her up in his arms. She linked an arm around his neck, so when he laid her down on the bed, she was able to pull him down to meet her mouth. He pulled away after a moment, stood and shrugged out of his shirt.

Her heart jammed in her throat. The emotion he usually sought to contain was unleashed. He undid the button and zipper on his jeans, then, as if he couldn't go without touching her any longer, joined her on the bed and covered her mouth with his. Passion flared, clean and bright, sending sharp darts of need throughout her system.

They clung, pressed, rolled on the bed. The light from the single lamp on her dresser slanted across the bed so they moved from brightness, to shadow, to light again. His hands swept over the silky camisole, then slipped beneath it, streaking over skin. He rolled to his back, pulling her on top of him without releasing her mouth. Edgy blades of lust pricked at her, and her hands were as ruthless as his as she wedged them between their bodies and went on a sensual discovery.

Once released, the emotions he sought to guard so closely were not easily restrained again. And before the night was over, she was determined to have every last one of them. With hot, voracious kisses and long, gliding strokes, she found what made him groan; what made his breath hiss and what caused shudders to rack his big body.

She sat astride him and tipped her head back, letting her hair brush her shoulders, running her hands down the sides of her camisole. With her gaze locked on his, she grasped the hem in her hands and pulled it over her head. The restless smoke of his eyes was enough to send fiery little demons of passion pounding through her veins. Then his hands came up to stroke, to touch, to claim.

His hand went to her nape, and he pulled her down for his kiss, his fingers shoving into her hair as his mouth ate at hers. Colors exploded behind her eyelids, fragmenting into a prism of brilliant hues.

This was what she wanted from him, she thought dimly. Passion, primitive and unchecked. A need uncensored, unchained. One she returned without reservation. Her hands danced up his spine, lingering over each individual vertebra. Bodies rolled, tongues battled, damp flesh pressed to damp flesh. Sensation zinged from his fingertips to pulse points under her skin. She turned her head to graze his shoulder with her teeth, desperate for the taste of him. He indulged his own appetite by moving down her body and taking her nipple in his lips. Each rhythmic pull of his mouth elicited a corresponding contraction of pleasure low in her belly. Clawing need burst forth, a desperate wanting for now, now, without another moment of waiting. She was slowly being turned inside out as she writhed and moaned beneath him.

She was too close to toppling from that towering pinnacle of pleasure that he built with each stroke of his tongue, each glide of his fingers. And she was determined not to fall alone.

Her hands went to his hips and began tugging at the heavy denim. To aid her frantic fingers, he lifted up, and she reared beneath him, rolling him over and fighting the jeans down his long legs.

When she'd freed him, she slid up his body and wrapped her fingers around him. She stroked her tongue up his heavy masculinity and a ragged groan tore from his throat. And then his hands were on her shoulders and she was flipped on her back. Her pants were swept away, and he made a place for himself between her legs.

Yes. She almost wept at the promise of imminent satisfaction. The urge to have him inside her was brutal, the need to bind with this man primal. Then he drove into her, and she unraveled in one violent eruption.

There was no time for muscles to relax, for sensations to calm. With a feral snarl vibrating deep in his throat, he yanked her legs higher around his hips, and thrust harder, faster, deeper.

The aftermaths of the first climax slapped into the rising waves of the next. Breathing was impossible as she madly scrambled for the next peak. Her gaze unfocused, her nails scored the tense shoulders above her, and they went over the next shattering precipice together.

His touch was less urgent, but no less possessive as he stroked her body back to calm. His heartbeat hammered against her ear, the sound solid and comforting. When he rolled away from her, she made a noise of protest but couldn't summon the energy to open her eyes.

"Don't go," she murmured.

"I have no intentions of going anywhere tonight." His voice was low, with the edgy rasp of satisfied male.

"Good." She smiled and snuggled more deeply into the pillow. "Otherwise I'd have to come after you and drag you back to bed, and that could prove tricky. I think I've gone blind."

There was a smile in his voice when he suggested, "Maybe you should open your eyes."

"Why, if you're not going anywhere?"

She could hear his footsteps padding across the room, the gentle click as the lamp on her dresser was turned off. Then the bed sank with the weight of his body, and she reached out and found his muscled thigh. He had the legs of an experienced horseman, she thought dreamily, pausing to caress the sleek bundle of muscles there. She stroked gently, neither of them speaking for a long time. But there was something she had to broach with him, because Jed needed pushing and he needed prodding. He'd be the first to admit that prodding was her forte. She'd always believed in going with her strengths.

"What are you going to do about your brother?" The question hung in the darkness between them. And although she still touched him, she felt a part of him, a part deep inside, shift away.

"Leave it alone, Julianne."

She wondered if he recognized the note of weary plea that threaded his words. It was enough to make her sorry she couldn't do as he requested. Her touch was not quite absent, her fingernails lightly scoring hair-roughened skin. "I've never asked you for anything, Jed. And I'm not asking for myself, I'm asking for you. Just promise me you'll think about it."

He didn't answer, and her heart split just a little. She'd always known the man was stubborn, and what she'd learned from him tonight told her that there was a seething cauldron of rusty guilt and pain oozing inside him. It was naive of her to hope, but she was helpless not to try.

He rolled away from her, and this time she didn't protest, thinking she'd pushed too hard, too fast. After several moments she became aware of something feather light fluttering to land on her sensitized skin. She smiled slowly, stretched, keeping her eyes tightly closed. Because Jed was here. He may have closed up again, but he wasn't running. At least not from her.

The scent of rose petals stung the air, and she drew in a sharp breath as his lips followed the path of the flowers he'd shredded. He kissed each inch of skin covered by the fragrant pieces, then she laced her fingers in his hair, drew him up to meet her lips.

"Promise me," she whispered against his mouth.

His lips hesitated against hers for an instant before kissing her deeply. And as the silken web of passion began to tighten around them once again, she was very much aware that he hadn't promised her anything at all.

Chapter 13

"What in heaven's name are you doin' in there, girl?"

Julianne started in surprise, banging her head on the inside of the refrigerator. Wincing, she withdrew from the appliance and faced Annie. The woman was carefully moving her walker toward a chair, where she sat down, breathing heavily.

"We're going to have to put a bell on that thing," Julianne observed. "It's getting downright dangerous the way you sneak up on a person."

Annie was flushed with exertion. "Never thought I'd see the day when just getting around was enough to wear me out. Why, it can't be more than twenty yards from my room to the kitchen, and look at me. Puffing and panting like a hound dog on a hot day."

"Maybe that should tell you something."

The housekeeper waved away the concern in Julianne's voice. "All it tells me is that I've laid in that blasted bed too long. Now." She fixed the younger woman with a steely look. "What was it you thought you were doing, climbing into that fridge?"

Julianne pointed with her wet rag to the countertop lined with the refrigerator's contents. "Cleaning it, of course."

"Don't suppose it ever occurred to you that those shelves and drawers are removable."

She blinked once, then turned, opened the door and peered inside. "Well, I'll be darned," she said, wonder tingeing the words. "That's handy, isn't it?"

When she looked back at Annie, the woman's eyes were twinkling. "Learn something new every day, don't you?"

"Sometimes too late," Julianne muttered. With quick movements she started replacing the food items in the freshly cleaned appliance. She caught the other woman's broad grin, and it elicited an answering smile. Whatever her feelings about taking over for Annie during her convalescence, she couldn't deny that the experience had been an education. When she'd been a girl, the housekeeper had never required Julianne to do more around the house than keep her room neat. And there had always been servants at the homes she'd shared with Andrew. She'd been kept too busy during her marriage, at any rate, trying to pull her ex-husband out of a bottle or the nearest casino.

But despite the aching muscles and the sheer drudgery of some of the tasks she'd taken over, Julianne didn't regret a moment she'd spent replacing Annie. Regardless of the tedium of some of the days, regardless of the missed hours for riding and the sometimes bone-deep exhaustion, there was an undeniable sense of accomplishment at being able to keep the household running smoothly. A quiet satisfaction that came from looking at a sparkling room and knowing she was responsible.

"Why don't you sit down for a few minutes?" Annie suggested. "Lord, the way you fly around the house these days is enough to make a body tired just looking at you. Take a break.''

"And when did you ever take a break?'' Julianne asked. But after a quick sideways glance at the clock, she slipped into a chair. There was still the laundry to finish, the upstairs to dust and a cake to bake and frost for dinner. But she'd always left time in her day to check on Annie, to fetch and carry for her and to stop in for a few minutes of chatter every hour or so.

"Don't worry. The way I've been feeling the last couple of days, I'll be on my feet again before you know it.''

"You'll be on your feet when the doctor says it's okay, and not a moment sooner,'' Julianne corrected her. "Jed and I aren't going to let you push yourself harder than you should.''

Annie's eyebrows raised. "Jed and you, is it? Think because you've got the big man himself on your side that you'll scare me into staying down for a few weeks more?'' She snorted, reminding Julianne vividly that this was the woman who'd raised her and kept both her and Jed in line for more years than she'd like to count. With effort, she suppressed a smile. Annie would be supremely unimpressed with anything either of them suggested.

Placatingly, she said, "Now, Annie. We just want you to follow doctor's orders, is all. Dr. Brierly said you're going to have to take it easy for a couple of months, at least.''

"That old fool,'' Annie sniffed, forgetting for the moment that the two of them were only months apart in age. "Once I get off this blasted walker, I'll be back to my routine again. I really could do more right now. There's no reason at all I couldn't dust a few things for you. I'm moving along well enough with this thing.''

The look of horror on Julianne's face had the other

woman allowing, ''Well, so maybe it will be a few more weeks, but I can't believe you'll be so unwilling to give up some of these tasks.''

''I promise to hand over dust rag and mop just as soon as the doctor releases you to work,'' Julianne pledged, hand over her heart. ''Satisfied?''

''Not that you aren't doin' a fine job around here, you understand. I've been right proud of the way you've stepped in and taken over for me.''

''Well, it did make me feel useful, and that's something I've needed for a long time.''

Reaching out to pat her hand, Annie said, ''You're a good girl, Julianne. None finer, and that's the truth. There's not a useless bone in your body.''

''Maybe not.'' Though the words warmed, they didn't quite dim the doubt. ''But I've had a lot of time while I've worked around here recently to think about my future, and what I want from it.'' Her eyes flashed to the other woman's. ''No offense, but I think it involves more than washing, cooking and cleaning.''

''None taken. Everyone needs to choose their own paths, and any job, when done with pride, is a responsible one in my book.'' Annie tilted her head and surveyed her. ''Did that time spent thinking result in any plans for that future you're talking about?''

''Well, I could ride out with Jed and the men every day, but—'' she shrugged ''—he doesn't really need me to help him run the ranch.'' The words struck an answering pang in the depths of her heart. Jed didn't *need* her on any level, none but the obvious. The knowledge shouldn't have had the power to wound, but it did. Deeply. Careful not to let emotion color her voice, she continued lightly, ''And let's face it, Jed and I working side by side daily would be the quickest path to homicide. No, I've been thinking of going back to college.''

Annie looked approving. ''That sounds like a good idea. Never did like the fact that you quit to get married before you got your degree.''

Julianne wondered if the other woman understood that quitting school had been just one in a long list of failures in her life. Some of them she had to chalk up to experience, but this was one she could rectify. *Wanted* to rectify, more every day. ''I've only lacked a year from getting my degree, but I'm going to change majors, so it will probably take me even longer.''

''What major are you thinking about?''

''I thought…counseling. I'd like to get a job in an elementary school. Jed will jeer at what he calls my bleeding heart, but there's a lot of need out there, and I'd like to be part of the solution.'' Her mind streaked to Jed's childhood. Who had been there to calm a little boy's devastation at the loss of his mother, his brother, his home? Her chest ached as she thought of all he'd endured when just a child. Surely someone had been assigned when he was taken from his mother, perhaps another when he'd been in foster care and then adopted. But the adults hadn't been able to ease the suffering from his injuries, hadn't freed him from his jail of guilt.

''Don't you worry none about what Jed will say. You've got a soft heart, but you're wise enough. You'll do fine. He isn't exactly an authority on the subject of letting others help him.''

Seizing the opening, Julianne told Annie of the call from John Sullivan, and Jed's reaction to it. The woman's face went slack with surprise.

''My, oh my,'' she murmured, rocking a bit in her chair. ''I don't know what Jed will do. I wish I could think he'd reach out just a little for the chance of family. But I have to believe that he won't.'' Her gaze rose, and she caught sight of Julianne's face. ''It won't do you no good to hope, I'm afraid. Something has burdened him for as long as I've known him. People have disappeared from his life too many times for him not to have built a mighty tight shield around his feelings. He's a grown man. Right or wrong, he's gonna make his own decisions.''

The woman hadn't said anything Julianne didn't know in her heart, but she couldn't prevent a fresh wave of disappointment. Last night Jed had given her a clue about the cause of his guardedness, and she was afraid that Annie was right. He wasn't going to contact John Sullivan, wasn't going to risk emotion on another, wasn't going to trust, even a little. She didn't want to examine the rush of pain that accompanied her certainty.

A door opened and closed somewhere in the house, and Julianne's gaze flew to the clock in panic. What was Jed doing in an hour before his normal time? And entering by the front door, at that? Wiping her hands on a dish towel, she went to the hallway to greet him, questions on her lips, and was confronted by the sight of her father.

Shock held her still for a moment, before welcome bubbled up inside her. ''Dad!''

''There's my Julie-girl.'' Harley Buchanan held out his arms. ''Got a kiss for your old man?''

She hugged him, words tumbling from her lips. ''I didn't know you were coming. Or, I guess Jed said you were planning a visit, but he didn't say when. How did you get here? Someone could have picked you up at the airport, if you'd let us know.''

''Oh, I just rented a car.'' He stepped back, an easy

smile sitting on his face. "I have to be getting back tomorrow. No use putting anybody here out."

Julianne's smile dimmed. "You're leaving tomorrow already? What's the rush? Take a few days and look at what Jed's done to the ranch. Visit the neighbors." *Spend time with me.* The words remained unspoken. She'd never come high on Harley's list of priorities. She wondered when that fact would lose its bite.

He patted her shoulder. "I would, but my motto is Don't Walk Away From the Table in the Middle of a Winning Streak, and honey, the streak I'm on is blazing." He winked at her, a tall, still-handsome man, long-limbed and broad through the shoulders. He didn't look any different from the last time she'd seen him, which had been—she mentally calculated the time—almost two years ago. She'd arranged to visit him when he was in Atlantic City. Other than a couple of dinners, they'd spent very little time together. She'd been unable to compete with the lure of the cards.

She tucked the hurt away with an ease borne of long practice. She'd never let him see it. Demands made Harley uncomfortable and changed nothing, except to leave her feeling ashamed and guilty when he left.

Pasting a smile on her face, she slipped her arm through his and led him to the kitchen. "Well, we'll have to make the most of the time you're here. Are you hungry? Dinner isn't ready yet, but I can make you a sandwich. You'll be surprised to learn that I'm well on my way to becoming a domestic goddess."

"Annie can get me something. I didn't eat on the plane. Got into a game of blackjack with the guy beside me." He winked, grinning widely. "He never knew what hit him."

"I'm sure not." Competently, she began to get fixings

for a sandwich out. "Annie had a fall a couple of weeks ago and I've been taking over for her until she gets better. She's sleeping right now, but I'm sure she'll be as tickled as the rest of us to see you."

"Don't know about everyone," he muttered, picking up the glass of milk she'd set before him and taking a long swallow. "Somehow I can't imagine Jed feeling tickled." He surveyed the thick roast beef sandwich Julianne set before him with pleasure, and began eating. "He sounded downright menacing the last time he phoned."

That snagged her attention. "Jed called you?"

The man nodded, making short work of the food on his plate. "He's getting to be a real nag, you know that?" Catching her eye, he hastened to add, "Not that I'd tell him so to his face, you understand. The man's got a slice of mean that doesn't bear crossing." He finished the rest of the sandwich in two quick bites. "Only people I've ever noticed him having a soft spot for were Annie and you."

"Me?" Julianne sank to a chair beside him, eyes wide. "I've never noticed that Jed had any particular soft spots, and certainly not one with my name on it."

Harley leaned back in his chair contentedly. "Well, you could fight like two tomcats on occasion, but he watched out for you. Still does."

"Too much, sometimes," she murmured. Then something else he'd said caught her attention. "Is Jed the one who gave you the idea to visit?"

The man's gaze shifted away. "Well, I've been promising him I would. Been meaning to for a while. I wanted to come check on you when your divorce went through, but I figured you needed some time to yourself."

Her face went set and still. What she'd needed at that time, she recalled, was someone, anyone, who cared about her, to just be there. Not to rescue her, not to chastise her, but just to *listen*. Her chin angled. She'd made it through without help, and maybe she was the stronger for it. But she wouldn't be thanking her father for that.

"And I was right." He beamed a smile at her. "Look at you—beautiful as ever. You're the picture of your mother. I've told Jed over and over that he worries too much about you." He nodded wisely. "You're stronger than he thinks. I've always known that. Don't know why he can't see it."

She rose and took his plate and glass, rinsing them and setting them in the dishwasher. It was too easy to imagine how Jed had pushed and prodded Harley to act like a father and go to her aid when she'd been at her lowest point. Irritation warred with the swift warmth that spread at the thought. The warmth won. Maybe Harley was right. It did appear that Jed had a "soft spot" where she was concerned. Wistfully she wondered just how deep that spot went.

She wouldn't have to wonder long. Harley was speaking again, expansive after satisfying his appetite. "I heard from your ex-husband, did I tell you that?"

Her attention snapped back to him. "Andrew? When? Why?"

He wrinkled his brow. "Oh, it must have been a couple of weeks ago. Called me up and asked for money, of all things."

Something twisted in her stomach then, a quick, nauseating turn. "He called me, too. When I turned him down, he must have been desperate."

Harley snorted. "Desperate is right. Never did care much for the boy and I told him so. As if I'd give him the time of day after what he did."

"Well." She drew in a deep breath. "I'm glad you

didn't agree to help him. Andrew is going to have to make some hard decisions and pay for the mistakes he's made.''

His hand slipped inside his pocket and he withdrew a slim cheroot. Putting it to his lips and lighting it, he inquired, ''Can you get me an ashtray?''

She raised her eyebrows. ''Annie still doesn't like people smoking in the house.''

He aimed a winning smile at her and blew out a stream of smoke. ''Let's not tell her, then.''

A laugh gusted out of her. He was incorrigible, always would be. The rules had never applied to Harley Buchanan. She'd passed the time when she believed they ever would. She rose and took out a small bowl to place in front of him. He reached for it, running a finger around the rim in a quick, restless motion that spoke of nerves or boredom. Since he hadn't been here long enough to max out even his attention span, she had to assume it was the former. Her eyes narrowed.

''Something on your mind, Harley?''

His gaze was startled, a bit guilty. ''Me? No. I do have something to tell you, though.'' He set the bowl twirling in a dizzying motion. ''I got myself married again.''

Of all the things he could have said, she thought this one was the most unexpected. Clutching the back of a chair, she said weakly, ''Married? When?''

''Last week. Mona—I mentioned her the last time we talked, didn't I?—she said let's do it, and I thought, why not.'' He shrugged and smiled sheepishly. ''I've been alone a long time. We enjoy the same things.'' He inhaled and expelled a line of smoke. ''That's why I have to hurry back. We're going on a honeymoon in a few days.''

Comprehension filtered belatedly through her shock. Mona must have been the bodacious babe he'd had to get back to, cutting short their last phone conversation. "Congratulations. When am I going to meet her?"

"Oh, soon," he said vaguely. "Since this was going to be such a quick trip there wasn't really time for her to prepare to come. And she's busy selling her business so she can travel with me. She has a liquor supply company. That's how I met her, at the Flamingo in Vegas."

"Well." Julianne sat down and took a deep breath. "I hope this works out for you. I want you to be happy." Sincerity laced her words. Harley had been searching for something for as long as she could remember. She hoped for his sake that he'd found it.

He looked relieved and reached over to pat her hand. "Exactly what I've always wanted for you. Now, why don't you tell me what your plans are. You're not going to hole up on the ranch indefinitely, are you?"

A sudden thought struck her then. "Why? Are you and Mona thinking of living here?"

"Us?" He looked amazed. "No. Of course not."

Of course not. She shook her head slightly to clear it. "I've decided that I'll be going back to the university to finish my degree. Then I guess I'll get a job."

"Well, that's fine then." He beamed at her, as pleased as if he'd made the decision himself. "You landed on your feet just like I knew you would. You'll do well in whatever you try. You're smart," he said, pointing the cheroot at her. "And you're lucky, too. That's a damn near unbeatable combination." He put the cigar back in his mouth and puffed furiously. "I told Jed he was worrying for nothing, but he insisted I tell you about the deal." Shaking his head, he leaned over and tapped the cigar's ashes into the bowl.

Something in the word made her go still. "The...deal?"

"To sell the ranch." He managed to look both abashed and charming. "I kind of had a slump for a while. Oh, I won some, but it just seemed like I lost it faster than I could win it back.'' He shook his head reflectively. ''I haven't had a streak that sour for years. Hope I never do again.''

His ruminations failed to penetrate her shell-shocked brain. She couldn't focus on any words beyond the first ones. Dimly she realized that Jed had stepped into the room, but her attention was focused on her father. ''You're...'' Her voice cracked, and she cleared her throat before trying again. ''You're selling the ranch?''

His gaze searched the room, couldn't seem to find a place to land. ''The fact is, Julianne...I've already sold it.''

His words punched through her with the force of a fist, sending her senses reeling. Her lungs constricted, couldn't seem to draw in oxygen.

''You promised.'' The words were strangled, all but inaudible. Certainly Harley didn't seem to hear them.

''I was in a real bad way, honey. And the fact was, I wasn't ever going to live on the ranch again. It was a business decision. You understand.''

She stared at him with no acknowledgment of his wheedling tone. *You understand.* The words could have been echoes from the past, back to haunt her.

''I know I promised I'd be back for your play, baby, but something's come up...I can't make it to your concert after all...I'm just not going to get back in time for your graduation, honey...you understand....''

''Who?'' She barely recognized the dull voice as her own. ''Who did you sell it to?''

For the first time Jed spoke, and his words completed her descent into utter despair.

''He sold it to me.''

Chapter 14

The only sound in the awful stillness of the room was the nervous tapping of Harley's fingers against the stoneware bowl. Julianne stared at Jed for long moments. His face was a hard, grim mask. There was no doubting the truth of his words. And no denying the rush of bitterness that nearly swamped her.

"When?" Her gaze swung back to pin Harley's, and he shrugged, clearly uncomfortable with the emotional-laden question. "Not long ago. Before the divorce, wasn't it, Jed?" He lobbed the ball neatly back into the other man's court and breathed a distinct sigh of relief when his daughter's attention shifted away from him.

"It was a few weeks before Andrew's arrest," Jed affirmed. His eyes were steady on hers, and she could read nothing in their gray depths. "Harley called and told me he was planning to list the ranch with a Realtor." His voice carefully blank, he added, "He took me by surprise."

Julianne pressed a hand to her stomach, hoping to quiet the nerves grinding there. "Yes. He's good at that." She made no attempt to mask her resentment. She doubted she could have done so, at any rate. It bubbled and churned inside her with violent intensity.

She looked down at the table and struggled to keep her voice level. "If you were that desperate for money, Harley, why didn't you come to me?"

"Now, Julianne." His voice was too hearty, too sincere. "What were you going to do about it? I didn't need a loan, I needed cash. A lot of it. And the truth is, I knew you wouldn't be able to get your hands on it. Andrew was losing it faster than I was at the time." He lifted a shoulder. "Word travels in my circle, especially about that kind of money."

Yes, no one knew better than she that word did, indeed, travel quickly. The fact that her father had heard before she had about the speed with which her ex-husband had spiraled out of control brought one more stab of pain in her chest.

"So you decided to put the ranch on the market."

He nodded, obviously pleased at her composure. "I was ready to do what had to be done, but Jed here was having none of it." He slid a quick, wary glance at the silent man. "He made me an offer I couldn't refuse."

"Yes, I'll just bet he did." The words tasted as bitter as they sounded. Once Harley had stated his decision to sell, Jed would have made sure he'd be the only buyer considered. His inheritance must have been sizable. The down payment alone on a place this size would have been a fortune. And she already knew how important the ranch was to him, didn't she? Her gaze traveled to the man watching her silently. It hurt to look at him. The shock of her father's announcement had settled into a throbbing wound that threatened to tear at any instant.

Harley slipped unnoticed from the room. "You should have told me." Her words were flat, cold.

"It was your father's decision," Jed said evenly. "I figured he should tell you himself. He owed you that much."

"How incredibly noble." Propelled to move, she rose from the chair and circled the table. "As if it would make a difference who I heard it from. It doesn't matter. The ranch is *gone*." She propped her hands flat on the table to steady legs that had suddenly gone weak. The deep breath she took seemed to rasp through her lungs. "It's gone. After all his promises, all this time…" She squeezed her eyes shut in an effort to keep the dangerous emotion caged inside.

"I told Harley you'd take it hard."

Her spine stiffened at the rough edge of sympathy in his words. Her eyes opened to flash at him. "You let me babble on like an idiot about Harley coming back here to live, and you never said a word about it. I should have guessed, I suppose, when you explained all the money you were putting into the ranch, but you said you'd taken care of it with Harley, and I thought…" She broke off then. What she'd thought, hoped, was that Jed had worked some magic on her father and found a way to keep the ranch safe. And in Jed's mind, maybe that's exactly what he had done. At least he'd kept it safe for himself.

Tears scalded her eyes and she longed to scream, to smash something. No doubt that was exactly what Harley had feared when he'd made his surreptitious exit. Never one to face the unpleasantries of life, he'd made his escape when he could.

Jed reached for her then, a gesture she avoided. She felt

as fragile as century-old glass, afraid she'd shatter at a touch. He seemed to be searching for words. "I know it's a shock."

She gave a slow nod. "I'll just bet you do. It came as a shock to you when he started selling off land, didn't it? Kind of shook that nice, secure little niche you have in the world." She saw his eyes narrow and was fiercely satisfied to have forced a reaction. "How convenient that he decided to sell after you'd come in to a substantial amount of money. Convenient for you, anyway."

The ice in his voice matched the chill in his eyes. "If you're suggesting that I pushed him to the idea, you're way off base."

"Am I?" she asked recklessly. The disappointment and bitterness frothed and crashed like white water within her. "Do you honestly expect me to believe that you're unhappy with the way things turned out? Now you have everything you've always wanted." She turned a blinding smile on him, all the more bright for being completely detached. "The whole place is yours now, and yours alone. If I'm not mistaken, that's precisely the way you like things."

Dawn was spilling soft pastels across the Montana sky. Julianne sipped her third cup of coffee, watching the hues bloom above the horizon. With a mental click she freeze-framed the image, storing the memory away, for a time when memories were all she had left of the H/B.

The thought sent sudden pain piercing the dull ache in her chest. Sleep had been impossible, so she'd had plenty of time to think last night. Plenty of time for regrets.

The hostility between Jed and Andrew had kept her from returning with her husband for another visit after that first disastrous one. She'd never trusted Andrew alone enough to chance a trip back by herself. But she'd always known the ranch was here for her. There had been comfort in that. Now even that was to be denied her.

She heard Harley's stealthy steps before she saw him. She let him reach for a coffee mug, pour it full before she spoke.

"You're up early, Dad."

He jolted, splashing the coffee over the rim of the mug he'd lifted halfway to his lips. "Julianne." Dismay was evident in his voice. "I didn't expect to see you up."

"I'm sure you didn't."

He wrapped both big hands around the mug and trained his gaze on it. "You didn't used to get up until full morning."

She didn't bother to remind him that he was no expert on her habits. They hadn't spent any amount of time in the same house for more than a decade. "I didn't sleep last night."

He peered at her. "And you look exhausted. Why don't you head on upstairs? Get yourself a nap."

She nodded toward the bag he'd dropped to the floor beside him. "Planning on leaving soon?" She already knew the answer to her question. He'd planned on sneaking out like a thief in the night. But unlike a thief, who would have only relieved them of their possessions, he'd stripped her of the one remaining illusion she'd still had about him.

Forced heartiness in his voice, he replied, "Got an early flight. Didn't want to bother anyone. I'll drive myself back to the airport. Next time we'll have us a nice long visit. Maybe you can come and stay with me and Mona for a while sometime."

Julianne traced the edge of her mug with a fingertip.

Her tone polite, she asked, "When, Dad? When should I come?"

"When?" Surprise filtered the word. "Well, sometime after the honeymoon, maybe. Of course, we don't really have us a place yet. Maybe when we get settled." His voice grew smoother. "I'll let you know. We'll have us a real good visit soon, though." He drained his coffee and stood up, reaching for his bag. "But right now I better run if I'm going to catch that flight."

Her words were level, but there was no mistaking their command. "Sit down."

His face went slack with surprise. "What?"

"I said sit down. I'm not going to make it easy for you this time."

Harley set his bag down again, but then didn't seem to know what to do with his hands. They opened and closed reflexively, before he wiped them down his pant legs. Slowly, gingerly, he reseated himself. "What's this all about, Julianne?"

She surveyed him with clear eyes and a heavy heart. This man was her father, although the occasions he'd acted like one were rare. He'd relinquished his parenting responsibilities so he could follow wherever his addiction had taken him. Yet, she knew he cared about her, in his own way. He'd always failed miserably at showing it.

"I love you." She watched the unease flicker on his face and felt an overwhelming sadness, for both of them. "I don't remember the last time I told you that. The last time I had a chance to."

He reached over awkwardly and patted her hand. "I know. I feel the same way. We don't need to talk about these things."

"Yes, I think we do." Fatigue was beginning to make itself known, but it was an exhaustion of the spirit and the mind, owing nothing to the physical. "I think we haven't talked about these things for too long now."

Squirming on the chair, he said, "Julianne, let's wait and do this another time. Sometime when you're not so tired."

She looked down. "You mean sometime when I wouldn't make the kind of scene you hate." She raised her gaze to meet his. "I don't think so. I've spent my whole life keeping my feelings from you, because emotions make you uncomfortable. I thought shielding you from them would draw you closer. It never did."

As if he finally realized he wasn't going to escape this time, his big body slumped a little in his chair. "You always wanted so much, Julianne. I could never give you enough. You always wanted more."

She'd thought there was no more room for hurt to spread through her. She'd been wrong. "Too much what? Too much love, too much attention? You made me feel that way. Don't make demands, don't make any unpleasant scenes. I think that's why I asked for so little in my life, from myself and from my marriage."

He raised his head. "You can't blame me for that."

"Yes, Dad, as a matter of fact, I can." The three cups of coffee weren't quite enough fortification for her to get through this. It took all the inner strength she had to continue. She knew if she didn't now, she never would. "I was so used to settling for the crumbs you could spare me, I got to where I didn't think I could ask for more. Well, that was wrong. *You* were wrong. It's not greedy for me to want to be loved unconditionally. We all deserve that."

She let her gaze drift away. If she had to look at him, she knew she couldn't finish. And if she didn't finish this, they could never start over. "You've disappointed me over the years. Time and again, when you'd put a game or a race ahead of me. But nothing has ever hurt me as badly as your selling the ranch. It was the one promise you'd made to me that you'd kept. Until now.''

There was a shake in his voice that reminded her that he was no longer a young man. ''Baby, I explained that. I had to have the money. You were a little girl when I made that promise. How was I to know you'd feel the same way now?''

''You couldn't.'' Tears burned behind her eyes, but she refused to shed them. ''Because you never asked. Don't pretend that you even considered my feelings. I know you too well. All you thought of was what you needed…your addiction.'' She drew an unsteady breath, glad this was almost at an end. ''But you can't hurt me anymore, Harley. The one advantage of hitting rock bottom is that there's nowhere left to fall. You can't disappoint me anymore because there are no more promises left to break.'' Her smile was wavery. ''That should be a relief for both of us.''

She didn't say anything else; she couldn't. She watched as her father rose, as if suddenly old, and hesitate. Finally, without another word, he reached for his bag and walked out the door.

The cloud of dust from his departure still lingered in the air when Jed stepped into the room.

''Was that Harley leaving?''

Julianne swallowed around the hard knot in her throat and nodded.

He poured himself some coffee and sipped at it, his gray gaze surveying her over the rim. ''He didn't stay long.''

A humorless laugh escaped from her. ''Did you expect any differently? He put this scene off as long as he possibly could. It will be months before I hear from him again.''

He sat down opposite her. "I take it you gave him an earful."

There was no stopping the tears now. A weighty knot of remorse lingered in her stomach. "I shouldn't have said what I did to him. What difference does it make, anyway? It doesn't change anything." Her breath hitched once, then she reached up and swiped the tears away with a furious motion. "Nothing will change what's been done."

He made a move toward her, then checked himself, as if knowing his touch would be unwelcome. One large hand clenched into a fist. "I didn't do it to hurt you, Julianne."

"I believe you."

He raised his gaze, met hers. "Really?"

She refused to consider the hopefulness tracing through the word. "Of course. You never considered how I'd feel about you buying the ranch, because you never considered me for a second when Harley approached you. Just as he didn't. All either of you concentrated on was what you needed." She felt purged, empty, as if the quick bout of scalding tears had flooded away all feeling. She welcomed the numbness. It was a relief from the jangle of emotion that had gripped her for the last twelve hours. She knew it wouldn't last. Nothing ever did.

"Tell me what I should have done," he demanded, his voice dangerously cool. "I knew damn well that selling the ranch would hurt you, but there was no convincing Harley. Would it be easier if you'd found that the ranch had been sold to Walter Larkin, or Jim Pooler? Maybe to one of those fancy Hollywood types who have been moving into the state and buying up the property?" Quick as a flash, his hand streaked across the table and caught her wrist. "Tell me, Julianne. Is it worse having me own it? Would you feel better right now if the ranch belonged to a stranger?"

"It already does." She tugged at her wrist to free it. "I don't know you. I thought I did. At least as well as you let anyone know you. But I was wrong." Her voice grew deceptively distant. "I can see that now. Maybe you really did think Harley should be the one to tell me. But I'll never understand how you could take me to bed and still keep this bit of news to yourself. That strikes me as a bit cold, even for you."

"Sleeping with you had nothing to do with the ranch."

That those low, smooth words still had the ability to send a fast skitter down her spine was surely due to system overload. The reaction was unexpected, and totally unwelcome. "I need no convincing that emotion didn't enter into the act."

He bit out a curse, rose and rounded the table. "That's not what I meant, and you know it." He came to stand behind her, his hands on her shoulders, sliding down her arms and up again in a skin-warming caress. "I saved the ranch the only way I could. I own it, and I won't deny I'm glad about it. But I didn't mean to hurt you, then or now." At her silence, his fingers tightened on her shoulders and his voice deepened to a rumble. "I don't pretend to understand what's between us, but it's there, and neither of us can deny it. I don't know what it means. But I know that I want you to stay so we can find out."

She slipped out of her chair, away from his touch. Busying herself making another pot of coffee gave her something to do with her hands. "I'll stay. At least until Annie gets back on her feet. I've made some mistakes along the way, but I've never walked away from a commitment. Once she's well enough, though, I'll be on my way."

She could sense the utter stillness that came over him, even without turning to see it. Could feel the air between them grow thick and charged. Like a coward she kept her back to him.

"Where are you going?"

"To school." She was proud of the steadiness in her tone. "I've been thinking about it for a while, and if I want to be registered for the fall semester I'll need to get signed up. Then I'll have to find an apartment, a job...." Her voice trailed off. The sheer weight of the decision, one that had seemed so right only yesterday, seemed intolerably heavy today. Because now when she left, it was forever. Now when she left, it was goodbye.

He seemed to be choosing his words carefully. "Are you...is Harley going to pay for it?"

She whirled around then, temper flashing. "As if I'd have asked him!"

He inclined his head. "I didn't figure you would. I just want you to know that I'll handle your bills."

"Like you handled the ranch?" The words were out before she could stop and think. A muscle tensed in his jaw, and his eyes went flinty. "No, thanks. I'll take care of it myself."

"With what? You don't have much money. You couldn't after the way Andrew went through it." He made a swift motion with his hand. "Don't be petty, Julianne. You need the money and I have it. Let me do this for you."

She set her teeth to keep from grinding them. "Petty and immature, that's me." Her fingers clutched the countertop in back of her to keep them from finding something, anything, and heaving it at his head. "How can I make you understand? I will not take anything from you. I'd rather dance barefoot on broken glass. When I leave here, I won't be your concern anymore. There will be no more Sir Jed to the rescue. I won't be coming back." She held up a hand to stem his words. "Save it. You don't need me for anything more than to salve your conscience." Her tone mocking, she reminded him, "You told me not long ago that you didn't need anybody. The biggest mistake I ever made was not believing you."

Riding fence was a meticulous, tedious job. There were miles of it stretching around the pastures of the H/B, and all of it had to be checked regularly. But working outside had its advantages, chief among them the scenery. The peaks were backdropped against the bright blue sky, the foothills of the mountains dotted with lush green trees. Somewhere a meadowlark sang its cheerful summer tune. The sound never failed to lighten Jed's mood. Until now.

He'd given Julianne several days to cool down and start thinking logically. He knew her temper. It was the type to flare suddenly, explode brilliantly, before vanishing. He'd known she'd be disappointed. But he'd seriously under-estimated her reaction.

It wasn't that she avoided him. She was still taking Annie's place in the house with ever-increasing competence. She fixed the meals and watched over the housekeeper's progress with an eagle eye. She was *there,* but she wasn't accessible. At least not to him.

Kneeing his mount gently, he urged it to a faster pace. He couldn't reach her on any level. She was civil, but frighteningly distant. She spoke to him about the meals, Annie's progress. But any attempt to turn the conversation to a more personal note had been met with complete failure.

There was no doubt about the depth of her hurt, but there was no hint of it in her voice when they spoke. It was in her eyes, though, in the deliberately blank mask she affected. Like a wound too deep to bleed, the hurt didn't show.

Her reaction only added to the load of guilt that had been growing inside him since she'd returned to the ranch. She'd been right, he hadn't thought about her feelings when he'd offered to buy the place. At least, not at first. He'd learned not to expect Harley to sink any money into the H/B, learned to weather those times when the man would attempt to drain it of major chunks of its operating capital. But it was when Harley had started to sell off pieces of prime bottomland that Jed had felt the first real stirrings of panic. For the first time he'd faced the fact that there was nothing to prevent the man from parceling the ranch off to support his gambling habit. The realization had been like a stake to his heart.

Finding a loosened wire on the fence, he signaled to the men and then worked with them to rewrap the wire and fasten it more securely. Thanks to the inheritance from his father, he hadn't had to stand by helplessly and watch Harley whittle the place down to a shadow of its former magnificence. He'd always considered that money as the grandest of ironies. The man who'd never really been a father to him had enabled him to buy the one place in the world he'd ever called home.

He remounted. Maybe it was true that Julianne's feelings hadn't been his first priority when he'd bought the ranch, but it was equally true that he hadn't stopped considering them since she'd come home.

And for some reason that scared the hell out of him.

The air of stillness in the house had all his senses on full alert. Instead of removing his boots and going upstairs to shower and change, he strode immediately to the kitchen. It was empty.

Jed stood in the center of the room and scanned the area with one narrowed glance. There was no sign of dinner preparations being made, and no sign of Julianne.

A cold sense of unease twisted his insides and he went to Annie's room. The woman's welcoming smile quickly turned to a frown when she saw his dress.

"Jed Sullivan, what in blazes are you thinking, wearing your boots in the house? I'm not so crippled up that I can't get up out of this chair and teach you a lesson you ought to have learned years ago."

"Where is she?" His quiet voice reflected none of the panic circling in his gut, none of the flat-out dread. But there was something in his tone that had Annie eyeing him carefully.

"If you're talking about Julianne, she went to Billings today. Took off early this morning, actually. She wanted to be home by dark, but wasn't sure she'd make it."

Relief rushed through him in a torrent, making him incapable of speaking for a moment. When he'd seen the empty kitchen, he'd thought... He mentally backed away from the fear that had flooded through him. Julianne was coming back. She'd told Annie so.

"I hope you're not going to ride the girl about her taking a few hours to herself. She's been working herself to a frazzle around here. Even after hearing the news that you and Harley had been keeping from everyone, she hasn't let up."

Jed exchanged a long, steady look with the woman. As usual, when faced with that penetrating stare, he felt like the recalcitrant kid he'd been at twelve. He jammed his fists in his pockets. "Dammit, Annie, I explained this once. I didn't want to tell you or anyone else until Julianne knew."

"And you wanted to force Harley to be the one who told her." The woman nodded. "So you said."

He looked away, his face grim. "You think I was wrong."

"I think you were right to force that old reprobate to take responsibility for his actions, for once," she said tartly. "About the other...buying the ranch..." She heaved a sigh. "I know he would have sold it to someone else if it hadn't been you. And there's no man who deserves it more than you do. But I can't parcel out my feelings for you and Julianne. I don't like to see either of you hurting the way she is right now. It about breaks my heart."

Her words were tiny daggers to his chest. If he'd thought it was impossible to feel any more miserable, he'd been wrong. He swung away, went to the window and stared sightlessly out at Annie's prize roses.

"This doesn't have to change anything." It took effort to keep desperation from leaking into his words. "There's no reason for her to leave the ranch. It's as much her home as it is mine. I've tried telling her that, but she isn't listening to me these days." He turned his head to look at Annie over her shoulder. "Maybe if you talked to her."

The woman looked away and began pleating the bedcover with her fingers. His eyes narrowed. "Annie?"

Stubbornly, she refused to answer. He swung around to approach her, a sudden thought occurring to him. "What did you say Julianne was doing in Billings today?"

There was a long silence before the woman released a breath. "Well, you'll find out soon enough, I suppose. She's been calling all the pawnshops in the area. I suppose she's making the rounds."

Surprise held him still. "Pawnshops?"

"There's no talking the girl out of an idea once she's decided on it. I told her I had money put away, money I'll never use, but she refused to borrow from me. She's going to finish college and she's bound to do it on her own. She's selling her diamond earrings.''

It was a moment before comprehension set in. "She's pawning her jewelry?"

Annie smiled sadly. "She didn't really have much, but she did set store by those earrings. I guess there's something she wants more.''

There was a pain in his gut, like the twist of a carefully placed knife. Yeah, there was something she wanted more. Like leaving the ranch. Getting away from him.

He swung away again, pacing in the room. He had a vivid memory of the earrings that Annie spoke of. Julianne had been sporting them the only time she'd visited the ranch with her husband, had worn them again the night of the Cattlemen's Ball. The first night he'd kissed her. He should feel no sorrow that the gift from her husband would be lost to her, but the thought of Julianne having to give up one more thing she loved made his throat go tight. "Little fool," he muttered. "I told her I'd take care of her expenses. She's got to get over her damned pride, Annie, and let us help her.''

"I'd say chances of that are slim. She's made up her mind to leave." The quaver in the woman's voice had Jed's attention jerking toward her. "I don't know of any way to stop her from doing just that.''

The panic was back, practically choking him. He clenched his hands and released them spasmodically. "She's hurt and angry. I know that. But she loves the ranch. College won't last forever. She'll be back.''

The woman firmed lips that were inclined to tremble. "No. Not this time. Believe me, I've tried. I've talked myself blue in the face.''

Desperation reared, with a ferocity that was alarming.

"She's left before. The ranch is part of her. She can't be in the state and not return."

"But what's to keep her in the state once she finishes school? She only has a year or so left on her degree. No, Jed, I think we just have to accept the fact that Julianne is going to leave us, unless we can convince her otherwise."

He wasn't prepared for the wave of helplessness that drenched him at her words. The power of the emotion stunned and terrified him. Violent desperation spilled out then, fueling anger. "What am I supposed to do, get on my knees? Well, screw that," he snarled, not noticing the shocked expression on Annie's face. "I'm not begging her to stay. If she wants to leave, let her go. I don't need this mess, I don't need her. I've got the ranch."

"Yes," Annie agreed quietly. "You've got the ranch."

There was a time when those four words would have been all he needed to fill the vast emptiness he carried inside him. Bleakly he contemplated the oak plank floor and wondered when having the ranch had ceased to be enough.

Chapter 15

Jed sat on the edge of Julianne's bed and watched as the smell of fresh coffee brought her awake in slow, involuntary increments. By sheer force of will he kept his gaze on her face, away from the soft skin and smooth silk bared by the bedcovers bunched at her waist. Her head burrowed deeper into the pillow, and there was a pang in his heart as he remembered a time when her head had rested on his chest. With little effort, he recalled the softness of her cheek, the feel of her pressing closer to him. Her eyes fluttered slowly open then, and the dazed, unfocused look in them reminded him of the look he'd seen on her face each time he'd slid deep inside her.

The mental images kept him tense as she stretched and yawned before propping herself higher in bed. He shoved a coffee mug into her hand with barely controlled violence and watched her eyes slide closed in appreciation for its hot, bracing flavor. And he knew the exact instant when sleep fully fled, when awareness and memory returned.

Her eyes flew open and her fingers clutched the mug more tightly. "You make an unlikely waiter. When did you add room service to your list of duties around here?"

He heard the wariness layered beneath the words, and his chest drew tighter. "We need to talk."

"Okay. All right." Her gaze lowered to the mug in her hand and refused to lift. "I'll meet you downstairs in fifteen minutes."

Something perverse inside him made him ask, "What's wrong with now?"

He watched her swallow hard and reach to pull the covers higher. "Well, since I'm not in the habit of sleeping fully clothed, I'm really not dressed for it."

His gaze flashed to her shoulders, bare but for bits of ribbon, all that held her short nightgown in place. She hadn't been dressed for it the last time he'd come to her bedroom, either, he remembered, though he'd come that time to talk, as well. To apologize for pushing her away when she'd been trying to help him in the only way she knew how. He'd almost told her then about the sale of the ranch. The secret had weighed particularly heavily after offering up that slice of his past. But before he could, she'd made an offer herself. One that had been impossible to resist.

She still wouldn't look at him. As she hunched her shoulders to sip at the coffee, one ribbon did a slow, sensuous slide off her shoulder. She shrugged at it impatiently, and it inched a couple of fractions higher.

He stared at the sliver of fabric, filled with a sudden need to reach out with one finger to hook the ribbon, to pull it lower. To bare the flesh that had not long ago been his to touch, to taste, to possess. The urge was so strong that he rose abruptly from the bed, shoved his hands into his pockets and propped himself against the wall. If there was ever a time to avoid temptation, it was now.

"I didn't know if you'd be around later. You took off yesterday without a word. Thought maybe you had plans for today, too."

"No, not really. Just the usual chores to do."

The silence stretched, thrumming with tension. "You didn't get back until late last night," he said finally. Not by a hint in his voice did he let on that he knew the exact moment she'd arrived home. The tide of relief that had coursed through him when he'd heard the front door open, heard her take the stairs to her room, had been short-lived. It had been too easy to imagine a not-so-distant time when he'd wait in vain for her return. The knowledge had made sleep impossible, and the Scotch too inviting.

"So, your trip to Billings was successful?"

She stiffened. "I did what I set out to do."

"Dammit, Julianne." The words exploded from him, and he pushed away from the wall, striding around the bed until its length was between them. Only then did she lift her gaze to his.

"Pawnbrokers? Some of those people aren't real trust-worthy. I can only imagine the parts of the city you were in. Alone."

She ignored the emphasis he'd placed on the last word and confronted his anger head-on. "It isn't your concern, Jed. Annie has obviously told you the whole story, so what do you want to hear? That I failed? Sorry to disappoint you."

Frustration made his voice harsh. "You're hardly a match for those predators."

"On the contrary." Her chin tipped up in a gesture of defiance. "I'm not stupid. I knew I'd be at a disadvantage, so I used my God-given talents of charm and persuasion.

I wore the guy down.'' At his silence, she added, ''I did my homework. I got the best price possible for them.''

It wasn't until that moment that he admitted to himself that he'd been hoping to hear a far different answer. He'd wanted to hear that she hadn't raised enough money, that she'd changed her mind. He should have known better. His palms went damp, and he stifled the urge to take them out of his pockets and wipe them on his jeans.

''You know it's going to be a couple of months before Annie's up to full speed. And even then someone should be watching her to make sure she doesn't overdo things.''

''I'll be here as long as Annie needs me.''

The words slashed through him like a keen-edged blade. As long as Annie needed her. But not Jed. He fisted his hands. He wasn't a man to know about need. He'd spent his life making damn sure that he never felt it for anyone. Why then did it feel like her words carved a deep, ragged furrow through his chest?

''I've been thinking about something you said before.'' At her words, his gaze went to hers and held. ''It still hurts, that Harley sold the ranch. I think it always will. But—'' she took a deep breath, as if forcing herself to continue ''—if the ranch has to be belong to somebody else, I'd just as soon it be you. I know what it's meant to you all these years.''

The words should have soothed. Instead they tangled with the guilt and frustration that seemed constant companions these days. ''What about what it's meant to you?'' he countered. He watched her closely, saw the spasm cross her face, saw the way her fingers clenched the mug, and pressed his advantage. ''Think about it, Julianne. Nothing has to change.''

A sad little smile pulled at her lips. ''Everything already

has. *We* changed it, Jed, you and I. We can't change back. At least I can't."

It took more courage than he cared to admit to utter the next words. "So you're just going to walk away from what's between us?"

"Actually, I'm going to run like hell." She tried for lightness, didn't quite pull it off. "Who are we trying to kid, here? I've spent my life wanting more, and you've spent yours making damn sure no one ever hurts you again. If anything good has come out of this situation, it's that I've been forced to take a hard look at myself. I won't be satisfied with crumbs anymore. Not from my selfish father. Not from my emotionally crippled ex-husband. Not from you."

His gaze shot to hers then, a protest on his lips, but she wasn't finished. And every word she uttered pummeled him with relentless force. "No one gets close to you, Jed. You make sure of that. I've made up my mind that I'm not going to *settle* for anything anymore, and that includes being content with the tiny fractions of yourself that you're willing to dole out." Her tone became wry. "Call it a delayed sense of self-preservation."

His eyes squeezed shut for a moment, and the words he spoke were torn from him. "You want me to admit that you matter to me?" He whirled on his heel to pace the room and wished savagely for a cigarette. "You *do* matter. I've told you that before. What else do you want?"

There was a sadness in her voice that tore at his heart. "Nothing from you. *Just for you.* I guess for a start I'd like you to have what I just got with Harley. If not satisfaction, at least a sense of closure. Until you put your past behind you where it belongs, you can't get on with your future."

She waited, but when he didn't respond she shook her

head. "Maybe Harley was right. I've always wanted too much."

He stood still while she slipped from the bed and entered the bathroom, closing the door behind her. His gaze fell to the rumpled sheets, and he swallowed hard. Memories of the two of them lying there lingered in the air, of tangled bodies and heated nights. Of silky hair, smooth skin and eager hands. Of Julianne, painted with moonlight and shadows, adorned with only rose petals.

Suddenly the air in the room was too thick to breathe. He tore his gaze from the bed, scowled and concentrated on moving oxygen in and out of his lungs. She had no right to look so hurt, so disappointed by his silence at her words. He didn't have the faintest idea what she was talking about, anyway. Closure? What the hell was that? He'd had little opportunity for closure in his life. People disappeared too fast. Keeping himself apart, shut off, was an acquired defense, one that had served him damn well. Until she had taken even that from him.

Wearily he scrubbed both hands over his face. He knew with an instinct that owed nothing to logic that if Julianne left, even a return to that safe, comfortable detachment would be impossible. He was in the middle of a crossroads, and both paths were equally terrifying.

When he heard her turn the shower off, he finally moved toward the door. He'd played it safe all his life, maintaining control, eliminating risks. Now he was faced with the greatest risk of his life. One false move would cost him Julianne forever.

The supper table had been cleared and Julianne had gone to Annie's room to beat the woman at gin. Uncustomarily, Jed had joined them, although not to play cards. Instead he was prowling the room silently, in a way that had Annie raising her brows and Julianne clenching her teeth.

"Land sakes, Jed. You're awful restless tonight," Annie commented as she discarded from her hand. "You don't have to keep us company, you know."

"What?" He looked at the women blankly.

"I said, either sit down or get on to your den. You're breaking my concentration. Playing with this one—" she nodded toward Julianne "—requires all my attention."

His gaze shifted to Julianne then. She could feel his piercing regard, feel the force of his will leveled at her, and couldn't quite control a shiver. It had been a week since he'd brought coffee to her room, a week since he'd accepted her decision about leaving the ranch.

She slid him a sideways glance, which skittered away under the force of his gaze. At least he'd seemed to accept it. But when the two of them were in the same room, the tension was palpable. He'd made no attempt to talk her into staying again, and she knew he wouldn't. The price she'd named had been too high, the demand too great. Maybe once she was one hundred miles away, in a new apartment, that fact might stop making her ache.

He'd walked in on her when she was calling to inquire about the availability of apartments within walking distance of the campus, and just the memory of the expression on his face still had the power to weaken her knees. Until recently, she'd had no doubt about her ability to co-exist with him until Annie was well. But she hadn't reckoned on the charged silences, the smoldering looks. She hadn't reckoned on the strength of her own feelings for him.

Because she was unwilling to examine those feelings too closely, she focused instead on her cards. She hadn't counted on the torturous nights alone, when the prospect of sleep was distant and the future stretched out before her, bleak and desolate. She hadn't counted on feeling like she'd lost every chance of happiness she'd ever had.

She drew a card and discarded it without thinking. Only when Annie made a pleased sound and pounced on it with barely disguised glee did she remember what the other woman had been collecting.

The next hand, Annie laid her cards down and crowed, "Gin! And I owe it all to you, Jed." She beamed a smile at him. "Your pacing must have distracted the girl. Maybe I'll keep you around every time we play."

Julianne didn't dare risk a glance at him. He was a distraction, all right, much more so than Annie could know. And she was rapidly beginning to accept the fact that he would continue to be a distraction no matter how far she moved, or how fast she ran.

The doorbell pealed then and she looked up quizzically. "Are either of you expecting company?" Annie shook her head, and Jed...she looked at him more closely. If she hadn't doubted he possessed any, she'd have sworn he was wearing nerves.

When he remained frozen in place, she rose and headed to the front door. "No, no, don't get up," she muttered under her breath. "Let me do it." Then she pulled the door open.

The couple on the porch were strangers to the area. She knew all the neighbors within a fifty-mile radius of the ranch. Yet there was something familiar about the man's still, waiting air, something recognizable in his enigmatic gray eyes.

Julianne's gaze shifted to encompass the dark-haired woman standing by his side, and she smiled tentatively. "Can I help you?"

It was the man who spoke. "We've come to see Jed. I'm John Sullivan, and this is my wife Ellie."

His words rocked her. Disbelievingly, her gaze swung from the man to the woman, and back again. Jed's brother. One part of her mind took rapid inventory, even as the rest struggled with comprehension. At first glance, they didn't resemble each other. Where Jed was dark, this man's hair was almost as light as her own. Jed was an inch or two taller, maybe a bit leaner. But upon closer examination, the similarities were there, too. That gray gaze that gave nothing away; the quiet aura of strength and purpose. It was more than the thin white scar tracing across the man's throat that told her that he could be as dangerous as his brother.

His brother. Foreboding flashed across her mind. What was Jed going to say? How was he going to react? He'd firmly rejected the idea of contacting this man, despite every hope she'd held to the contrary. His brother's unexpected appearance was going to force him to face his past, and her throat tightened in anticipation of the scene to follow.

Then Jed's voice sounded behind her, and his words completed the sense of unreality that encompassed her. "Well, don't just leave them standing on the porch, Jules. Invite them in."

She stared at him for a long moment. From the lack of surprise on his face, it was clear that he'd invited the couple. The sense of unreality gave way to utter amazement.

Pushing open the door, Julianne said, "John and Ellie, please come in. Jed forgot to inform us of his plans, but I'm frankly delighted that you're here."

Ellie smiled then, and her husband slipped an arm around her waist as they entered the house. "Actually, my husband prefers to be called Sully. If you call him John, I'm afraid he won't answer." She slanted a glance at the man beside her. "We enjoyed the trip from the airport. It's beautiful country.'' As she made small talk, one hand was stroking Sully's arm soothingly. ''Neither of us have ever been west of the Mississippi. I can't wait to see more of the ranch.''

In a heartbeat, Julianne realized what the woman was up to. Jed and Sully were silent, watching each other with the wary air of two stalking predators. She'd thought before that they shared a similar sense of danger, and the air was charged with it now. Without conscious decision, she joined forces with Ellie Sullivan.

''I'll make sure you both get to see as much of the ranch as you like. There won't be time for it tonight, but tomorrow...'' As she chattered, she led the couple further into the house. ''You'll have a choice going by horseback or truck. Going by horse you'll see more of the spread, of course. But the truck will save your backside.''

Sully finally spared her a glance. ''I'm not sure how long we'll be here.''

She aimed a winning smile at him, one fashioned to charm. When it had no appreciable effect, her estimation of John Sullivan went up a notch. ''Certainly you'll remain long enough to see a few sights. Jed meant for you to stay for a while, didn't you, Jed?''

His voice devoid of welcome, he replied, ''Yeah. Sure. For as long as this takes.''

At his flat tone Julianne's smile bumped up in wattage and she resisted the urge to kick him. Hard. She was still struggling to comprehend that Jed had invited his brother here, despite his earlier decision not to. Now wasn't the time to figure out what the act meant. And it certainly wasn't the time to allow a tender sprig of hope to grow roots and bloom. She shifted into hostess mode and guided the group into the kitchen.

She brought out refreshments and introduced the couple

to Annie. When the tension between the two brothers didn't lessen noticeably, she decided it was time to forget finesse and resort to bullying. She was equally adept at both.

"Jed, why don't you and Sully go to the den. Ellie and I will get acquainted out here." She gave him a look that was forged with steel, and she hardened herself against the fleeting panic on his face. The flash of emotion was quickly replaced with annoyance.

"I don't need herding."

"I know that. If I thought you did I'd get the cattle prod." Ellie's laugh behind her was quickly disguised by a cough. But Julianne's gaze never wavered from Jed's. After a long moment he looked at Sully and muttered, "Follow me." Turning on his heel, he exited the room.

"Wait." Sully turned back at his wife's voice. She reached into her purse and withdrew a manila envelope, holding it out to her husband. "You'll probably want this." He reached to take it from her, sliding a finger over her wrist in an intimate caress. Then he followed Jed from the room.

Ellie's voice was tinged with worry. "Do you think it's wise to leave them alone?"

"Wise?" Julianne debated the word as she began to make coffee for what would surely prove to be a long night ahead. "Maybe not. But definitely necessary. Nothing is going to get resolved with either of us providing a buffer between them."

The other woman hesitated for an instant, then sank into a chair. "I suppose you're right. But I can't help worrying. Sully doesn't exactly trust easily." The two women shared a look filled with understanding.

"Then that's something the two of them have in common."

* * *

Jed motioned Sully to a chair and circled the desk to the portable bar. "Drink?" he asked in a clipped tone.

"Whiskey, if you have it. Neat."

He splashed some liquor in the glass, then poured a Scotch for himself. When he'd made the call to John—no, he corrected himself—to *Sully,* he'd been operating on a combination of exhaustion and desperation. Now he wondered what the hell he'd been thinking of.

He turned and strode to the man who claimed to be his brother. Something inside him dodged admitting to a relationship, *any* relationship with him. Julianne had spoken of closure, and that's what this meeting was about. He downed a swallow of the Scotch in one burning gulp. That's what this meeting was *supposed* to be about.

Sully sipped from his glass, watching him expressionlessly. "Julianne is who I talked to on the phone when I called?"

"Yeah."

"Seems like a determined woman."

All his frustration was loaded into his next words. "What she is is a pain in the ass."

Hiding his slight smile in his glass, Sully inquired, "And what else?"

Jed speared his fingers through his hair and took another drink, welcoming the liquor's warm explosion in the pit of his stomach. "Damned if I know."

The genuine bafflement in his tone had Sully's face lightening a fraction. "I think I've been where you are not too long ago. You'll figure it out soon enough."

"Right now we have a few other things to figure out," Jed reminded him. His gaze met the other man's and held. "As far as I know, I don't have any brothers." *Alive.* The word whispered across his mind. With an ease born of long practice, he shoved it away.

"We're half brothers, I suspect. Though there's no way of telling, short of medical tests, we most likely had different fathers." Sully reached into the envelope Ellie had given him and withdrew some documents. Without a word, he handed them to Jed.

Jed perused them one by one. It was a stack of birth certificates, and his was on top. With a curious sense of detachment he scanned the information on it. It read the same as the copy he had in his lockbox, with the exception of the parental information. The mother listed was Marcy Elaine Sullivan. Father...unknown.

He stared at the document in his hand for long moments, expecting to feel something. Anything. But there was no emotion to bubble to the surface, no long-forgotten bit of memory to burst forth. The absence of either would have comforted him if he didn't believe that they would pounce when he least expected it.

He flipped to the next document, a birth certificate for the man before him—a second brother he never knew existed. With a feeling of dread he went to the last document, already knowing the name it would carry.

Cage Sullivan. Birth date just twenty-two months after his own.

The emotion that had been missing just moments earlier flooded through him now, great crashing waves of it, pounding him with relentless urgency. His brother's name whispered across his mind, dragging unwanted memories in its wake. Memories that wouldn't be banished. And a guilt that wouldn't subside.

He shoved the documents back to Sully, who took them and handed him a sheaf of papers. "County record copies of our births,'' he said. With a sharp gaze he watched Jed carefully. "They can be checked out, if you want to."

Jed stared at the papers blindly. "You went to a lot of trouble."

Sully lifted a shoulder. "Figured you might need convincing." He shifted in his chair, his first outward sign of unease. "I would, if I was in your shoes." When Jed didn't respond, he went on. "I found most of this stuff when I cleaned out my...*our* mother's apartment. She died eight months ago. The birth certificates were there, some legal papers and these." He reached into the envelope again, this time drawing out a handful of photographs.

Jed took them slowly, reluctantly. And with a feeling of dread he forced himself to look at them, to read the notations on the backs.

The first photos were of a young Sully, pictured with a blond woman whose good looks seemed to deteriorate in each successive shot. The next photos pictured the same woman, a little younger, this time with two boys. There was no mistaking the older of the two for himself. He had pictures taken only a couple years later, after his adoption, and the resemblance was too great. He handed the pictures back blindly, and rose to pace around the desk, to the window. And wished he could retreat from the dogging memories as easily.

"I don't want to hear a peep out of you two, you hear?" Why was it he'd had no memory of his mother's face, but the sound of her voice lingered in his mind like a persistent ghost? The memory beckoned others, and it was too late to slam that mental gate shut. They wouldn't be denied.

The door closed, and the total darkness of the closet seemed to swallow them up. He and Cage huddled in the shadows, clutching each other, and tried to block out the noises in the bedroom.

He tipped his glass to his lips and swallowed the remaining Scotch. Somehow the darkness had been the worst of it, he remembered. Worse than the hunger, worse than the beatings that would follow the slightest misdeed. At least it had seemed to be until that last night in the apartment.

Swinging away from the window, he went to refill his glass. Without asking, he brought the whiskey bottle to Sully and splashed some more inside. "You're right," he said bleakly, meeting the other man's gaze. "At least I figure you must be. That's me in the pictures."

"I was as surprised as you are. Marcy never mentioned any of this."

Jed's smile was humorless. "I'll bet not. I didn't live with her long, at any rate."

"Yeah, I found the court documents in her things. I know her parental rights were severed." At Jed's nod he continued, "I've pieced together some of it. We can probably compare notes."

There was a not-too-distant place inside him that would have liked to pull away from the whole scene now, a part that was every bit as cowardly as Julianne had accused him of being. He said nothing. It was too late, too late to do anything but play this bitter scene to the end.

"I don't know much," he said. He lowered himself to a chair opposite Sully's. For the first time, he let the memories play out. "My adoptive mother told me some, when I asked."

Surprise sparked in the other man's eyes, eyes too much like his own. "You were adopted?"

Jed contemplated the amber eddies in his glass as he nodded. "When I was six." In a cynical understatement, he added, "It didn't work out."

"With your last name of Sullivan I just assumed..."

"I took my birth name back when I was nineteen."

"That made it a whole lot easier to find you. What about Cage? Was he adopted, too? Do you know where he is?"

The question was expected, but that didn't seem to lessen the punch of emotion that coursed through him. The tidal wave of guilt was never more than a heartbeat away, threatening to drag him into the darkness.

"Cage is dead."

The words were too sharp, too sudden, but he knew of no way to pretty up the truth. He saw the shock on Sully's face, saw the way he put the glass to his lips and took a long swallow.

"Hell." The two men drank in silence for long minutes, both wrapped in regrets, each stemming from a different place.

Finally Sully heaved out a sigh. "How did it happen?"

"There was a fire in the apartment. We were alone. Cage didn't make it." The words were succinct, the feeling behind them wasn't.

Sully's gaze snapped to him, a frown on his face. "Are you saying he died in the fire?"

Fingers gripping the glass in his hand tightly, Jed responded, "Yeah."

The other man shook his head. "That doesn't make sense. I've got records of the proceedings in which Marcy gave up her parental rights. You and Cage are both mentioned by name. Details of the injuries both of you sustained in the fire were documented, I suppose to support the county's case. They said you were treated for serious burns, and Cage for smoke inhalation. There's no mention of his death."

There was a haze in Jed's mind that owed nothing to the alcohol, and everything to a cautious, blooming hope. "What are you saying?"

"I'm saying that I have every reason to believe that our brother is alive."

Chapter 16

The first thing that struck Julianne when she descended the staircase the next morning was that the door to the den was still closed. She paused midway down and contemplated it. It was early, at least an hour before she usually rose. That didn't seem to matter since she hadn't done much sleeping last night, anyway. When she and Ellie had finally retired, her mind had refused to shut off and let her rest, despite the lateness of the hour. She couldn't tear her thoughts away from what was happening in the den between Jed and his brother.

And Sully and Jed *were* brothers. What Ellie had told her had persuaded her of that. She wondered if Jed had been convinced. She wondered if he would let it matter.

She continued down the stairs slowly, her gaze fixed on that door. There hadn't been any noise from the den last night, and she'd know, she'd been listening. Surely the fact that the two men had been locked up together for hours was a good sign, wasn't it?

Hesitating outside the door, she mentally listed several reasons for continuing into the kitchen. She didn't need to get drawn any closer into that dark and dangerous place in which he hid his feelings. Didn't want to fall deeper into the trap of wishing to help. The only one who could help Jed was himself.

Her hand reached for the doorknob and turned it. Someday, she acknowledged, she really would have to start listening to that wise inner voice.

She took only two steps into the room before she saw him behind his desk. His gaze rose from the glass in his hands and fixed on her.

"Either you didn't get to bed last night or you've come up with a new morning routine." Her approach was cautious and she surveyed him carefully. The hours since she'd last seen him had been rough ones. His hair was falling forward on his forehead in the way he'd always hated, and his jaw was unshaven. From the looks of the half-empty bottle next to him, Scotch was at least as much to blame for his heavy eyes as lack of sleep.

"Are you drunk?"

"No." He raised the glass before him and contemplated its contents. "But it's an option I've been seriously considering." He watched the way she scanned the room and his brow arched. "Looking for bodies?"

Her attention snapped back to him. "Of course not. I just…I mean, it was late when I went up. I assume you showed Sully to his room?"

"A couple of hours ago."

He said nothing else, and for a sudden aching moment she doubted he would. Was this just one more experience then, for him to shove into a forgotten corner of his mind, one he would do his best to avoid dealing with?

She edged further into the room and perched gingerly

on the edge of the couch. "So how long will Sully and Ellie be staying?"

"They're leaving today."

She bounced from the couch with the energy of a launching rocket. "I knew it! I just knew it!" The anger flooded, as much at herself as at him. She despised herself for the fragile bud of hope that had blossomed inside her. Hated to admit that her desire for things to be different could still blind her to the reality. A couple of paces took her away from the desk, then she whirled to stride over to it. Shoving her face close to his, she accused, "You did everything you could to push him away, didn't you? You just couldn't hold out one tiny particle of faith that Sully could actually be something to you. *Mean* something to you. Because you're scared. Scared and selfish."

He replaced the glass on the desk without taking a drink. He watched as fury pushed her away from the desk, carried her across the room and then back again. "Selfish?"

"You're damn right, selfish. That's exactly what it's called when you hoard parts of yourself like a miser, as if by opening up you chance someone sneaking in and stealing them."

"Actually," he said slowly, "that's a fairly accurate description of what's happened."

She didn't stop to listen. Disappointment and nerves rasped fresh, raw wounds inside her. Furiously she called herself every kind of fool. For believing that things could change. For *wanting* to believe it.

"I didn't kick him out, if that's what you're thinking."

"No," she agreed caustically. "You rolled out the red carpet, right? Made him feel right at home like a member of the family? Oh, I forgot. You don't have any family. You won't let yourself."

The glint in his eyes could have been temper. In the

next instant it was gone. "Sully couldn't take much time away from work right now. He told me that when I called him. He's in the middle of a case."

Not entirely pacified, she stopped to eye him suspiciously.

"He's a DEA agent in Florida."

"Oh." The memory of the pale scar that stretched across Sully's neck flashed into her mind, and a shudder worked through her. No doubt the man was as tough and hardened as Jed. There was absolutely no reason to be encouraged by the fact that the two men had exchanged such rudimentary information as their occupations. She wouldn't allow herself to be.

He took out a cigarette and lit it, causing her brows to climb. "Taking a liking for living on the edge?"

"After the last few hours, one more cigarette isn't going to matter." For the first time, she noticed the heavy cut glass on the desk filled to overflowing with cigarette stubs. "I'm going to arm Annie with the wooden spoon myself."

He inhaled deeply and released a narrow stream of smoke. "She'll have to take on two of us, and I'm betting I can outrun her."

"So, Sully smokes." Calmer now, she sat down again. "Something you have in common."

"A bit more than that, it seems." Pensive, he blew out a smoke ring. "It appears we share the same mother."

It was so little, but more, much more than she'd begun to expect. "You believe him, then?"

At first she didn't think he'd even heard her. He was watching the smoke that drifted between them reflectively. His answer, when it came, seemed directed as much to himself as to her. "I really don't remember much about her. But the life he described seemed like a long-forgotten echo. The poverty, the men.'' His gaze slowly lifted to hers then, and held. ''The drugs.''

His voice had a rawness to it that made her wish she could leap in and save him from the scars inside that had never quite healed. She remained motionless. There was no rescue from feeling, no escape from emotion. It was a lesson Jed had learned from the most bitter experience.

''I'm sorry,'' she said, and meant it. Sorry that the memories he had of his childhood were ragged bits of hurt and despair. And sorry he seemed intent on letting them ruin any chance of happiness he could have in his future.

He seemed to find the glowing tip of his cigarette fascinating. ''Sully did some research before coming here.''

''I wondered how he found you.''

He lifted a shoulder. ''Since I took back the name Sullivan it probably was simple. He had my original birth certificate. Mine and Cage's.''

Her heart was a dull knot in her chest. ''Did you tell him about the fire?''

''He already knew. Seems he has copies of the court proceedings to sever custody.'' His gaze finally lifted, as if drawn by an invisible force. His voice was deceptively detached when he added, ''The proceedings were for two children.''

She blinked, comprehension slow to dawn. ''But you said Cage was…''

''Dead.'' He completed her words when her voice trailed off. ''I thought…I was always sure…''

Hope unfurled inside her. Understanding came on wings. ''Oh, my gosh. Oh, Jed.'' She sprang to her feet and moved, unconscious of doing so. She rounded the desk and came to stand before him. ''You were told Cage was gone, and to your traumatized mind that meant dead. But he must have been alive, had to have been, to have been named in the court proceedings.'' The prospect dazzled; relief flooded her. ''There's some other explanation. He was placed in a different foster home, he was adopted....''

''You're way ahead of me,'' he warned. ''All we know is that Cage survived the fire. We don't know what happened to him, or if it would be possible to find him.''

She surveyed him with eyes suddenly brimming. She wondered if he even realized how naturally he'd just said *we*. ''But you're going to try.'' The words were a dare, one she could only hope he'd take her up on.

''Sully intends to.''

When he said nothing else, she could have wept with frustration. ''What about you?''

Slowly, meticulously, he stubbed the cigarette out and dropped it in the glass with the others. ''I told him I might be tied up for a while.''

''What can be more important than reaching out for your first chance of family?''

''We've got things to settle. You and me.''

Her gaze streaked to his and her nerves stumbled. ''You and me?''

''I've been thinking about what you said.'' He rubbed his fingers across his palms in a nervous motion that was curiously unlike him. ''About the last few weeks. About...everything.'' With restrained violence he pushed away from the desk to pace. ''I hate that you're leaving because you've lost everything that's meant something to you. Because Harley hurt you...again.'' His eyes were flinty with suppressed emotion. ''I hate that I was part of that.''

She shrugged awkwardly. At that moment she knew exactly how bitter pity felt, when it was directed at her. ''Like you said, if you hadn't bought the ranch, someone else would have.''

"You don't have to leave." The words hung like fragile crystals between them, as if the slightest force could shatter them.

She released a pent-up breath. "Yes." She forced the word out and struggled to mean it. "I do."

He wasn't looking at her anymore. He dragged his hand through his hair and stared at the floor. "You're only leaving because you think there isn't a place for you here anymore. You're wrong. You could stay." The words began to pour from him in a deluge. "The place belongs to you as much as me, in a way."

She struggled to keep the ache from her voice. "Not in any way that matters."

"It could. Legally. If you married me."

Shock shot her spine with steel. "Married you."

His gaze was so fierce, she felt scalded by his regard. "It's not such a bad deal. You'd get to live here. I know you love the ranch. Half of it would be yours. You'd be close to Gabe, to Annie. You could still finish school. Hell, I'll even teach you to fly."

Taking advantage of her stillness, he strode over to her and took her shoulders in his hands. "Think about it." His voice was a warm river of temptation trickling through her mind. "I can give you exactly what you want."

"Can you, Jed?" she asked in an aching whisper. "Can you really?"

His hands rubbed up and down on her arms in a heated glide, bringing a shiver to her skin, a heaviness to her heart.

"It sounds like you've thought this out. You've managed to appeal to my love for this place, my need for security and my sense of adventure. Too bad I recently decided that I deserve more."

A muscle worked in his jaw then. "You mean the ranch

isn't enough for you.'' He dropped his hands and moved away. "Well, that shouldn't be so surprising, I guess. I never thought the day would come when I'd feel the same way.''

She went completely still. "What?''

Driven to move, he paced the room, away from her, back again. He didn't seem to have heard her. "It should have been enough. It would have been…'' He shook his head in frustrated bafflement. "You changed everything, Jules. You said you deserve more. And damn you, you've made me want more, too. I want it all. I must be crazy. I know I'm crazy about you.''

That stopped her breathing for a moment, but just for a moment. Then heat suffused her, and her pulse began to thrum. "Nice touch, Sullivan.''

"You could walk away at any time. I realize that. I know a wedding isn't a guarantee.''

"I could walk away from the ranch,'' she agreed. "It isn't the land that would hold me.''

He hadn't seemed to have heard her. "You talk about taking risks. Well, this is the biggest one I can imagine. But there's no other way for me, Jules. I love you.'' He stopped, seeming as shocked as she at hearing the words. He reached for her, ran a finger down her throat. "I love you. And I'm willing to take a gamble that given enough time, you'll love me back.'' She noted the tension in his jaw, the control it took for him to relax it again, and her heart turned over at his show of nerves.

It was difficult to swallow around the boulder in her throat. "Still going for the sure thing, Sullivan?''

His eyes brightened, and he slid his hand up her neck to cup her jaw. "What are you saying?''

"Just that I love you, too.'' His eyes squeezed shut for a moment in a display of emotion that made her heart stutter and swell. Then they were reopened, trained on her intently.

"Say it again." He pulled her up and into his arms, demand implicit in his touch, in his words.

She complied willingly. "You, too." Her hand tangled in the hair at his nape. "I'm getting a taste for even odds, myself."

"I need you." His mouth pressed against the pulse throbbing at the base of her throat, cruised up her neck. "I'm not letting you go." He took her earlobe between his teeth. "I'm willing to bet we're for keeps."

She twined both arms around his neck and smiled brightly. "That's one bet I'll take you up on, cowboy."

* * * * *

The Sullivan men are falling for the only women who can tame them. But will Cage be found in time for the next family reunion?
Stay tuned to Intimate Moments for the next Sullivan story!

INTIMATE MOMENTS®

Silhouette®

presents

MARCH MADNESS

featuring four captivating new authors whose page-turning stories will keep you anxiously awaiting their characters' every move.

CULLEN'S BRIDE, #914
Fiona Brand
This outlaw needs the love of a good woman, and Rachel is more than willing to oblige.

A TRUE-BLUE TEXAS TWOSOME, #915
Kim McKade
When the small-town sheriff laid eyes on the woman he'd never stopped loving, he thought he *must* be dreaming.

THE MAN BEHIND THE BADGE, #916
Vickie Taylor
Finding love and passion in the line of duty can be dangerous—especially when Jason and Lane are working together to catch a notorious crime boss.

DANGEROUS CURVES, #917
Kristina Wright
Being wrongfully accused of a capital crime was not something Samantha was proud of. And then she met Jake…!

Available at your favorite retail outlet.

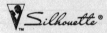

Silhouette®

If you enjoyed what you just read,
then we've got an offer you can't resist!

Take 2 bestselling
love stories FREE!
Plus get a FREE surprise gift!

Clip this page and mail it to Silhouette Reader Service™

IN U.S.A.
3010 Walden Ave.
P.O. Box 1867
Buffalo, N.Y. 14240-1867

IN CANADA
P.O. Box 609
Fort Erie, Ontario
L2A 5X3

YES! Please send me 2 free Silhouette Intimate Moments® novels and my free surprise gift. Then send me 6 brand-new novels every month, which I will receive months before they're available in stores. In the U.S.A., bill me at the bargain price of $3.57 plus 25¢ delivery per book and applicable sales tax, if any*. In Canada, bill me at the bargain price of $3.96 plus 25¢ delivery per book and applicable taxes**. That's the complete price and a savings of over 10% off the cover prices—what a great deal! I understand that accepting the 2 free books and gift places me under no obligation ever to buy any books. I can always return a shipment and cancel at any time. Even if I never buy another book from Silhouette, the 2 free books and gift are mine to keep forever. So why not take us up on our invitation. You'll be glad you did!

245 SEN CNFF
345 SEN CNFG

Name	(PLEASE PRINT)	
Address	Apt.#	
City	State/Prov.	Zip/Postal Code

 * Terms and prices subject to change without notice. Sales tax applicable in N.Y.
** Canadian residents will be charged applicable provincial taxes and GST.
   All orders subject to approval. Offer limited to one per household.
 ® are registered trademarks of Harlequin Enterprises Limited.

INMOM99   ©1998 Harlequin Enterprises Limited

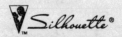

Silhouette

SPECIAL EDITION ™®

In March 1999 watch for a brand-new
book in the beloved MacGregor series:

THE PERFECT NEIGHBOR
(SSE#1232)

by

#1 *New York Times* bestselling author

NORA ROBERTS

Brooding loner Preston McQuinn wants nothing more
to do with love, until his vivacious neighbor, Cybil
Campbell, barges into his secluded life—and his heart.

**Also, watch for the MacGregor stories
where it all began in the exciting 2-in-1 edition!**

Coming in April 1999:

THE MacGREGORS: Daniel—Ian

Available at your favorite retail outlet,
only from

Silhouette®

Look us up on-line at: http://www.romance.net   SSEMACS2

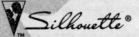

invites you to join the Brand brothers,
a close-knit Texas family in which each
sibling is eventually branded by love—
and marriage!

MAGGIE SHAYNE
continues her intriguing series

with

THE BADDEST BRIDE IN TEXAS, #907
due out in February 1999.

If you missed the first four tales of the irresistible
Brand brothers:
THE LITTLEST COWBOY, #716 (6/96)
THE BADDEST VIRGIN IN TEXAS, #788 (6/97)
BADLANDS BAD BOY, #809 (9/97)
THE HUSBAND SHE COULDN'T REMEMBER, #854 (5/98)
You can order them now.

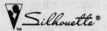

Available at your favorite retail outlet.

#913 ROYAL'S CHILD—Sharon Sala
The Justice Way

Royal Justice knew he would do anything to make his daughter happy. So when she insisted that a lone hitchhiker needed *their* help, he went against his better judgment and told Angel Rojas to climb on board. After that, it didn't take long before his two favorite females were giving him a few lessons on how to live—and love—again.

#914 CULLEN'S BRIDE—Fiona Brand
March Madness

Sexy Cullen Logan thought he had no chance for a happy family—until he met Rachel Sinclair. She was everything he'd ever wanted in a woman, and now she was about to have his child. Cullen knew that being a father was a full-time job, but given his dangerous past, was he qualified for the position?

#915 A TRUE-BLUE TEXAS TWOSOME—Kim McKade
March Madness

Toby Haskell was perfectly content with his life as a country sheriff. Until his one true love, Corrine Maxwell, returned to town. Losing her had been hard—and accepting it even harder. Now she was back, and he knew he had a second chance. But was his small-town life enough for a big-city girl?

#916 THE MAN BEHIND THE BADGE—Vickie Taylor
March Madness

The last thing FBI agent Jason Stateler needed was to get too close to his sexy female partner. But Lane McCullough was part of the case, and he knew she wasn't going away—and, secretly, he didn't really want her to. Tracking down a criminal was easy—it was their unexpected passion that was going to be the problem.

#917 DANGEROUS CURVES—Kristina Wright
March Madness

Samantha Martin knew she was innocent of murder—she'd just been in the wrong place at the wrong time. And so was Jake Cavanaugh, because he had been foolish enough to pick her up when she was making her escape. But now there was no turning back, and before long she was trusting him with her life…but what about with her heart?

#918 THE MOTHER OF HIS CHILD—Laurey Bright
Conveniently Wed

The moment Charisse Lane most feared had arrived: her child's father had found them! More disconcerting was her immediate, intense attraction to the tall, dark dad—an attraction Daniel Richmond clearly reciprocated. But Charisse knew that a legacy of lies—and secrets—could very well prevent the happily-ever-after she wished could be theirs….